The Compound

ALSO BY ROBIN MAHLE

REMY FONTAINE THRILLERS

Book 1: Orleans Avenue

Book 2: Terrebonne Bay

Book 3: Baton Rouge

Book 4: River Ranch

STANDALONE

The Chef

The Man In My Attic

The Compound

THE COMPOUND

ROBIN MAHLE

Joffe Books, London
www.joffebooks.com

First published in Great Britain in 2024

Cover art by Nick Castle

ISBN: 978-1-83526-906-0

To my fierce and fearless daughter.
Your strength, determination, and unshakable spirit inspire me every day. This book is for you — a testament to your courage and the boundless heights you will reach.

CHAPTER 1

Kylie

Flames licking my back. Screams echoing from those trapped inside. Running for my life. My mind's eye conjures these images as I stare out the plane's window, touching down on the tarmac. Maybe it was a mistake — taking this job. What was I thinking, coming back here?

You needed the money, that's what you were thinking. And working on my first big-budget movie as the lead production assistant — it would have been career suicide to pass it up. Besides, all that happened a long time ago. Twenty years, in fact. I was only thirteen. Just a kid. I'm not that young girl anymore and those people — they're gone. Most of them.

"You okay, babe?"

I feel Jesse's hand on my shoulder, and the sound of his baritone voice soothes me. I pull away from the view of the blurring landscape of greens and yellows. "Yeah . . . fine." He doesn't know — about any of it. When Jesse and I met, I was still in my late twenties. We were hired to work on the same film. He was a cameraman, still is, and I'd just moved up to production assistant. That was five years ago. We've been inseparable ever since. Although, if he knew what had happened here, I'm not sure we'd be together. The thought terrifies me.

I moved to Los Angeles when I was thirteen, after spending my childhood in Iowa. The film is shooting in a small town between Denison and Carroll. Both are southeast of Sioux City. And only miles from where it happened.

I don't know if the area around here looks all that different now from back then. We weren't allowed out much. And the day I left, well — I do remember the smell of the cornfields. Earthy and sweet. Until harvest, that is. Then it turns musty. Corn is kind of a big deal here. That, and hogs.

I see the portable staircase rolling to the door, and the flight attendant push it open. Am I prepared to be here again? So close to where it all happened?

Down the stairs, I bolted, taking the steps two at a time in my desperate escape. The terrifying echo of my mother's screams were carried in the air. My baby sister, once vibrant and full of life, had already been silenced.

The living room loomed ahead, shrouded in a darkness that seemed to swallow up the moonlight. As my foot found the final step, I slipped. The slick sensation underfoot was unmistakable — blood. My brother's blood. His body, a lifeless shadow at the end of the hall.

From upstairs, the man's voice resonated through the house. "You think you can get away with what you've done?" His threat hung in the air like a promise as I made my escape, leaving everyone else behind to die.

"Kylie, we're deplaning," Jesse says.

I clear my throat, as though that might help turn off the movie of my past as it plays on repeat in my head. "Huh?"

"Everyone's getting off the plane, hon. Come on. Let's go."

"Yeah, sorry." I grab my bag from under the seat and shimmy out into the narrow aisle.

The oppressive summer heat clings to my skin as I step off the plane. It's the corn sweat. People in L.A. have no idea what I'm talking about when I say that. They're clueless as to the amount of moisture that comes off all the corn. When one acre of it adds four thousand gallons of water to the air in

July, I tell them to imagine how much water is added from the 2.7 billion bushels produced every year in this state. It's a hot, sticky mess in the summer. And it's only just begun.

"Holy shit, it's hot," Jesse says as he takes my bag from me. "Here, let me carry that."

Jesse's a big guy. Used to be a surfer. Yep, he's the blond-haired, blue-eyed, Southern-California-surfer type. Exactly the kind of guy I never thought I'd end up with. But he has his uses. I smile at him. "Thanks. To be fair, it is lighter than the equipment you carry."

"Just barely," he replies with a smirk. "Does this heat get any better?"

"Oh, no." I laugh. "It only gets worse from here, buddy."

He knows I'm originally from Des Moines, but that's it. That's all anyone knows about me. Other than the fact I spent my so-called formative years with Aunt Grace in her craftsman-style home in Garden Grove, a suburb of Los Angeles.

One of the producers, who's several feet ahead and walking toward the gate's entrance, looks back at us. We are a group of twelve, with more coming. Some, we'll hire on-site. Locals and others who know how to put a few pieces of wood together to help enhance our sets.

"Okay, kids," he begins. A slicked-back suit with tons of money named Monty Cummins. "We'll get checked in at the Radisson, then drive out to the location for our first meeting. No time to waste, people. We're burning money already."

I check the time. It's 3 p.m. and the long day of travel isn't over yet. The location we're filming at is still fifteen miles away. An old farmhouse with lots of land. Many of the interior shots were done at the studio, but several take place outside. So, the location scouts chose this place. Lucky me.

* * *

We arrive at the hotel, where several cars line the parking lot. No way is there that many guests here. It's the middle of summer, in the middle of nowhere.

“We have six cars rented for the production,” Monty says from the front row of the shuttle bus. “Plenty to go ’round. So, I want everyone to get checked in. We’ll huddle up shortly and drive to the location.”

After dropping off our things in our room, Jesse and I prepare to head out. And, yes, everyone knows we’re together. It’s kind of how things go in this business. We’re a tight circle and we all know each other. For better or worse.

Jesse offers me the car keys. “This is your town, not mine.”

I flinch for a minute as we stand in the lobby. “No, it’s not.”

He tilts his head and creases his brow. “It’s just an expression. So, you want me to drive?”

“Actually, that’d be great. I’m already feeling the jetlag.” I hear footsteps rush up behind me and turn around. “Lucy, hey.”

“Mind if I hitch a ride with you guys?” She’s out of breath and flicks her red locks from her neck. “My ride left already.”

“Sure. No problem,” I reply.

We head outside. Several of the crew are already pulling away, and we step into the sedan. Lucy Marks is my closest friend and was the one who told me about this job. We met a couple of years ago on the set of a sitcom, which aired for only ten episodes. Our mutual dislike of the lead actor after he’d hit on us led to an unbreakable bond between us. We protect each other. I couldn’t do that for my siblings, so I make sure to do it for Lucy.

She’s an incredible makeup artist who excels at special effects and was nominated for an Academy Award last year ago. Didn’t win, but who cares? You have any idea how hard it is to get recognized at all, let alone for an Oscar, in this industry?

I see her through the sideview mirror as she closes the rear passenger door. Lucy’s about my age, mid-thirties. The sweat’s already consuming her as she raises her long hair to let the air conditioning cool her neck.

I want to tell them about this place, but I can't. I've lived with this secret for twenty years. But being back here, well, it's hard not to think about it. Impossible, if I'm honest.

"I believe this is the spot," Jesse says, making a right turn into the gravel parking area. Ahead is a beautiful farmhouse surrounded by fields and rolling hills that are covered in yellowing grasses.

"When's the cast due to arrive?" Lucy asks.

"Don't know." I look out to see several people standing around. No sign of our illustrious director, Caroline. "I'm sure Caroline or Mason will tell us. There's still a lot of pre-production stuff to take care of first." Mason Rivers is our set designer. "Can't pay the talent to just stand around looking pretty."

I step out, feeling the sharp stones under the soles of my black Converse sneakers. I almost forget how clean the air is here, taking a long deep breath. The clear blue sky. Grassy hills waving at us in the distance. The stunning old farmhouse with a wrap-around porch stands alone in all its glory. Gleaming white siding with black shutters. Little herb or vegetable gardens planted on the sides. "I see why the scouts chose this place."

Lucy moves in next to me. "It's beautiful. Kinda makes me want to leave the city and go off-grid."

I look at her, a tight smile on my face. "You wouldn't like it for long."

"Oh, I don't know, Kylie," she says, hands on her hips as though assessing the possibility. "The isolation. The peace and quiet."

"That's right. Out here, no one can hear you scream," Jesse says with a chuckle.

I feel sick at his comment. He doesn't know any better, of course, but he has no idea how right he is.

"You watch too many movies, Jess," Lucy replies, swatting her hand at him.

We walk on, heading to the porch with the rest of the crew. And that's when I feel it. My chest. It's in a vice grip. I cough, hoping to loosen it.

"You need some water?" Jesse asks.

"No, I'll be okay." Several more moments pass when Mason, the set designer, hands me a bottle of water. "Well, maybe a sip." I twist off the cap, drinking down a large gulp of it. "Thanks. Don't know what happened. Must be all the clean air."

"Lungs aren't used to it," Mason replies. "We should get started."

Everyone finds their seats on the shady, but still-warm front porch. I stay back a moment. Jesse stays with me. "Go on. I just need a second."

He eyes me with suspicion. "You sure?"

"Yeah. I'm sure."

"Okay."

I step down to the bottom of the porch. I can't stay here long because I have a job to do. But I need to know if it'll stop. The memories. The thoughts of that day, and the days leading up to it. I survey the vast farmland before closing my eyes and concentrating on slowing my breath. It's what my therapist said I should do whenever the memories take over.

I feel a hand on my back and open my eyes to see our director. "Caroline."

She smiles, warm and comforting. In her late forties, she's known as 'Mom' onset. I hadn't worked for her before this, so I'm excited to get to know her better. I hope she feels the same.

"Whatchya doing over here?" Caroline asks. "Meeting's on the porch." She walks back toward the others.

I force my feet to move. "Yeah, of course. Right behind you."

***

There's not much to do around here, so the crew sits in the hotel bar as night arrives. Location shoots are always a lot of fun. Like a sleepaway camp. Or like what I'd imagine a sleepaway camp might be like.

Mason Rivers raises his glass as we all huddle around a couple of tables we pushed together. "Caroline and Monty put together an amazing cast and crew for this shoot. I can't wait to get started. Cheers!"

"Cheers!" the rest of us say in unison.

It's true. Monty is the money man. The suit. Caroline is the visionary. The crew, as I look around, we're all here for one reason . . . because we believe in this film.

I toss back another shot of tequila, my third one, and quickly realize I've hit the proverbial brick wall. I don't drink much — anymore. I look at Jesse, who's in a conversation with the other production assistants, or PAs, as we're called. There's three of us here. I'm the lead, and I hope after this shoot, my work will get noticed.

I sort of fell into this job. Growing up in L.A. . . . it's hard not to gravitate toward this business. I didn't go to college. Instead, I started as a runner for the studios. Getting coffee, driving talent to and from soundstages. Eventually, I worked my way up to second PA. And now this. It's my shot. And I swear, if I mess this up . . .

"Hey, babe," I say to Jesse as my head starts to spin. "I'm going to head up to the room. We have an early start tomorrow."

He sets down his shot glass. "You want me to come up with you?"

"No, no," I insist. "Have fun with the guys. I'm exhausted. See you later." I kiss his lips, almost intending to draw the attention of the other women on the crew. Yeah, it's petty. But I couldn't bear to lose him. I need Jesse far more than he needs me.

I wave my hand to the crew. "Night, everyone."

Lucy walks over to me. "You want me to walk you up?"

"I'm good. See you in the morning." I carry on toward the elevators, riding up to the third floor. There are only three floors in this hotel. Stepping off, I walk along the red and gold carpet, worn in some spots. A musty odor lingers.

At the end of the hall is our room. A swipe of the key card and the lock clicks. I walk inside, tossing the card onto the dresser, where a TV is mounted above.

Shedding my clothes and shoes, I pull on one of Jesse's T-shirts. It falls just below the top of my thighs. I've always been petite, just like my mother. Got this thick brown hair from her, too. But what I lack in size and strength, I make up for in tenacity.

I fought to be here. Harder than anyone should. I pick up the phone as I note the time. We're two hours ahead of L.A. I wonder if my aunt will still be awake. I press her contact and listen while the line rings. She'll answer, even if she was sleeping.

"Kylie, sweetheart. I'm so glad you called."

"Hi, Aunt Grace. I wanted to let you know that I arrived safely. We've already been out to the location and had a meeting."

"Oh good. How was the flight? All right?" she asks, her tone cheerful and positive.

I would never have made it this far without her. She was my literal life saver. My mother's younger sister, Grace, always worried about her sister, and about us kids. Said she should've brought us all to L.A. to live with her, rather than let Mom and Dad take us away from Des Moines. But that didn't happen. Instead, her sister was murdered. Her niece and nephew, too.

"The flight was fine. A little long, but uneventful," I reply. "I didn't wake you, did I?"

"Honey, it's only eight o'clock here. I know I'm old, but give me some credit." She laughs the wonderful, charming laugh that I adore.

"Yeah, I guess so. Anyway, I just wanted to let you know it's all good here. They say we're scheduled for four weeks. Hopefully, we won't have any overruns."

"I hope not," Grace says, her tone turning serious. "I don't like that you're there, Kylie. I don't like it one bit."

"I'm not crazy about it myself, but it's a great opportunity for me. The pay's good. And besides, Jesse's here too. We'll be fine." We fell silent for a moment. "I should hop in the shower. Goodnight, Aunt Grace. I love you."

"I love you too, baby."

I smile, ending the call. I'm thirty-four years old, but when I talk to Aunt Grace, I suddenly feel like I'm thirteen again. I know she worries, but I'll be okay. I can handle being back here. After all, twenty years is a long time.

* * *

Crew call is at 5 a.m. The one downside to this job . . . long hours. And since it's growing warmer with summer having arrived, the days are already getting long. So, here I am, five in the morning. The sun not quite over the hills.

I help get the lights set up. Help with equipment. Print call sheets. Pretty much do whatever the director asks of me. And I love it. I wouldn't have it any other way. Jesse is already at work setting up the cameras. Lucy is in the lead actor's trailer, putting on his makeup. Mason is ensuring all the props are set out, and everything is on its mark.

The dozen or so other people here all have their tasks, and everything seems to be running smoothly. A good start for the first day of filming. Being here helps keep my mind off other things. Things that kept me up for a good part of last night. Never mind.

I run around, putting out little fires as we prepare for action. The heat rises along with the sun. At least it's not raining. The whole day would be ruined. The number one cause of budget overruns? Weather.

It takes another two hours for the actors to rehearse, to block. For the cameras to move into position.

"Quiet on the set," the assistant director calls out.

"Roll sound." The second AD claps the slate board. "Call it."

Finally, the first AD gives the command. "Scene twelve, take one. Roll Camera."

Caroline waits a moment, staring at the small screen before her. "Action!"

I stand far away from what's called a hot set. My job is finished for the time being. I watch the scene unfold inside the quaint living room of the farmhouse, through the window, of course.

The set decorators captured the essence of the film in their design. I see an old sofa with a crocheted throw on the back. An oak coffee table in the center. Worn wood floors and a brick fireplace. Most of the pieces were brought in for the movie. Whoever owns this house . . . this land . . . they've kept it up.

The film is about a retired couple whose daughter has come home after leaving her husband, a troubled man. Only, he doesn't like that she left him. Things go south from there. Not exactly an original story, but a relatable one, for sure. And it's all in the execution, the direction. That's what will make this stand out.

Jesse operates one of the cameras. Lucy is nearby, ready to blot away any unsightly patches of oil from the actors' faces under the hot lights and hot sun.

A cool breeze kicks up from the west. I feel it brush against my skin and look outward. Nothing is there. No houses. No buildings. Just fenced-in farmland. In the damp air, I get a whiff of manure. It takes me back. And as I look beyond this place, to the west, I remember what used to be there. Oh, it's several miles away, but I can feel it. And it knows I'm here.

CHAPTER 2

Day three of filming and things are going smoothly. Good weather. Great cast and crew. Though I do think they're starting to understand what I mean by the corn sweats. I tried to warn them. Sleep hasn't been easy, but I manage. Even when Jesse says I look a little tired, I wave him off, insisting it's simply jet lag. But he senses something isn't quite right.

Today, more crew are scheduled to arrive, and a few locals, from what I understand. A rewrite of the first act now includes another building, so it has to be constructed. It happens from time to time. Always a good idea to hire a local who knows the area and can get contractors or materials easily.

I head down from our room into the hotel lobby to meet with Mason and Caroline. It's early. The sun isn't up yet. But when I arrive, I see a man with them. He looks local. That probably sounds meaner than I intend for it to, but I lived in Iowa for a long time. I can tell one of my own.

"Morning." I offer my hand to him.

Caroline gestures to me. "Dale, this is Kylie, our lead production assistant. You'll coordinate with her on the construction."

"Nice to meet you, miss." He shakes my hand.

"It's just Kylie," I reply. "Nice to meet you too, Dale." He looks away, almost as if he's embarrassed. Did I say something weird? He's older than I expect. Fifties, maybe? A little scruffy. Light brown hair and deep lines, folds, almost, that go right down the middle of each cheek. But he appears strong, rugged. His hand is calloused. I feel the rough skin in his greeting. Yeah, he'll do.

"Why don't you two drive out to the set?" Caroline begins. "Most of the crew is out there now. Make some introductions and help him get started."

"Of course." I smile at Dale. "You ready to go now?"

"Yes, ma'am. I got everything I need in my truck."

"Okay, then." I glance at Caroline, feeling uncertain about getting into this man's truck. She senses my apprehension.

"You know what?" Caroline says. "It's probably best you two drive separately. I may need Kylie to run some errands later."

"Suit yourself," Dale replies, and looks at me, gesturing outward. "Lead the way, Kylie."

* * *

I arrive on location. Dale pulls up next to me in his old Ford truck, painted white with a red stripe along the body. Faded, of course. A shiny metal toolbox lies across the bed. He steps out and opens the lid.

"I got quite a few tools in here, so I'm ready to get the ball rolling," he says.

"Great. Let's go up and I'll introduce you to our set builders. Mason will be here soon, so any other questions you have, he'll be able to answer for you."

"Sounds like a plan." He walks next to me. "So what do you think of this part of the country? Beautiful, isn't it?"

"Yes, it is." I look around as if seeing it for the first time. "You must live nearby."

He grunts. "Not too far away. A few miles. Been here most of my life. You?"

"Oh, I don't live here."

"I figured that," he replies.

I don't really want to get into my life's story with this guy, so I see the key grip and call out to him. "Hey, Brian."

He catches sight of me and nods. A moment later, he and his assistant, Brandon, walk over to us.

"Kylie, how's it going?" Brian asks.

"Good, thanks. This is Dale. He'll be helping out with set construction." While Dale offers a nod and a handshake, I take a moment to assess the assistant, whom I've never had the pleasure to work with. Brandon's a young guy in his mid-twenties. Muscular, stout. It's sort of a requirement for a key grip or one of the grip crew. They rig lights, move heavy equipment, set up lighting. It's a labor-intensive job and those guys are pretty easy to pick out, given the physical demands. In fact, these two look like they could be brothers. Both are sizable men.

"Is this your first location shoot, Brandon?"

"Yes, ma'am. How'd you know?"

I don't like that he calls me ma'am. Makes me feel old, but I smile. "Because you look happy to be here."

"Gee, thanks, Kylie." Brian laughs. "Don't listen to her, kid. It's not all bad."

"I'm only giving you grief," I say. "It's good to meet you. Hey, I don't suppose anyone's seen Mason yet?"

Brian scans the area. "Mike's over there. He might know." He thumbs back. "We'd better get at it. Catch up with you later?"

"Sure thing." I start out and Dale follows. I see the crewman ahead and call out to him. "Mike? Hey, you have a minute?"

He heads our way. "Sure, Kylie, what's up?"

"This is Dale, uh . . ."

"Coleman," he says. "Dale Coleman. Pleased to meet you, Mike."

The two shake hands, then Mike turns back to me. "Is he helping us out today?"

"Today, and for however long you need him, I believe. Better to check with Mason when he gets here. I'm only here to take notes. See what it is you guys need and help put together a plan and a schedule. You know Caroline."

"Oh, I do," Mike says. "No overages on her sets." He turns to Dale. "We should get started."

The two walk away and I stand there, watching Dale. Every person he meets, he offers them a smile and a tip of his head. I'm quickly reminded that this isn't L.A. People are far nicer in other parts of the country. However, I can't help but feel as though I already know him. That I've met him before. Maybe it's just me creating some amalgam of every Iowan I'd ever known, or who I thought they were. He's friendly. I can say that much.

The actors are off filming in another location today. A nearby diner. That leaves us crew to prepare for the next scenes here, which include the new building. Dale gets to work, taking measurements, jotting down notes. He slips the pencil behind his ear, making his shaggy brown hair stick out, and walks over to me.

"Everything all right?" I ask.

"Sure. But I'm gonna need a few things, so I thought I'd run out to the hardware store. Wondered if I could bring back lunch for everyone."

"Everyone?" I do a quick head count of the crew. "Well, the producers usually have lunch catered, but with the split session today, I suppose lunch will fall to me."

"Fantastic. I know a great spot not far from the hardware store."

There's that smile again.

"Come on. Take a drive with me. I'll show you 'round and we'll stop to grab food for everyone," Dale says.

I look ahead and see Mike. Jesse's at the other shoot. And while I feel slightly more at ease around Dale, trust doesn't come readily for me. "Hey, Mike." I call out. "Dale and I are going to run to the hardware store and pick up some lunch. Be back in less than an hour."

He waves at me. "All right. We got things under control here."

Great. I think to myself. At least someone will know where I am.

"Well, let's go." Dale marches on toward his truck. The driver's door creaks as he opens it.

The passenger door groans just the same as I climb inside. The vinyl bench seat is a faded red and ripped in some spots. Dale turns the engine and reaches for the floor-mounted stick shift. I never learned how to drive a stick. Aunt Grace knew how, but when I moved in with her and eventually got my driver's license, her nerves were shot. She still doesn't care for me driving her around. Never mind. Soon enough, no one will know how to drive. Everyone's car will drive all on their own. Although I'm not sure I want to be around for that either.

We head down the dirt driveway and back onto the two-lane road headed toward town. "So, tell me, Dale, what else do you do for a living?" I ask.

"Just the local handyman, mostly."

He turns to me, wearing that smile again. I'm starting to warm up to it. "Sounds a lot less stressful than my job."

"I imagine so, Kylie," he replies. "But you should be proud of your accomplishments. Folks who face adversity and such, well, they don't always have it in them to succeed. To fight for a better life."

I cast a wary eye at him. "I don't mean to be rude, Dale, but you don't know a thing about me, or what I've been through in my life."

He raises a hand in surrender. "I apologize, Kylie. I was making a general statement, more than anything else. Guess what I mean to say is that it's clear you had to fight to get where you are now. I imagine a young woman, such as yourself, had to work hard to be the big shot that you are today."

"Big shot?" I laugh. "Hardly, but . . . thanks." I see the main street up ahead. I haven't been here in years. Not that I spent much time here in any case, but it doesn't look like how I remember. Times change, thank God.

Dale pulls up into the parking space in front of the store. As he shifts into park, the gears grind. "I have got to get that looked at. A mechanic, I am not." He cuts the engine. "Want to run in with me or are you okay to wait here?"

"I'll come in. It's too hot outside." I open the door and step down. The air smells better. No scent of farm animals, just a hint of barbequed burgers and fresh cornbread from the diner across the street. The very same one where they're shooting a couple scenes.

I look over, and through the window, I can see Jesse inside. I smile.

"You know that fella?" Dale asks.

"I sure do. That's Jesse. Lead cameraman. He's my boyfriend, actually." I feel strange saying that. Not because Jesse and I are together, but because I just told a stranger we were.

"He's a lucky man," Dale says, walking inside the store.

The bell above the door dings as we enter. I get a whiff of automotive oil, sawdust, and fresh paint. Still better than the cow manure. I cast my gaze out over a few of the aisles. "What are we looking for, exactly?"

"I'll tell you what." Dale takes out a slip of paper with his list on it and rips it in half. "I'll get what's on my half. You get what's on yours. It'll go quicker."

"Fair enough." I examine the items, having no idea where to find them, but heck, I'm willing to give it a shot.

"Let me know if you two need any help finding something," the man behind the register says.

I offer a polite nod and carry on down the aisle, while Dale heads farther down the store. It's not a big place. A fraction of the size of any big city's Home Depot. I see hammers. Nails, all sizes. Duct tape. Wood glue. "Here it is." I pick up the first item — staples for a staple gun. I double-check the size and carry on to the next thing.

But at the end of the aisle, I stop on a dime where hunting knives hang all in a row. My pulse quickens and my throat dries. I blink hard, trying to stop the memory from coming, but it's a persistent invader. All-encompassing and overwhelming. Beating me into submission. Forcing me into a deep dark hole that can take days to come out of.

"Kylie?"

I gasp, spinning around. It's Dale, wearing a look of concern. How long have I been standing here? His little basket is already full of items.

"Hey, you okay?" he asks.

I look down and see one of the knives in my hand. "Jesus." I drop it. Luckily, it's still in its sheath, or I might've just lost a toe.

Dale reaches down to pick it up and return it to the shelf. "You know what? We have enough here. I can make do for now. Why don't we go and get that lunch for everyone?"

My feet feel like they're stuck in concrete. Dale's hand is on my shoulder, trying to gently push me along. The eyes of the man behind the counter are fixed on me. I take a breath, looking at Dale's face. *I know you.*

"Come on now. Let's get going," he says again, matter-of-factly.

This time, his words click in my head. Like he unlocked a door, and it's safe for me to go through it. I nod, and my feet are once again under my control.

We breeze through to the checkout counter. I stand there while Dale prepares to pay, then remember that the producers should pick up the tab. "Wait. You don't need to—"

"We'll sort it out later," he replies, handing over his credit card to the cashier.

Soon, we're back in the truck. I'm a little unsure of how I got here, but I'm starting to feel better now. It's been a long time since I felt that pull. Like something grabbed me by my ankles and tried to yank me down into the earth. And how the hell did the knife get into my hands?

"There's a little barbecue place down the end of the road here." Dale starts the truck. "Since your people are filming in the diner, I figure that'd be a good place to grab a filling lunch for the crew."

"Yeah, that sounds great," I reply.

As we drive on, I can feel Dale's glance. I'm afraid of what he might say next, fully expecting it to be related to my little incident inside the hardware store.

"Hey," he begins. "What did the exasperated man serve at his barbecue?"

I return an inquisitive gaze.

"Sheesh kabobs." He slaps the steering wheel.

The tug on my lips is unavoidable, and I can't help but laugh. Dale Coleman isn't what I expect, and I'm grateful he doesn't ask questions.

He gently elbows me, though it doesn't quite connect. "You got a good hearty laugh, Kylie. It's nice to hear."

CHAPTER 3

The mood of the shoot had changed in an instant. Filming at the diner had gone off the rails, according to Jesse. One of the actors wanted to change the script. The other got offended. The extras weren't cooperating. The entire day had been a disaster.

"What did Caroline do?" I ask, as we're sitting in the hotel bar. I'm nursing a glass of red wine, mindful of my shaky history with booze. Jesse's gone all in, drinking a shot of whiskey.

"She pulled the actors aside and knocked their heads together till they got back in line," he replies. "I'm just glad it's over."

"Tomorrow will be better," I assure him. "You know what's it like."

"Oh, I do." He looks up, the lobby doors sliding open and a few of the crew walking inside. I admit, they look worse for wear.

"How'd your day go?" he asks, returning his attention to me.

"Fine. The secondary structure is coming along, which made Mason happy." Telling him what happened in the hardware store isn't important right now. And it's not like he'd understand anyway. Better to leave it alone and move on.

Since we've been together, I've had maybe a handful of similar instances. Not quite as pronounced as what happened today, but it had thrown him for a loop, nonetheless. I would make up some excuse or other for it.

I told him I'd lost my parents in a car crash when I was a kid and that was how I ended up living with my aunt. And you know, PTSD and all that. They say the best lies are mostly true. I didn't venture too far off the fine line.

"How's that local guy working out?" Jesse asks, throwing down his second shot.

"Good. Great. He's a . . . he's a funny guy." I smile, recalling Dale's terrible dad joke. "Fast worker. Nothing I wouldn't expect from the people around here."

Jesse holds my gaze a moment. I recognize the flirty look and jerk my thumb back. "Should we head up to the room? Maybe order some room service?"

"Caroline and Monty won't pay for it," Jesse says.

I shrug. "Eh, we can swing it. Come on." I slide off the raised bar stool and offer my hand. He willingly accepts and we walk toward the elevators, passing by a few of the crew. "Night, guys. We're heading up. See you in the morning."

A few rumbles of acknowledgment and we were off. Yeah, the mood had changed, but I've been around this long enough to know that tomorrow, all will be forgiven.

We arrive at our room on the top floor. Jesse swipes the key card and opens the door for me. Stepping inside, he secures the lock and stops, fixing his gaze on me again.

"What?" I ask, suddenly feeling self-conscious.

"I love you, Kylie. You know that, right?"

My heart softens at his words. "Of course I do. And I love you, too." I wrap my arms around his neck. "Tomorrow will be better. I promise."

"It always is."

He lifts me off the ground until only my toes brush the low-pile beige carpet. I feel weightless in his arms as he walks us toward the bed. We've been together a while, and we're not twenty anymore, so that initial period of lustful lovemaking has transformed into something deeper.

He gently lays me on the bed and climbs on top. His hand cups my breast over my shirt, and he presses his lips firmly against mine. God, I love this man. I actually think he's the one. Yet how can I have a life with him if he doesn't even know my real name?

* * *

Is that the sun hitting my eyes? I snatch my phone from the bedside table and look at the time. Holy shit. "Jesse?" I shake his arm. "Babe, wake up. We're late."

"What?" He rubs the sleep from his eyes and squints at the time on his phone. "Damn it. How the hell . . ." He jumps up from the bed, pulling on his clothes.

There's no time for a shower. Caroline will be pissed that we're late. How did that even happen? I had my alarm set. Never mind now. We have to hustle. "Jesse, let's go," I call out to him while he's in the bathroom.

I grab whatever clothes I can find that aren't completely wrinkled and toss them onto the bed. As I pull off my night-shirt to change, I see my sneakers by the door. Thinking back a moment, I was sure I'd put them in the closet last night. I did have a couple glasses of wine, so I could've been mistaken. Except . . . they're dirty. Dried mud on the soles.

The bathroom door swings open, and I whip around to see Jesse, who's already dressed. "I need five minutes," I tell him.

"You have two," he replies, stepping out of my path.

I walk into the bathroom and splash water on my face, pushing aside the shoe distraction. My phone is next to me, and it pings with an incoming text. I only glance at the notification, but see that it's Caroline. "Jess, she's texting. We have to move."

"You're the one still in the bathroom," he shouts back at me.

He's right. I quickly pull back my thick brown hair, wrapping it into a low bun. I look at my makeup bag. "Screw it." But on second thought . . . I reach for it, taking it in case I have a few minutes when we're on set. "Okay, I'm ready," I say, stepping back into the room.

"Me, too." Jesse shoves his wallet into the back pocket of his jeans and opens the door. "You look great. Now, let's go."

"Sure I do." I smirk, heading out the door.

We drive together today, knowing the shoot is back at the farmhouse. Several text messages arrive on both our phones, but we ignore them. "We'll be there soon enough," I say to him.

Jesse has his foot pressing so hard on the gas, it's practically on the floor. The landscape of fields and grass flies by my window, and the high clouds whisk overhead. My nerves begin to settle when I see the house appear in the distance. I check the time again. "We're only half an hour late. Hopefully, Caroline won't freak out."

But I notice something as Jesse makes the turn, heading up the long dirt driveway. "Why is everyone standing around?"

"Maybe we're not the only ones who are late," he replies.

That's always a possibility. Actors are notoriously temperamental. Maybe someone's still holding a grudge. But as we reach the parking area, I realize this is something else. When Jesse stops, we get out of the car. I can hear the rumblings, but can't make out any words. Too many people are talking. And the look on their faces . . . "What the hell's going on?"

Jesse takes my arm. "I don't know."

I feel my pulse quicken, because I begin to recognize the look on the crew's faces. I see Dale off to the side, talking with the other set builders. Lucy stands there, alone, clasping her arms as if she's cold, yet it's almost eighty degrees out here.

"Sorry we're late," I say as we approach Caroline.

"I texted you," she replies, her tone unyielding.

"Yeah, sorry about that." I didn't bother making up an excuse because I don't think it would've mattered anyway. "Caroline, is everything okay?"

She looks at me, then at Jesse. Her red-rimmed eyes glisten. "It's Brandon . . . he's dead."

Brandon? The key grip's assistant? I tilt my head, skewing the world around me as my vision narrows. "Oh my God. What happened? Was it an accident?"

Jesse wraps his arm around me, pulling me close. "Caroline, for God's sake. How did this happen?"

Sirens wail in the distance. The crew peers out at the road, anticipating the arrival of what I assume are the police. I watch their faces, but all I see is shock cloaking their expressions like a mask.

"He was murdered, Kylie," Caroline says in a whisper. "Inside the house. Someone killed him."

Her words ring in my ears. I've heard them plenty of times before. Murder. Death. Killings. I've heard them all, but not in a very long time. Something propels me forward. I brush past everyone as they simply stare at me. No one says a word.

"Kylie, don't."

I hear Jesse's footfalls, trying to catch up to me.

"Babe, what are you doing? Come back. The police will handle this. You don't need to . . ."

"Stop." I whip around to him. "Yes . . . I do. I need to see him. I have to know what happened." He concedes, and I press on, walking up the porch steps. The front door is open.

"Kylie, what the hell are you doing?"

It's Mason. I stop only feet from him. "Have you seen him?"

"Yeah, and trust me, you don't want to. Jesse's right. Let the cops take care of this. There's nothing you can do for him now."

I step over the threshold, seeing Dale from the corner of my eye. He says nothing to me, so I walk inside. Two crew members stand over the body. Brandon, a goddam kid. Barely twenty-five. He's on the floor in the kitchen, lying in a crimson pool.

"Don't come any closer, Kylie."

I turn my head toward Brian, the key grip.

"You shouldn't be in here. We can't risk messing things up for the cops."

I look down at Brandon. His mouth is hanging open. His throat is sliced from ear to ear. My stomach turns as nausea swirls. The sting of fresh tears forces me to blink. "Oh my God." But it's his eyes that make me want to gag and sob all at once. "Who did this to him?"

The other crewman, Holton, takes me by the arms and ushers me outside. "Come on, Kylie. You don't need to see this."

I need the fresh air. Jesse rushes to me. "I got you, babe. Come on." He takes over for Holton, helping me back down the porch steps. I hear their cries . . . the rest of the crew. The actors. Everyone. They echo in my ears, growing louder and louder.

The police are here. The lights flash on their cars. No more sirens, though. Four of them step out, all in uniform. And then, another man emerges, dressed in a suit. A detective? Probably.

Caroline and Monty approach them. They're all talking. Caroline aims a finger toward the house.

I stand there, Jesse at my side, watching their conversation, but unable to hear the words clearly. Then I feel something, or someone. I look to my right. Dale is staring at me. We lock eyes.

My gaze breaks off when I see Caroline walking toward us. She extends her arms as if trying to pull us all together.

"Okay, guys." She waits while we all form a tight circle around her. "The cops are going to take statements from all of us. They said we need to stay here for as long as necessary to make that happen. And we'll do that . . . for Brandon."

"What about the shoot?" Neil, one of the sound engineers, seems to regret asking the question by the look on his face.

"That's not our top concern right now," Caroline says. "The safety of this cast and crew is my top priority. We'll do as the police ask." She looks at Monty and Mason. "We'll figure out the rest later."

We all stay in the circle. No more words. Only cries and soft sobs. I see Lucy dabbing her eyes with a tissue. I haven't said a word to her yet. She must be terrified. They all look terrified. I know I am.

I feel Jesse's warmth as the heat of the day rises. It's like he's holding me together. I'm afraid if he loosens his grip, I'll fall into pieces on the ground. The thing is, he doesn't know how much I need him in this moment. Because what I saw in there . . . Brandon's eyes. I've seen it before. This can't be happening. Not again.

CHAPTER 4

The body is taken away in an ambulance. I watch it drive off into the distance, not fully believing any of this is real. Police are inside, keeping us at bay with strips of yellow caution tape wrapped around the porch columns. I'm numb to the heat and humidity as I turn my attention to the others. Tears streak their faces. Their bodies tremble amid restrained sobs.

Standing here now, outside the farmhouse, the green grass brushing against my ankles, all I see is Brandon's face. And his eyes. Someone knows I'm here, and this is how they've chosen to make themselves known to me. But then, why not come for me directly? Why kill an innocent man?

I glance down and catch sight of my shoes, then recall my sneakers and the mud on the soles. The ground around me is dry. Not sure when was the last time they had rain here, but it must've been a few days. I still don't understand how . . .

Jesse rubs my arm. "You okay?"

I look up again, the setting sun glaring in my eyes. "Yeah. I mean, no, but I guess I'll be okay."

We're all still here. Each of us, giving our statements to the police. And now, I see the detective approaching. I'm next.

"I'm staying right here with you," Jesse insists. "I don't care what the cops say."

I shake away my lingering doubts. "Thank you."

The detective holds a small spiral notebook. He's old school. Tough exterior. The kind of cop I'd expect to hail from New York or Boston, not from here.

"Ms. Forbes? Kylie Forbes?" the detective asks.

"That's me."

"You mind if we have a word — alone?" He side-eyes Jesse.

"I'd prefer to stay close," Jesse says. "If you don't mind, Detective . . ."

"Burns," he replies. "Doug Burns. And, respectfully, I do mind. It's important for me to speak to all of you individually, just so there's no undue influence, even unrealized."

"It's okay, babe." I squeeze Jesse's hand. "I'll be fine."

With obvious reluctance, Jesse steps away, walking toward Lucy and a few others who've already been crossed off the cops' witness list. I look at the detective. "Better?"

"Sorry, miss. It's just the way it has to be." He reaches into his pocket for a pen and opens his notebook. "Kylie Forbes."

"Yes, sir." I fold my arms, a chill running through me that has nothing to do with the weather.

"I understand you and your . . . friend, Jesse Cooper, were late today. I asked around, seems it's unusual for you . . . for both of you."

"Yeah, uh, my alarm didn't go off this morning," I reply. "Or I didn't hear it. Jesse was with me. I woke him up and we hurried down here. About half an hour late, I guess it was."

He put pen to paper, jotting down something. "You from around here, Kylie?"

"No, sir. I live in Los Angeles. Most of us here do. We're filming a movie. I'm a production assistant."

"I gathered." His eyes seem glued to his notebook as he continues to scribble. Finally, he looks up again. "Have you ever lived here, Kylie?"

What kind of question is this? And why does it matter? I hesitate, considering making up a story, but instead, I choose to leave out a few details. "Yes, sir. My family is originally from Des Moines. I moved away when I was thirteen. Why do you ask?"

He frowns, shaking his head. "No reason." Burns casts his gaze toward the house, studying it for a while.

I shift my weight from one leg to the other, knowing damn well he has a reason. Cops aren't known for their idle chit-chat.

"Did you know the victim?" The detective keeps his gaze ahead as if avoiding me. The question hangs in the air until he returns his attention. "Ms. Forbes?"

"Brandon was a good person, Detective. I didn't know him well, in fact, this was our first film together, but it didn't take long to notice he was always the first to offer help. I can't imagine anyone wanting to hurt him. Especially in that way."

Burns raises his brow. "You saw the body?"

"Uh, I did, yes." I glance down for a moment.

"I was led to believe the three people inside the house were the ones who called it in. You were late. You'd been told what happened. So, why did you go inside? Did you touch anything?"

I feel like I'm in trouble now. "No, sir. I didn't get that close. I just . . . I don't know, I guess I needed to see him." He jots something else in his little notebook. I can't see what it is, but I imagine it doesn't put me in a good light.

Burns puts away his notebook and pen. "Can I see your phone?"

"I'm sorry?"

"You don't have to give it over. I'm just asking." He extends his hand, palm upturned. "Can I see your phone, Ms. Forbes?"

"Yeah, I guess so." I reach into my back pocket to retrieve it.

"Unlock it, please."

"Sure." I hold it to my face to unlock the screen, then hand it over. "Here you go."

He opens my messages. He's looking for something. What? Was it because I saw Brandon's body? I don't recognize him. I have no idea who this guy is, other than a local cop. I'm not even sure what jurisdiction. We're nearest to Carroll, but I'm pretty sure it's county sheriff's territory out here. Then again, I'm no expert, and I don't intend to ask him.

"Thank you." Burns hands back the phone.

I want to ask him if he found what he was looking for, but being a smart ass right now would be a mistake. "Of course. Is that all, Detective?"

"Go on," he says. "We're good here. For now."

* * *

It's late. The cops have finally finished talking to everyone. We're all back at the hotel bar. No one says much, except the occasional ordering of more drinks. I'm on my third, and I feel myself sliding down that slippery slope once more, not really caring about that at the moment. Shock has turned into grief. We all feel Brandon's loss.

Caroline clears her throat, drawing everyone's attention. "We've been asked to halt production for the foreseeable future," she says. "I don't know what exactly that means, but I'm guessing the next several days, at least."

"Several days?"

All eyes turn to Lucy, who asked the question we all want the answer to. She sets down her glass of wine. "You mean, we're actually going to keep filming?"

"At some point," Caroline says with reluctance. "Lucy, we've got millions on the line here. The backers . . . they want . . ."

"Do they know what happened?" Lucy cuts her off, disgust in her tone.

Caroline glances at Monty. "Yes, they do. Look, guys, we're going to take this day by day, all right? We need a little time to figure things out. Monty and I will be talking to the accountants. The cops, well, I don't know what their plan is, other than to figure out who did this to Brandon."

"Are we in danger?"

I'd had my attention on Caroline and didn't see who asked the question, so I look around. That's when I see Dale. His eyes are on Caroline. Why is he chiming in at all? He's an outsider. Well, technically, he's not; we are. But he's not part of this. He didn't know Brandon.

"The police are looking into Brandon's history," Caroline says. "I don't know any more than that. Do I think we're in any danger?" I see a flash of hesitation in her eyes before she answers. "No. And our goal is to get back to work as soon as they let us."

Chairs screech on the floor as some of the crew begin to leave. I don't think any of us want to be here now. Caroline's going to have an uphill battle keeping the production going. We could all leave and she'd have no choice. But that's not how we operate. We're a family, and one of our own is gone.

In the back of my mind, I know I should say something to the cops, but it simply can't be connected. They're all gone. In jail or dead. But that Detective Burns . . . I wonder how long it'll take for him to figure me out. And what will happen when he does?

* * *

A sliver of moonlight cuts across my eye. The glare comes through our hotel room window. Jesse snores gently, the way he does when he's had a little too much to drink, like tonight. I didn't get on his case for it, though. After all, who am I to judge?

The heaviness in my chest still weighs me down. Guilt. Sadness. Fear. I don't know what to think, so I get up. My mouth is like cotton. Too much wine, but I'm sober now. I grab my phone, cupping my hand over the screen to shield the light. It's one in the morning. We don't have to be up early tomorrow. There's nothing to do. No scenes to shoot. We'll all be sitting in the diner or in the hotel bar, wondering what the hell is happening. But I can't do that. I have to try to make sense of this, if that's possible.

Dale Coleman enters my thoughts. Who is this guy, really? He acts like he's everyone's best buddy. He's been on set . . . what, a couple days? Then Brandon is brutally murdered? Maybe he didn't do it, but is it possible he knows who did?

I stand in the darkness, glancing over to see Jesse still asleep. It only takes a couple of beers, and he'll be out for the night. I like that he's not a big drinker. There was a time when I was. Not anymore, though I have to remind myself of that. My clothes lay folded over the desk chair. I take them in my arms.

Quietly stepping into the bathroom, I close the door, cringing as it clicks shut. The light stings my eyes when I flick it on. My reflection looks back at me, judgmental as hell. *Yeah, I know.*

Once dressed, I run a brush through my hair before turning off the light again. Darkness envelopes me. Tears spill down my cheeks. It's time.

The hotel corridor is dead silent. The velvety carpet feels soft on my bare feet till I slip on my shoes. I don't think Jesse heard me leave. The lights on the walls burn low as I walk by, heading toward the elevators.

Making my way to the lobby, I see it's empty, so I keep on walking until the doors part and I step outside into the darkness. Warm, damp air penetrates my skin. There's that moon again. Bright and full. And a clear sky. There's a convenience store not far from here. I feel a little hungry, so I drive there and run inside for a bag of peanuts and a Diet Coke. It's then I realize I hadn't eaten at all yesterday. Or is it still today? I don't know, and it doesn't really matter.

I want to go back. I want to see the farmhouse. Maybe the cops missed something. Maybe whoever killed Brandon is there, waiting for one of us to show up again. Who am I kidding? Waiting for *me* to show up. I don't know what the hell I want, except that I don't want to return to the hotel.

I could go back to where it happened. It's not far from here. The place where my life was ripped apart. Jesus, why the hell would I put myself through that?

I don't know. But I can't sit here and do nothing. Brandon's dead and it might be my fault.

The two-lane road is pitch-black. Not a streetlight to be found. Nothing but a full moon and my headlights. Jesse will be pissed if he finds out.

Don't tell him, then.

I could turn on the radio. Fill the car with meaningless noise to help keep my mind off where I'm going, and what I'm doing. Instead, I mull it over in dead silence. Rethinking every detail. I know now it was a mistake taking this job. When Lucy told me about it, I was excited. Until she mentioned the location shoots. Four weeks, maybe less. No biggie, right? And I needed not only the money, but the experience. I'm on my way up, or so I tell myself. And really, what were the odds? I scoff, never imagining someone else I knew would be murdered, and in a strikingly similar way to . . .

Still fighting back the tears, I wipe my eyes with the back of my hand, blurring my vision for just a moment. And then . . . a flicker. I glance into the rearview mirror. No one's there. Ahead of me . . . no one. I'm alone out here, right?

My phone's GPS shows I'm getting close now. I struggle to remember exactly where it is. I was just a kid when it all happened, but I sense a heaviness around me. The road sign reads only another mile. And when I arrive, I pull onto the dirt road. Ahead of me . . . nothing.

I get out of the car, leaving on the headlights to see. They shine far into the distance, illuminating the concrete and burned wood remnants. My feet crunch on top of the gravel as I walk on.

The air feels thin, like I can't suck enough of it into my lungs. A shiver crawls up my spine, tingling the back of my neck. I'm not alone out here, after all. The dead are with me.

Muffled shrieks pierce the walls inside the study room. I get up from my chair. The other kids do, too. We were supposed to be studying for a math test, but something's happening. "What was that?" I ask.

My friend, Michelle, grabs my arm. "Is someone hurt? Should we get your dad?"

I look around. "Where did Ms. Franchuk go?" I start to walk out of the room by myself.

"I'll come with you," Michelle insists.

"No. I'll go. Stay here with everyone else. I'll be right back." They all look up to me. I'm Clarence's daughter, after all. So, I walk into the hallway, craning left, then right. No one's around, but I hear the commotion, and more screams inside the sterile building.

I run toward the sound, heading straight to the grown-ups' meeting room. It's coming from that direction. When I arrive, I stop as the door flies open. "Dad?" He emerges. Wild-eyed. Erratic. Blood on his hands. Blood everywhere. "Dad, are you okay? What happened?" I try to peek around him, to see inside the room, but he grabs me, spinning me around. "Kayla . . . run."

I pull in a sharp breath, staring off into the distance at the building that's no longer there. Dad had called me by my real name. The sound of it . . . almost foreign to me now. But I did run that day. I ran as fast as I could. So did my dad. But eventually, someone came for us.

I turn around, my tears, uncontrollable now. I'd spent years in therapy trying not to think about this place, yet I return. What a stupid, stupid thing to do. What did I hope to gain? Did I think I'd find Brandon's killer out here?

"Maybe," I say.

I return to the car when I hear a sound. My heart jumping into my throat, I spin around, searching for the source of the noise. "Who's there?" I yell into the void.

Just get in the car and go.

Without awaiting a reply, I jump inside, turning the engine. Thrusting the gearshift into drive, I slam my foot on the gas pedal. The car lurches, the tires spin on the gravel, until finally, it moves, driving right through the plume of dust it created.

The steering wheel feels loose in my hand, so I try to regain control of the car as I reach the roadway again. Still, no one else is around. No other headlights, but I'm certain someone was watching me. I know I heard something. But I also know not to stick around long enough to find out.

CHAPTER 5

Dale

If there's one thing this town needs, it's money. And those movie folks . . . they were spending it like there was no tomorrow. I was grateful they offered me work, but there's no work for me today, or for the foreseeable future after that tragedy. So I'm sitting in the diner, sipping on a cup of coffee that's not nearly strong enough for my liking. Place is damn near empty. Then again, it usually is. We're just far enough away from Sioux City and Des Moines to have little in the way of jobs in this town. Even less in the way of population. It's mostly farmland. Not sure why I've stayed here as long as I have. But who am I kidding? I know I have to stay.

Taking another sip from my mug, I see that detective outside the window. The one who talked to all of us yesterday. Burns, was it? Manning PD covers our little outpost. They sent him to investigate the murder. And I doubt any one of them over there ever seen a dead body, except that guy. We look about the same age. All these other officers are young kids, though most have grown up around here. Doubt they remember what happened twenty years ago. But this guy, Burns? I'll bet he does.

He's still sitting in his car, looking at his phone. The damn sun's reflecting off the hood, so I squint, keeping my eyes on him as he finally steps out, adjusting that cheap black jacket he's wearing. *It's summer, you idiot. You'll roast in that thing.*

The little bell dings as the door opens and he steps inside. He pulls off his sunglasses like he's Tom goddam Cruise. A little long in the tooth for that kind of swagger, you ask me. Man looks more like Sipowicz from that old cop show, *NYPD Blue,* than he does Tom Cruise. By a whole country mile, as a matter of fact. And when his gaze lands on me, I figure I'm the reason he's come. No one else in here. No one else part of the movie, anyway.

My fingers wrap around the handle of my coffee mug, and I raise it to my lips, my eyes never leaving his as he walks on over. I set it down again, swallowing the black coffee I know's been sitting in the pot for a few hours. Just has that old taste to it.

"Morning," I say.

"It's Mr. Coleman, right?" He shows me his badge. "Detective Burns."

"I remember." Gesturing across the table, I continue, "Have a seat, Detective. You want a coffee or something?"

But before he has a chance to answer me, the server, a young girl who looks like this is her summer job, approaches wearing a forced smile. "Good morning. What can I get you?" With her pen and notepad in hand, she eyes the detective.

I already said I wasn't hungry. Truth be told, I don't really like the food here. Only came here cause I got nothing else to do.

"Just a coffee for me, thanks. Cream and sugar, please," Burns replies.

"You got it. I'll be right back." She looks at me again. "You need a refill, sir?"

I shake my head, placing my hand over my cup. The universal sign for 'no thanks.' She walks away, and I swear I hear her mumble an obscenity, but I'm not bothered by it. She's just a kid working for tips, and she won't get much from this table.

"So, Detective Burns, you figure out what happened to that young man yet?" The question comes off a little colder than I mean for it to. Like I don't really give a shit, but that's not true. Not true at all.

"Not yet," he says, eying the girl as she returns with his coffee. "Thank you, miss." He grabs a couple of sugar packs and dumps them in. When she walks away, he sets his gaze on me again. "You've lived here a long time, haven't you?"

"Yes, sir, I have."

He frowns while stirring his coffee. "You remember about twenty years ago . . . what happened at the New Hope compound?"

I grunt. "Course I do. And what happened after."

"Yep," he says. "Mind you, lots of bigger happenings around the world at the time sort of drowned out much of the press in the aftermath. Small town. A few deaths. They had bigger fish to fry, I suppose."

I'm not sure what he's getting at, but I decide to wait it out, keeping my mouth shut.

"I bring this up because, well, not many people know how Lucas Shaw died," he continues. "So imagine my surprise seeing that poor kid yesterday with his throat slit and his eyes gouged out . . . with a fork, no less."

"Suppose you can find just about anything on the internet, though, huh?" I ask, taking a sip of my coffee.

"Sure. That's probably true. Seems a lot of work to dredge all that up again," Burns adds. "Can't for the life of me figure out why. Any thoughts?" He raises his brow and draws his mug to his lips, slurping on the coffee.

The sound grates on my nerves, and I know he's doing it on purpose. Burns is trying to get to me, but why? "Got no clue, Detective. Far as I know, all those people — Shaw's followers — either died, killed themselves, or are in prison right now."

"That's my understanding too. Makes me wonder, though." He pauses, licking his lips, drawing out the suspense, by the look of it. "Why now? Why those Hollywood types who aren't even from around here? They have no idea about any of this, I suspect."

"Probably wouldn't have chosen to come here to shoot their movie if they did," I say. "You planning on telling them?"

"Don't know yet. I'm still trying to piece this together." He eyes me again. "You?"

I raise my hands. "Look, Detective, no one in this town or the next town over wants to relive what happened back then. As far as I'm concerned, that shit's in the rearview, you understand? Now, as far as this murder goes, I'd be focusing on the fact it's probably an inside job. Someone who did a little bit of research on the internet. Can't put anything past those Hollywood folks, you know?" I sip on my coffee again. "Cause you can be certain, no one from around here wants New Hope's past to be resurrected. Not a chance in hell."

"So you think keeping quiet about it is gonna help with this investigation?" Burns asks.

"I have no idea if it'll help you or not. Fact of the matter is, if those movie folks were smart, they'd shut it all down and get the hell out of Dodge. Lord knows there's plenty of old farmhouses in Nebraska or some shit where they could shoot this film."

Burns reaches into his back pocket and pulls out his wallet. Opening it up, he stares at it, flipping through the bills inside. Finally, he takes out a twenty and drops it on the table. "Appreciate the company, Mr. Coleman. Have yourself a good day."

I watch him scoot out of the booth with some effort. He's not a man who's in shape. As he takes to his feet, he looks at me again. "Do you happen to recall whether those who died had any other family that lived here?"

I raise my eyes to the ceiling, trying to harken back to those dark few days. "No, sir. Not that I can recall." I return my gaze to him. "If they did, I can guarantee you, those folks would've changed their names by now."

He chuckles. "Probably right about that. Thank you again, Mr. Coleman."

He walks outside, stops, looks around, and then returns to his car. I look at the twenty-dollar bill on the table. Two cups of coffee run about seven-fifty, so that little girl got a good tip after all.

I lean back in the booth and watch him drive away. No telling what today is going to bring. And it's hard to imagine those producers are going to be willing to hang tight just to see if the cops, Burns among them, let them start filming again. But to be honest, who the hell would want to get back to work after what happened?

Money spends the same here as it does in Hollywood, and they do still owe me. So, I get up and nod to the server. "Have a good day, miss." She smiles in return. I head outside, straight to my truck.

I drive to the hotel where they're all holed up. I feel kind of bad for asking, but they do owe me a couple hundred bucks, plus materials. And I'm retired, gotta watch those pennies, so I'm gonna need to collect.

It's the only chain hotel we have nearby. Good location, right by the entrance to the highway that leads straight out of town. No real reason to come here, other than to break up a long drive to Des Moines, maybe northeast to Chicago.

I walk into the lobby and see a few of the crew hanging around, drinking at the bar. Christ, it's barely noon. Then I remember what happened to their friend and cut them some slack.

But I'm not here to see these people. I need to see Mason or Caroline. They run the show and get the checks signed, no doubt. I don't see them hanging around and figure they're probably in their rooms. So I approach the front desk where I recognize the lady behind it. I smile and nod.

"Dale," she says. "What are you doing here?"

"Hey there, Amy. How you doing?"

"Well," she looks around. "Given what's happened, okay, I guess. What can I do for you?"

"I need to see Caroline or Mason. You know if they're here?"

She looks at her computer, punching a few of the keys. "I think they're all here, to be honest. Such a shame what happened."

"Yes, ma'am," I reply.

"It does appear they're still in their rooms. Cleaners were told to come back later, so I figure that's where they are."

I consider how to go about this. "I don't suppose you can call Mason for me? Tell him I'm down here and need to have a word."

She picks up the phone. "I'll give it a shot." Amy waits with the phone at her ear. I can hear the ringing. She must have it turned up pretty loudly. "Yes, sir. Sorry to bother you, but Mr. Coleman is here in the lobby. He asked if he could speak to you." She nods. "Okay. Great. Thank you so much. Uh huh, bye-bye now." She looks at me. "He asked if you could give him a couple minutes, and then he'll be down."

"That's great. Thanks, Amy. I appreciate it." I set my sights on the bar. "Maybe I'll go grab myself a pop." I walk over to the small bar area that could hold maybe twenty people on a good day.

A few of the crew are sitting at the high-top tables, sipping on some cold brews. I pull up a stool and nod to the bartender, who I figure isn't used to working in the middle of a weekday. "Can I get a pop, please?"

"Yes, sir."

I scan the room in search of Kylie, but I don't see her. Don't see her boyfriend either. Jesse . . . something or other.

"Here you go."

The bartender sets down the glass and right away I see the pop's flatter than a pancake, but am I gonna say something? No, course not. This is Iowa. We're not a confrontational people. "Thank you." I take a sip. Yep. It's flat. But as I smile at the barman in appreciation of this joyless beverage, I see a sizable bruise on his upper arm. Fresh, too. "Yikes. Where'd you get that thing? Fall down a flight of stairs?"

"Oh, yeah." He glances at it and chuckles. "Something like that."

I hear some chatter behind me and turn around. It's Kylie and her boyfriend. She and I lock eyes for a moment, then she starts walking toward me.

"Dale, hi. What are you doing here?"

"Needed to see Mason. He's coming down in a minute. How are you? Holding up all right?" I see hesitation in her eyes. She's preparing to lie to me.

"Yeah, I'm okay. Feel like we're all in limbo around here."

"I can see that," I reply. "Still no decision on whether you're gonna keep filming?"

"No, nothing yet. Monty's getting anxious, though."

"He's the money guy, isn't that right?" I ask.

"That's right."

She smiles at me, polite, friendly. But it's a front. Doesn't take a genius to see it. "Do you want to go back home? Back to Los Angeles?" *Oh, shit.* Probably shouldn't have said that.

CHAPTER 6

Kylie

For a moment, I wonder if I'd heard him right. He did ask if I was going back to L.A. The thing is, I never once mentioned where I live. On the other hand, it's a perfectly logical assumption, given my job. Why wouldn't he think I lived there?

I'm still tired and chalk up my concern to paranoia. This morning's ill-advised drive out to the compound is making me question everything, including whether or not I was being watched out there.

"I'm not sure what I want right now," I say, brushing off his comment, which will stick in the back of my mind until I can make sense of it. "My heart's just broken over what happened."

"I have no doubt," he says, sipping on his drink.

I think it's a soda, but for all I know, there could be some whiskey in there. I don't smell it on him, but I wouldn't blame him if there was. Neither of us is working today. Hell, maybe I should have a drink too. Then I remember . . . I need to reel that in.

I see Mason out of the corner of my eye and glance over. He looks like shit. We all do. Dale catches sight of him too as he swivels in the bar stool.

"Mason." Dale offers a hand. "Sorry to bother you today. I imagine you got plenty on your plate to deal with."

Mason shakes Dale's hand and looks at me. "Kylie."

"Hey." I'm a third wheel, so I nod politely. "Take care, Dale. See you soon." I turn to Mason and offer a closed-lip smile before walking away.

Jesse's waiting for me at one of the tables. I sit down next to him. "What do you think?"

"About what?" he asks.

"About whether or not we're going to keep production going. I mean, I need to work and if not here, then we should think about going home." I look around, feeling like going home would be the best thing anyway. And as my gaze reaches the elevators, I see the doors open. Caroline steps off and Monty is next to her. "Hang on. Look who's coming."

Jesse spins around. "She's with Monty. That has to mean something."

I feel a hand on my shoulder and look to my left. "Lucy. Hi."

"Hi. I see Caroline's coming. You think she has some answers?"

"I think we're about to find out." I pat the seat next to me. "Sit down."

"Thanks. Hey, Jesse," she says.

"Hey, Lucy. You get any sleep last night?"

"Not much. I doubt any of us did." She leans over the table and drops her tone. "Do you guys know who ended up telling Brandon's parents what happened?"

"I haven't heard," I reply. "But it was probably the cops. Maybe Caroline." I set my sights on Caroline and Monty as they walk toward those of us sitting in the bar. Probably half the crew is in here. All of us waiting for the same answers.

"Guys, if I can have your attention." Caroline scans the room. "Where's everyone else?"

"Probably in their rooms," Jesse blurts out.

"Right. Okay, so Monty and I have been talking with the studio. The banks. Pretty much everyone involved in our production. I told them we got approval from the local police to continue shooting at the farmhouse. They've cleared the scene and tell us we can go back to work while they continue with their investigation."

A scattering of whispers sound all around me. Everyone seems just as surprised as I am. I peer over my shoulder at Mason, who's still talking to Dale. It doesn't look like he's aware of this development either. Then I look at Dale again. He doesn't seem happy, which is strange, because he should be. Work for us means work for him. Still, I understand. He looks like the type of guy who's seen a lot. I know a little something about that. So maybe he doesn't think this is such a good idea. To be honest, I don't either.

* * *

I step out of the shower, wrapping the towel around me. Steam covers the bathroom mirror while Jesse stands at the vanity, brushing his teeth. He can't see his reflection, but it doesn't seem to bother him.

It turns out, Caroline didn't want to waste any more time, so she scheduled scene blocking this evening. Jesse and I went back to our rooms. Everyone did. And we started getting cleaned up.

Neither of us are in much of a mood to talk. The idea of going back inside that house . . . well, I'm glad I don't own it, or have to live there. Not sure I could stomach it.

Jesse turns back to look at me. His blond hair is still wet, the curls dripping onto his shoulders. He's also wrapped in a towel from the waist down. I drink in the view. His firm chest. Broad shoulders. Warm and gentle blue eyes. But then I sense he wants to ask me something. I can practically see the question forming on his lips.

Impatiently, I jump in, "What is it?"

He leans back against the vanity sink. "Did you . . . go somewhere last night after I fell asleep?"

I guess I wasn't as stealthy as I thought. If he knew where I went, he'd want to know why. And that part . . . I simply couldn't tell him. Ever.

"I was going to ask earlier, but I don't know . . ." He takes in a deep breath. "This has all just been so hard to take, you know?"

I did know. Better than most. "I went for a drive, yes. I couldn't sleep." So far, I think he believes me. Like always, the best lies are rooted in some truth. "I knew you'd worry, so I didn't bother waking you. I'm sorry. Please don't be upset."

"I'm not upset. Worried, sure." He walks toward me, sliding his hands on my hips. "But Kylie, we have no idea what happened to Brandon, or who killed him. Going out for a drive in the middle of the night?" He shakes his head. "It's not safe. Not until they catch whoever did this."

"You're right," I concede. "I won't do it again."

"I'm not saying you have to stay here, I'm just saying . . . maybe next time, let me come with you, yeah?"

I nod and smile. "Of course. We should finish up. We're due to start in an hour." I can feel his disappointment as he turns back to the sink. He doesn't believe me. Not fully. He thinks I'm holding something back, which, of course, I absolutely am.

Dad told me to run, but all I can do is stand here, staring at the blood on his hands. Chaos erupts around me, and I can hear men shouting. Women screaming. "Where's Mom?" I ask him. He looks crazy to me. "Dad? Where's Mom? Is she okay?" I have to yell at him because there's so much noise around me.

"Kayla, you have to leave. Right now. Go home. Take your brother and sister," Dad says, looking back into the room.

I finally listen to him and spin around, running back to find the rest of my family. We're all here. Somewhere. In the halls, I see men running by me. They hardly notice I'm there. Everyone is panicking. I push through the door, into the room, where my brother and sister are. "Katie, Kyle, Dad says we have to leave. Now." I'm the oldest, so I round them up, ignoring the kids around us. If Dad says to go, then that's what we have to do. "Come on. Hurry." I get them out the door, taking each one by the hand. We run. Fast.

Outside, the sun shines in my eyes. It's quiet out here. They're all inside, trying to figure out what's going on. I wish someone would tell me. Dad . . . he's done something terrible, I just don't know what. And then, thank God, I see her. "Mom!"

She's running toward us. "We're going to be okay now. Mom's here," I tell my siblings. But the look on her face . . . "Mom, what's going on?" I ask when she reaches us. "Dad said to leave. Where?"

"Go home," she says in a panic. "Pack a bag."

"Why?" I hear Katie start to sob. I look at my mom again. "What did he do, Mom? What did Dad do?"

Black tears stain her cheeks. She's trembling and looks at all of us. "Lucas is gone. Now, go. We're leaving this place. For good."

* * *

The sun is low, almost set. It looks beautiful behind the old farmhouse. The sky, painted in orange and red, is dotted with a few puffy clouds. It almost feels normal. But as Jesse and I get out of the car, I see everyone else. They're just standing outside, milling around like they don't know what to do.

"Caroline should've at least waited until tomorrow," I say. "Look at everyone. No one wants to be here."

He walks over to me. "She might not have had a choice, Kylie. We both know how this business goes. Money is everything."

"Yeah, I know." We start walking up to the house. Jesse holds my hand. "But I have to think that the studio is shitting their pants right now, afraid of being liable for what happened to Brandon."

"They might be," he says. "But that's up to the lawyers to figure out." Jesse stops and squares up to me. "Look, babe.

We don't have to do this. We can go home. Yeah, I get the money's good, but if this is too much . . ."

"No," I cut in. "I don't want to abandon these guys. I didn't know Brandon that well, but I imagine he wouldn't have wanted that either. We all believe in this project. I want to see it through." We start walking again. "Besides, we won't be here for too long. Then, we can go back to L.A. to wrap up." He squeezes my hand, a reassuring gesture that gives me the strength I need to push through this.

I see Lucy sitting on the porch steps and we stop in front of her. "Hey."

"Hey," she replies. "I can't get myself to go inside."

I look beyond her. The front door is open. Brandon's lifeless body flashes before my eyes. "Is she in there? Caroline?"

Lucy nods. "I don't even know why I'm here. No one needs me tonight. We're only blocking."

I shrug. "She probably just wants everyone together. I don't know."

"Hey, babe," Jesse interrupts. "Sorry, but I gotta get set up. You'll be okay?"

"Yeah, of course. Go on."

He glances at Lucy. "Stick close to her, would you? I think you both could use each other right now."

Lucy stands up, shoving her hands in her pockets. "I will." We watch him leave when Lucy continues, "You're lucky to have him. He's a good guy."

"He is. A great guy, actually." I feel even guiltier now, but how am I going to tell the love of my life that I'm not who he thinks I am?

"Places, everyone."

I see the first assistant director walking around the porch. "Sounds like we're getting ready. Come on. We can't stand here." I lead Lucy away from the house when I see Dale's truck pull into the parking area. "What's he doing here?"

"Who?" Lucy asks.

"Dale Coleman. One of the set builders Mason hired. A local guy."

"Caroline or Mason must've asked him to come. Don't know," she says, seemingly uncertain of how else to answer.

But I start to feel unsettled by the fact he's always hanging around. First, I see him at the bar earlier today. Claims he's there to talk to Mason. Ever hear of a phone, buddy? Now he's here? Sure, Mason might've asked him to come, but why? We aren't building anything tonight.

"Hey, Kylie, you still with me?" Lucy asks.

"Huh? Yeah, sorry." I pause a moment. "Actually, could you excuse me for a minute?"

"Sure."

I walk over to Dale. He sees me coming. Before he has a chance to say anything to me, I jump right in. "How'd you know I live in L.A.?"

"Sorry, what's that now?" he asks.

I stop in front of him. "I asked how you knew where I lived."

"Uh, I figured you were from there, seeing how you work for the movies and such." He tilts his head and gives me a suspicious look. "Everything all right, there, Kylie?"

I look back at his truck. A blanket of dust covers the front grill, tires, and most of the hood. "Your truck's dirty."

He glances back and then hooks his thumbs into his belt loops. "Yeah, is that a crime? We haven't had any rain lately. Tough to keep clean driving these back roads." Dale eyes me up and down. "Are you all right? You seem agitated."

"Well, one of my co-workers was murdered, so there's that."

"Gosh, I'm real sorry, Kylie. I truly am." He turns down his gaze. "I can't imagine what you're going through right now. All of you. But I'm only here to help."

"Help?" I cross my arms, suddenly feeling offended by his presence. "Did the cops talk to you?"

"You know they did," he says matter-of-factly. "They talked to all of us. Look, I don't mean to upset you. I'll let you be."

He starts to walk away, but I call out to him, and he turns back. "Dale, you're from around here, right?"

"Of course, but I think you already know that."

I nod, feeling certain I was followed last night, and maybe he was the one doing the following. But why? Who is he, really? I can't tell him what I suspect, though, because that would expose my truth. I can't afford that.

"Anything else, Kylie?" He thumbs back. "Mason needs me to fix something on the new building before tomorrow's shoot."

I swallow the unspoken question. "No." He grunts at me and walks away. I almost lost it. Almost blew up my whole life. He's lived here a long time. He has to have heard about what happened or remembers it. Hell, it was only ten miles down the road from here. But this isn't over. Something's not right about Dale Coleman. And I'm going to find out what it is. I owe it to Brandon.

CHAPTER 7

Detective Burns

Dinner smells great, and I'm starving. Didn't get a chance to eat lunch, and I only had a cup of coffee for breakfast. Sitting in the diner with Dale Coleman this morning, listening to him try to weasel out of telling me what he knows — I should've ordered eggs and bacon, but I didn't want to be the only one eating.

"Hon, I'm home." I take off my suit jacket and hang it over the hook at the entrance. I should've made better progress today, but I got tangled up in dealing with the victim's family in Los Angeles. Fighting them on whether they could have their son's body transported yet. Don't they know we need to do the autopsy first? Not that the cause of death wasn't obvious. Still, it's protocol.

My wife's voice calls out from the kitchen: "Dinner's ready, Doug. Get warshed up." She's originally from western Iowa. Me? I grew up in the central part of the state where we pronounce 'wash' as it should be. Oh well. I love her for all her faults.

I walk into the kitchen and see her standing at the stove. Our kids are grown. Flew the coop a few years ago, so it's just us two now. And Beth's retired, so she's taken to cooking dinners on most nights. She used to be a nurse and worked second shift. Most of our marriage has been either me gone all the time, or her working nights. Honestly don't know how the kids managed, but they did a lot of the raising themselves.

I grab a couple plates from the cabinet and set the table. "I need to do a little bit of work after dinner tonight. Hope that's all right."

Beth turns to me. "That poor boy who was murdered at that movie location?"

"Yep."

"Well, I'm sorry you have to be the one to take that case," she says, dishing out mashed potatoes onto our plates.

"Me too." I pull out a chair to sit. "You know, it's strange, because there were only a handful of folks who knew about Lucas Shaw. I mean, the way he died."

"Is that so?" Beth asks as she takes her seat across from me. "What makes you want to think about all that? It happened so long ago."

I grab my knife and slice into the chicken breast. "Because that boy? He died the same way. Only thing missing was the cut on the arm. He didn't have one. So, I don't know if that means whoever did it wasn't aware . . ."

"Meaning they might've heard about all that mess second-hand?" she asks.

"Could be. Maybe heard it from one of the followers in prison, but I didn't think any of them knew either. The person who did it is long dead. So is his family."

Beth takes a bite of her chicken and shakes her head. "Well, you might oughta ask whoever was on that original investigation."

With my fork in hand, I pile on another scoop of mashed potatoes. "Unfortunately, he's long since retired. All I got is what's in the file. Except for one thing."

"And what's that?"

"Dale Coleman. He's a local resident who was hired to work for the movie. Building something or other, I don't know. Point being, that boy died a couple days after Dale was hired. It's worth a look-see. That's for sure."

* * *

The house is quiet now. Beth's gone to bed. I'm in my study, which used to be our son's room. Blake moved across the country for work, and we don't see him much, so Beth went ahead and got all this set up for me. I know she did it so I wouldn't spend so much time at the station. And I can't argue that it isn't handy to have a place here to work. Beats the shit out of hanging around them young cops, speaking a language I hardly recognize. All their Tik Tok'ing bullshit.

Now, I gotta figure out how Dale Coleman fits into this kid's murder. I wasn't here when that cult imploded on itself. One of the members — a top guy, from all accounts — did the deed. But I read the file. I've seen the crime scene pictures. Damn gruesome sight.

And they left that final detail out of the press — the cut on Shaw's arm. But to find the kid with his eyes gouged out, same as Shaw, makes me think there's someone else out there. Someone who was at least at the compound when it happened, but maybe hadn't seen the whole thing.

I run a background check on Coleman. He's got a clean sheet. Holds a weapons permit. "Interesting." Though, not exactly uncommon around here. No steady employment, which strikes me as odd. Man's in his fifties, he should have a decent job. Unless he's semi-retired.

But I see nothing that stands out. Owns his home. I guess that's something. Single. "Oh, what's this now?" I lean in to read the note at the bottom. "No records prior to '04." I pull back in my chair. "The hell does that mean?"

* * *

This morning, I'm up and out the door early. I need to dig into this shit about Coleman. Guy was a damn near ghost before showing up in this township twenty years ago. I'm not the smartest man on the planet, but I ain't the dumbest either.

Man keeps to himself, works odd jobs, finds himself on a movie shoot. Then *Bam*! Someone's dead. Come on now. That's not how this works.

I head to my desk, a paper cup full of shitty coffee in my hands and take a seat. It's quiet this morning, which I appreciate the hell out of. The kid's file is on my desk, so is the Shaw murder. In fact, we dug up a whole thick mess of archived files regarding that New Hope cult. I got my work cut out for me. Could I be wasting my time, thinking there's a connection? That's a strong possibility. But what are the odds we get two psychopaths, some twenty years apart, kill someone by slitting their throat and gouging out their eyes? In this town? Pretty damn long.

CHAPTER 8

Kylie

Jesse and I were both up early this morning. Caroline scheduled the shoot for 6 a.m. She was trying to make up some time on the schedule. And probably trying to get us all the hell out of here as soon as possible. She'd get no argument from me.

I'd pondered calling Aunt Grace again. Telling her that I thought Dale Coleman was following me. But what would be the point? It'd only terrify her. She was getting old, and had suffered enough, having spent years trying to get us all out of that nightmare of New Hope. Of course, I didn't realize it at the time. It was only after I moved in with her . . . when it was all over . . . that she told me how she'd tried to help. Oh, and she'd also lived there for a while.

She blamed my dad. My mom? She was a victim, like the rest of us. And Aunt Grace wasn't wrong on that count. Dad dragged us away from our home in Des Moines to live there at the New Hope compound. I was eight, and it all went up in flames just before I turned thirteen.

But what happened after . . . when we were hunted . . . that was, well, Aunt Grace doesn't like to talk about all that. I don't blame her. I was just lucky enough to have gotten out. Still not sure how I managed, but I did.

This was her fear, though, with me coming here for work. Dredging up this nightmare again. I really thought I could handle it. That I'd be fine. I suppose I would've been, had Brandon not been killed.

I check the time as the actors step out of the farmhouse. I need to head out and grab lunch for everyone. I nod to Jesse, who walks over to me.

"What's up, babe?" he asks.

"I've got lunch duty today, so I'm going to head out."

"What are we having?"

"There's a sandwich shop a few doors down from the diner. I put in an order with them earlier this morning. That place Dale talked about."

"Okay." He looks at me with concern. "Are you going by yourself?"

"Yes, I think I can handle a run into town. I won't be long," I say. "Go on. I'll see you in a few."

He kisses my cheek. "Okay. Hurry back, but drive safe."

"I will," I tell him with a feigned confidence as I head toward the car. It's the only way he won't worry about me. I slip behind the wheel and drive away, the farmhouse shrinking in the rearview.

Dale Coleman isn't working today, which puts me at ease. I was, admittedly, hard on him yesterday. But until I figure out his angle, I don't know if I can trust him. So, rather than head straight to the deli, I make a slight detour, because I did my homework. Mason hired him, so he had an address to set him up as a contract employee. Now, I have that address. I'm not feeling great about how I got it, but never mind that part.

I have to drive through town to the other side, but it's not far out of my way. I mean, shit, there's barely four hundred people who live here. So, I carry on, passing the main street where the shops and restaurants are, driving by the hardware store where we'd stopped. And as I drive on, a signpost appears on the side of the two-lane road.

I slam on my brakes. "Oh my God." I quickly check the rearview, grateful no one's behind me, or I would've just caused a crash. But this sign. Jesus. It's faded, barely standing, but it's there, nestled among overgrown prickly bushes. 'New Hope is just around the corner,' it reads. And then the symbol. I'd recognize it anywhere. It's a pyramid with a rainbow shooting out of the top.

A horn honks, drawing my attention. "Shit." I press on the gas and wave my hand in the rearview mirror. "Sorry." *It's just an old sign,* I tell myself. *It doesn't mean anything.* And then, aloud: "Screw it. What the fuck am I doing, anyway?"

I turn around at the next intersection. *This is crazy. Just go back and get lunch. Do your job so you can leave this place.* So I head back to the main thoroughfare and pull into the parking spot in front of the sandwich shop. I see the sign on the window. *We serve Maid-Rites.*

Oh man. I haven't had one of those in years. I chuckle, knowing it's an Iowa thing. It makes me a little sad. I spent a good part of my life living like a regular kid. Going to public school. Eating as many Maid-Rites as I could. It's a lot like a sloppy joe, but without the sloppy part. Loose meat sandwiches, they call them everywhere else. And then it all changed.

I step out of the car and lean over to grab my purse. When I raise up again, I see it — Dale's truck. He's at the diner, is my best guess. Maybe the hardware store, but the diner's closer.

I slip back inside the vehicle, lowering myself in the seat. I want to see him walk out. Where's he going to go? Do I have the time to follow? No, I don't. I sit here for a while, pondering what to do.

A thump rattles the passenger window. I flinch, whipping my head to see a man pounding his fist on it.

"Hey, lady, this is a fifteen-minute zone. Shit or get off the pot, yeah?" he yells through the glass.

I look around, my heart in my throat. There are three parking spots nearby. What the hell is this guy doing? "Seriously?" I say to him, gesturing to those spots.

He pinches his lips and creases his brow. "Whatever." Then he walks away. And when I turn around again, I realize Dale's truck is gone. "Son of a bitch."

I get out of the car again and head into the deli. The smell of ground beef fills my senses, and it takes me back. "Hi," I say to the man behind the counter. He gives me a look. The one that says, *You're not from around here.* Except, technically, I am.

"What can I do for you, miss?" he asks, scratching his double chin.

"I'm here to pick up the order for Kylie Forbes."

"Right. The large order." He's all smiles now, realizing this order is probably going to pay for his rent this month. "It's in the back. Hang on just a sec."

When he disappears into the back, I study the items in the display case. Cookies. Cakes. Freshly baked bread. Meats of all kinds. Carved turkey and ham. It all looks delicious. My shoulders start to relax. I feel the tension in my neck loosen. It's only a momentary phase because I remember . . . Brandon's dead.

"Here you go, miss." The man returns with several bags of food. "That'll be six hundred, forty-six dollars and twenty cents."

I hand him Caroline's credit card. "Here you go." He swipes it and hands me a receipt to sign. "Thanks very much."

"Thank you," he replies.

Telling Detective Burns what I know would be the right thing to do. The scenario runs through my mind as I step outside, arms full. I mean, can I really live with myself wondering if Brandon's death is connected to me? But the thing is, no one knows I survived. Everyone involved, including the original detective, thinks I'm dead.

I pop the trunk and set down the bags of food inside. Long shadows cross the pavement below me. Legs? Someone's near, I can feel them. I close the lid when I hear footsteps. A tingling sensation climbs up my spine and I whip around. But all I see are near-empty sidewalks. An old couple walking across the street. A construction worker stepping out of the diner. A car drives by, and I peer into the window, hoping to see who it is. But of course, I don't recognize them. I can hardly make out who it is. "Stop. Shake out of it. Shake out of it," I repeat to myself.

And as I take a breath, trying to push aside my suspicion, something on the ground catches my attention. I cast out my gaze, ensuring no one is near before bending down to pick up the round piece of paper. It's a . . . sticker? I stand again and turn it over between my fingers.

My breath catches in my throat, and I spin around again, searching for whoever dropped this onto the ground. I swear it wasn't here when I parked. But there's no one nearby. I'm alone. And as I stare at the sticker, I'm reminded of what we all had to do to earn this so-called badge of honor, this sticker.

Why are you doing this to me? Who are you?

I get back into the car, locking the doors. Fear takes me in its grip. My hands shake as I look at the sticker. I never thought I'd see this symbol again and now, I've seen it twice in one day. "This can't be happening. No one knows I survived. No one."

In the darkness, I see Aunt Grace get out of her car. She searches for anyone who might be waiting. But it's only me out here, hiding in the bushes. I ran for miles through cornfields, down into the gullies, finally making it to the next town.

From a payphone, I'd called her, telling her what happened through my uncontrollable sobs. My family was dead. Murdered — slaughtered, but I made it out. I ran, just like Dad told me to.

They'd come for him, wanting to make him pay for what he'd done. But they made us all pay. I'd seen a hint of faraway light rising in the sky. Flames. My house. The compound. Everything I've known for the past five years is burning to the ground.

I've been hiding here for hours, but now, she's here, Aunt Grace.

"Kayla, where are you?" she calls out, almost in a whisper. "Come on, sweetie. I'm here. You're safe now."

Am I? I have no one now. No one, except Aunt Grace. So I run out. Run right into her arms.

"Oh, baby." She pulls me close, squeezing so hard, I can't breathe. "I've got you now. I've got you."

How did I make it back to the farmhouse? I was in a trance, and somehow, I'm here. Back in the moment. I park the car and pull down the visor, gazing into the tiny mirror. "You look like shit. Pull yourself together."

I dab a bit of powder on my nose and press a tissue against the bottom of my eyes, trying to wipe away the smudged eyeliner and mascara. In this moment, I feel more alone than I have since that night Aunt Grace found me, and I'm not sure how long I can keep this secret.

CHAPTER 9

Detective Burns

If it wasn't for the fact this Brandon kid got his eyes gouged out, I wouldn't have given a connection a second thought. The New Hope cult burned to the ground some twenty years ago and now I'm thinking they're probably connected. More importantly, I'm trying to figure out why the kid was targeted in the first place. Why him?

Come to find out from the folks on that film crew, the kid had been the first to arrive on set that day. No one else turned up for a solid hour. So who outside the production knew he was there? Or was this an inside job, like Dale Coleman suggested?

So now, I'm driving along the road to the farmhouse. The kid's phone was tracking his location, so I can confirm that the timing tracks. Seems strange the killer didn't take the phone. In this day and age, that's the first thing I'd do if I was gonna murder someone. So what does that tell me? It tells me, whoever got to him was either sloppy, or didn't give a damn if he got caught. I'm not sure which is worse.

I drive nice and slow, taking in the scenery, hoping to hell something might jump out at me. Tire tracks, a food wrapper . . . hell, anything would be welcome.

The young man's parents gave me the code to access his phone. They'd arrived late yesterday to identify their son. I can scarcely recall the last murder investigation I was on, but it's been long enough that I forgot how tough it can be, seeing the family in such pain.

On the side of the road, I see a spot that looks all dug up or something. Muddy and wet. Though I know it hasn't rained in days. I glance into the rearview before pulling off onto the shoulder and stepping out of my car. The sun heats up my suit jacket, turning it into a damn electric blanket, so I take it off and toss it in the backseat.

Now that I'm getting a little closer, I see the disturbed ground, but why is it muddy here? I look around for a source of water. Fields surround me. Could've been some kind of flood irrigation nearby spilling out onto the roadway. And when I look back, a smile spreads wide on my face. "Well, what have we got here?"

I grab my phone and squat low, aiming it at the shoeprints embedded in the mud. "This'll do me." Standing up again, I raise my hand to shield the glare from my eyes and look far ahead. Nothing. And then far behind me. Still nothing. No homes or buildings as far as the eye can see. Just corn.

The kid was here according to his phone, but why? Did he pull over on his own or was he being followed? Someone was out here, that's for damn sure. But Brandon was killed at the farmhouse, so did he have some kind of car trouble, and someone happened to stop by and help? Hence, the shoeprints? Multiple ones, by the look of it. Was he then followed back to the farmhouse, and that help wasn't the kind of help he needed? "More than one perp?" I ask myself, cause I usually prefer my own answers to anyone else's. "Maybe." But again, my mind fills with one word. "Why?"

There's one thing I need to do now, given these footprints, and that's go and have another word with Dale Coleman. I can't ignore the timing, and he's a local. Probably knows this area like the back of his hand. Course, let's not forget the fact that the man was non-existent before 2004. Tell me that's not a big red flag.

I stand there a moment longer, the sweat dripping from my hairline now. What's left of my hairline, anyway. So I get back inside and turn on the air conditioning full blast. Turning the car around, I make my way back toward town. Toward Dale Coleman.

It's midday, so I wonder if he's working on that set, now that they're filming again. Must be damn hard for them to get back to work. Back in that damn farmhouse. Not sure I could do it.

Dale's place isn't but down the road a little ways. I'm almost there, making the final left turn into the neighborhood. "Damn it." I don't see his old white and red Ford truck in the driveway, and it isn't gonna fit in that small single-car garage he's got. "Must be on set."

Going down there, though . . . I really don't want to raise alarm bells more than what's already sounded. Who can I call to find out if Dale is there today? The bosses. I try Caroline's phone and it goes to voicemail. "Son of a bitch." I try the other one next, but as the line's ringing, I see a vehicle ahead. Sun's in my eyes, so I can't tell what it is . . . oh, hang on. All right, here we go. Dale's back. I hang up the phone and wait. I'm parked out front of his house, so he's gonna see me straight away. What's he gonna do?

Oh yeah. He sees me. Dale stops on his driveway and steps out, heading right toward me. I get out, pulling back my suit jacket so he sees my badge . . . and gun. He's gonna know I mean business today. "Afternoon."

"Detective Burns, I'm surprised to see you here. What can I do for you?" Dale asks, hooking his thumbs through his belt loops.

I make my approach . . . cautiously, because I've been a cop for too long, and I've learned to never underestimate anyone. "Sorry to bother you at home, Mr. Coleman. I was wondering if we could sit down a minute and talk."

"Again?" He shrugs. "Sure. Come on in."

I wait for him to unlock his door and as I step inside, I smell the musty odor. Course, it is humid today.

"You want some water or pop?" he asks.

"Nah, I'm good." I get out my notebook and follow him to the kitchen, where we take a seat the table. It's evident the man lives modestly. The table's a little old and worn. Old oak cabinetry and beige appliances. I mean, I'm not a rich man, so I don't judge. Just making observations, trying to figure out motives.

"What did you want to talk about, Detective? I thought you were done with me."

"Why aren't you working on that movie set today?" I ask.

"They don't need me. Probably won't from here on out."

I nod, scribbling a few words I won't be able to make out later. "Got any other work lined up?"

"No, sir. Not yet," he replies. "I don't mean to be rude, Detective, but I sure would appreciate you asking whatever it is you came here to ask."

"All right." I set down my pen and notebook on the table. They're really just for show. I don't need them. I remember a whole lot. Things that people forget they even tell me. "Where were you between the hours of 2 and 6 a.m. day before yesterday?"

"You mean, when that kid was murdered?" he asks.

"Yes, sir. That's precisely what I mean. Now, I know I already asked you something similar, and you said you were here sleeping. But we know a little more now. Narrowed down the timeframe to the early hours of that morning. Possible location where he might've been. So, I'm gonna ask again, where were you?"

"And I'm happy to answer — again," he says. "I was here. Sleeping."

I wasn't expecting a different answer, so I keep going to the reason why I'm really here. "You're an interesting person, Mr. Coleman."

"Is that a question, Detective?"

"Nope. Just an observation," I say with a small chuckle. "Seems I can't find anything about you prior to 2004."

"Is that so?"

"Sure is." I lean in, my forearms resting on the table. "That was right around the time of that cult dust-up."

"I suppose it was." He rubs his square chin. "And your point?"

I lean back again. "Well, I sure would like to scratch you off my list, but I can't really do that until I get the whole story. So, I'm asking . . . by the look of you, you weren't born in '04. So where'd you come from, Mr. Coleman, and why can't I find anything more about you, sir?"

He smiles at me, like I caught him with his hand in the cookie jar. "You'd have to know my former name, Detective."

"Former name?"

"That's right. I changed it from Reese to Coleman when my father died. Best thing I ever did."

He glances through the kitchen window for a moment. I'm not sure if he's making this up as he goes along, or if he's being honest. But he did mention before about relatives of those cult people probably wanting to change their last names. Funny he didn't mention he'd changed his. "And why'd you do that? If you don't mind me asking."

Coleman looks back at me. "Cause Reese was my mom's husband's name. He adopted me when I was a baby. And then when I found my real father, I got to know him. He died after a short battle with cancer. That's when I decided to change my name to what it should've been all along — Coleman." He leans back, tilting his head. "Good enough answer for you?"

"Well, I suppose it is, Mr. Coleman." I push up from the chair, taking a glance at his feet, just to cover my bases. Hard to say if he's a match. I'll need to get back to the station and have Tech analyze what I found first. "I apologize for wasting your time, but I do appreciate you speaking with me." We shake hands and I follow him to the front door.

"You need anything else," he says, opening it. "You let me know."

"I will, and thank you again, sir." I step outside and swear it's gotten ten degrees hotter than when I entered. I hear the door close behind me as I'm walking back to my car. But I stop at his truck, and, curiosity getting the better of me, decide to peek through the driver's side window. I see a hunting knife on the floorboard of the passenger side. Now, the man could be a hunter, for all I know. But one thing I do know for certain? Brandon's throat was sliced with a hunting knife.

CHAPTER 10

Kylie

Lunch turned out great. Everyone loved the food. Even while the mood was still somber, we had moments, blissful moments, of light-hearted banter. But we're back at work now. I didn't bother telling Jesse about what happened in the parking lot of the deli. How could I? He wouldn't have any idea why a sticker would bother me. But it wasn't just that. Things are stacking up that I can't explain, and if I try to . . .

Of course, I ripped that sticker into pieces and threw it away before I even returned to the set. But now I know — someone knows me. The real me. And I can't deny it any longer: whoever it is, has to be the one who killed Brandon. I'm not so naive to think it's a coincidence.

"Hey."

I turn around and see Lucy. Boy, am I glad to see her. "Hi. You get enough to eat?"

"Oh, yeah." She pats her perfectly flat stomach. "I'm stuffed. You?"

"Sure." I'm lying, because I didn't eat anything. Couldn't bring myself to take a single bite. My head's so full of memories and fears and . . . I'm scared.

"Listen, I was talking to some of the guys." Lucy thumbs back toward the house. "And we're thinking about maybe asking Caroline to relocate. What do you think?"

I think it's the best idea ever. Even so, I say, "Monty will have a hard time convincing the financiers to scrap all the footage we've taken so far. I don't know, Lucy, that's a tough call for her to make."

"Seems an easy one to me." She looks back at the house. "I mean, come on. There must be a million farmhouses just like this one. We can't find another one?" Lucy turns back to me, her eyes pleading. "We can make the interior exactly the same. Kylie, no one wants to be here. The actors, the crew. No one. They have to go inside that place and see where it happened? Jesus, it's too hard, you know?"

"Yeah, I do." I close my eyes a moment, thinking maybe this could work. "What does Mason say? Have you talked to him about this?"

"Not yet. Thought I'd get your take on it first," Lucy replies.

I look over at the front porch. Caroline is standing there, talking to her assistant director. I want nothing more than to leave, especially now. "All we can do is present her with the option," I say. "It'll be up to her to convince the people with the money."

Lucy nods. "No doubt. But they can't think we're going to turn out some great piece of cinematic art with this hanging over our heads."

"Look, I'll side with you guys. I have no problem with that. We can ask her. The rest, she'll have to decide."

"Then we do it tonight," Lucy continues. "After today's shoot. When we get back to the hotel. We'll present her with some options."

I lay my hand on her shoulder. "It could work. I doubt Caroline wants to be here anymore than the rest of us."

* * *

We return to the hotel and it's already dark. The shoot ran long. It's clear that Caroline is pushing everyone so we can get the hell out of here. I'm grateful for that. I never want to come back to this town. To this state. Ever.

"Babe?"

Jesse comes up behind me while I'm looking inside the hotel room closet, trying to find something to change into. "Yeah?"

"You sure you want to lead the charge on this one?" he asks.

I turn around to face him. "What do you mean?"

"The whole changing-locations thing. Everyone's talking about it. I mean, Caroline probably already knows at this point."

"I'm not leading the charge," I say. "What gives you that idea? I told Lucy I'd back her and the others on the suggestion, but I'm not the one making it."

"Sounds to me like you might be," he says. "From the rumblings I've heard today."

"Well, I'm not." I feel annoyed now. Why the hell is this falling on my shoulders? "Where's Caroline now?"

"Not sure, but I think everyone's heading down to the bar in a few."

"Yeah, okay." I look back at the closet. "I'll meet you down there. I'm not sure what to put on yet."

"It's not like there's a dress code here, babe," he says.

I spin back around to him. "I know that, Jesse," I say, in a harsher tone than I expect. "I'll meet you down there in a few minutes, all right?"

He licks his lips, and I can see he's trying to hold his tongue. "Yeah, okay. I'll see you down there." He walks out the door, letting it close hard.

"Damn it." I look down and see my still-muddy sneakers. I grab them and head into the bathroom, setting them down beside the sink. I examine them for a moment, still having no idea how they got dirty.

Letting the water run, I clean them, scrubbing the soles with my fingers, not wanting to dirty one of the towels. Can't afford to raise more questions. My thoughts race, unable to recall why my shoes look this way. Am I making more of this than necessary? Probably. But I've blacked out before, losing swathes of time, not unlike what happened at the hardware store. It's usually caused by a trigger, and I've been surrounded by them lately. But if I did black out, where the hell did I go?

I'd told the detective I was here sleeping when Brandon died, and that Jesse was here with me. But what if I wasn't? *Stop. Please, stop.* I take a deep breath and return the now-clean shoes to the closet.

If I don't get down to the lobby soon, questions will be raised, so I snatch a shirt from the hanger and toss it onto the bed. Then I grab a pair of black pants and do the same.

While I change, my thoughts turn back to Jesse. We don't fight often. If we do, it's usually over something stupid. Just like this was. He's a good man who deserves to know the truth. To be honest, I should've already reached out to that detective and told him what I know. Who I am. But I'm terrified of what will happen.

It's selfish, to be sure. But if I come clean about my past, everyone will blame me for Brandon's death. Hell, I blame me. And my job, my career that's only just starting to get off the ground. What happens to it? How will I earn money? Jesse will leave me, I'm sure of it. Some crazy bitch whose family was in a cult? Whose father was a killer? For God's sake, I wouldn't want to be with me.

I can't put it off any longer. I have to go downstairs and at least try to solve one problem — get everyone the hell out of here. The rest . . . I'll figure it out.

The room's key card is on the dresser. I grab it and head out the door. The corridor feels cold, like they have the air conditioning set at sixty. Maybe it's just my nerves. When I arrive at the elevators, I press the button and wait. Seconds tick by like minutes. *Come on.* I shift my weight from leg to leg, growing impatient.

I hear the ding and the doors open. "Finally." Inside, I press the lobby button and the doors shut again. The car lurches, forcing me to latch onto the bar behind me. The numbers above illuminate as it descends to the lower floor.

But then, the lights flicker. The elevator abruptly halts. I stumble, but still cling to the bar for support.

What is going on? I press the lobby button again, though it's still lit. "Oh for God's sake."

The lights go off. It's pitch-black. "Great." I press the flashlight feature on my phone and aim it at the panel, looking for the emergency call button. I press it. After a few moments, nothing happens, so I press it again. Still . . . nothing.

The car drops a few feet, sending my heart into my stomach. "Oh my God!" I'm clutching the bar when it stops again, the force nearly causing me to fall. My chest is pounding now. My breaths come in short gasps. "Calm down. You're okay. Just stay calm."

But I can't. I check my phone and have zero bars. I try anyway, try to call Jesse, but it won't connect. Panic rises in my gut, filling my lungs, tightening my chest. I hate dark places. Tight, dark places. Here it comes. Faster and faster breaths. My head is light . . . I'm about to . . .

"Why'd you do it? Why'd you kill him?"

The slats of my closet doors block most of my vision, but I can see into the hall a little bit. I hear him yelling at Dad. My mom is screaming, but I don't hear Kyle or Katie. Where are they? Are they okay? I don't understand what's happening, but I know he's here because of what Dad did.

He killed Lucas, but why? Why would he do that? Just like the man yelling at him now, asking the same thing. But I'm too scared to come out. I don't want him to hurt me. I see my bag on my bed. We were getting ready to leave this place. To leave the compound where I'd lived since I was eight. Since Katie was born. Mom told us to pack, so I did.

Her screams stop. "Mom?" I whisper.

"All you had to do was let him take her, Clarence. Those are the rules. You know that."

"No." Dad's tone is firm, an underlying rage coming through. I hardly recognize it. "Not my Kayla. He can't have her."

"What, you think you're special?" the man spits back. "How about I take your eyes first, huh? Do to you what you did to Lucas, you son of a bitch."

"It's the only way I could be sure."

I don't understand what they're talking about. Eyes? What did he do to Lucas' eyes? I want my mom. I thrust my hand over my mouth, tears spilling down my face, trying to be quiet because if he knows I'm here . . .

"Be sure of what, Clarence?"

My dad doesn't answer for a moment. I hold my breath, still peering through the slats, but I only see my bed, and the nightlight coming from the hallway.

"I had to destroy his power. Don't you see that? It was the only way."

What is Dad talking about? But my thoughts cease when a crash sounds, like something fell. A piece of furniture? I strain to listen, but there are no more voices.

"No!" Dad yells out. Then another scream . . . then . . . silence.

"Dad?" I whisper, trembling inside my closet. "Mom?" A shadow crosses in the hall, catching my eye. I hear footsteps on the carpet. He's coming. He's coming for me.

The ear-splitting screams force my eyes open, and I realize they're coming out of my mouth. The elevator doors part. I scramble backward, still screaming.

"Hey. Hey." Jesse reaches out. "Kylie, it's me. It's Jesse. Babe, you're okay. You're fine."

He helps me to my feet. I'm out of breath. My throat feels sore. "The elevator . . ."

"It stopped. I know. You've been trapped in here for almost half an hour. But you're okay now."

He wraps an arm around me, helping me out. I see that everyone's staring at me. The entire cast and crew are looking at me like I'm crazy. Even the bartender and manager.

"She's okay, everyone. She's all right," Jesse says. "Kylie's not a fan of closed spaces, but she'll be fine. Come on, babe. Let's get you some water."

He ushers me through the huddled mass. I feel their eyes on me. Worry, fear, concern. I love these guys, I really do, but right now, I don't want to be anywhere near them. Any of them. But I'm here now. I don't know what happened with the elevator and I swear to God, I'm never getting inside it again.

We sit down at one of the tables. Jesse brings me a glass of water. I drink all of it in one go and set down the glass.

"I'm sorry that happened to you back there," he says. "We heard the screams. I ran and got the manager. He was able to do something. I don't know what, maybe he reset the thing or whatever, but it started working again."

"Are you embarrassed?" I ask.

"What? No. Why the hell would I be? You're not the only person who gets claustrophobic, honey. Trust me. You were just in there a long time, so I can't imagine what that was like for you."

I sigh, reminding myself how grateful I am to have him. "I'd love to just forget about it, okay? Can we not mention it again?"

"Mention what?" he says with a smile. "So, listen, one good thing happened while you were upstairs."

"What's that?"

"A bunch of us talked to Caroline and Monty. Mason, too. She's totally on board with us getting out of here."

Relief swells in my chest. "She is? That's great. That's the best news I've heard all day."

CHAPTER 11

Dale

It's clear to me now that Detective Burns is going to dig until he gets what he's after. So I'm going to have to do my best to get a step ahead of him.

Inside my kitchen, I sit at the table with my laptop in front of me. It's time to create Dale Reese, at least, the man I want Burns to see.

My fingers hover over the keyboard as I contemplate where to begin. How do I craft an identity that will stand up to the scrutiny of a seasoned detective? I know Burns will dig into every facet of this Dale Reese's life. Some of the work's been done for me. I still have it.

I open the archived file, clicking on the birth certificate. I haven't gone by Reese in a long time. In fact, if Burns scratches below the surface of what I do have, it'll all unravel pretty quickly.

The birth certificate, social security card, driver's license, it's all here. Now, it's time to craft an employment history, lease agreements, utility bills. That will take a little more time.

Slowly but surely, Dale Reese returns to life on paper. I open a PDF of an old bank statement. "This will do." I alter the name and date, ensuring it reflects just enough detail to convince Detective Burns I'm telling him the truth.

The good news is that I don't need to bother with an online persona. Before 2004, we didn't have social media. A blessing if there ever was one.

It's meticulous work. But if I do this right, I can satisfy Burns' curiosity, buying myself time. All I need is for him to believe that I was Dale Reese. Just a simple guy, living a simple life. He'll buy it. This isn't my first rodeo.

The memories flood my head as I'm forced to go back twenty years. I try to push them away, but the images slither through my brain right up to the surface. I'm back at the compound, the day everything changed forever. I don't like thinking about those days. *The day.*

Lucas Shaw was charismatic. Everyone loved him. He had a way of making you feel special. Like you were part of something big and important. I remember the energy in the compound that morning. I remember the pride in his voice as he spoke of our growing numbers, the fervor in his eyes. But that all changed when Clarence walked into the meeting room that day.

The hallway's empty, which is unusual for this time of day. The kids should be getting out of class, filling the halls with their chatter and laughter.

I stop just as I round the corner and see Clarence appear in the hall. He's holding a knife, looking at me, staring with dark eyes I'd never seen in him before. "What in the hell?" I stand there a moment longer, watching as Clarence yanks open the door to the meeting room. "Oh my God." Something bad is about to happen. I can feel it.

I know Lucas is inside that room. I glance around for anyone else who might be near, but it seems I'm alone. It takes me a minute, running through how I can get myself out of whatever predicament lies in wait.

Finally, I run down the hall toward the room. But before I get inside, the door flies open. I stop in my tracks and see Clarence. Blood covers his shirt. His arms and hands, too. My lips part, and my gaze lands on the knife. "Clarence, what did you . . ."

He runs past me. I see his daughter in the distance. He stops to tell her something, but before I can do anything, they're both gone. I run inside the room and see the carnage. "Oh God."

Lucas is on the floor. Blood spreads all around him. I run to his side. His eyes. "Jesus. God. What, what . . . Lucas, Lucas, can you hear me?" He doesn't move. He doesn't speak. He can't. Blood spills from the opening in his neck that runs ear to ear.

I try to press on it to stop the bleeding, and I can't stop looking at his face. I see the fork on the ground next to him. Covered in blood. "Help! Someone get some help!" I yell.

One of the teachers runs inside, but she stops cold. Her hand clamps down over her mouth. "Maggie, call the police. Now!" I yell again. But looking at Lucas, I know he's gone.

* * *

The sun beats down on my face. My cheek is stuck to the kitchen table as I open my eyes. It occurs to me that I fell asleep out here last night. And as I try to sit up, my back screams at me, aching from being hunched over for so long. Finally, I sit up straight in the chair, rubbing my spine with my fingers. And that's when I see the time. It's barely 6 a.m.

Neck stiff and back sore, I slowly rise. There's no time to do more than splash water on my face and change into fresh clothes. Movement seems to help loosen my joints and relax the muscles. I can just about function normally again as I snatch my keys from the living room table and head out the door.

Outside, I shield my eyes from the sun as it bounces off the chrome on my truck. The air is sticky, and droplets have collected on the windows. So when I step behind the wheel, I use the wipers to clear away the damp morning, and then I turn the engine.

I think I've taken care of the Dale Reese situation. Burns should be satisfied with what he sees. This gives me the cover I need, but for how long, I can only guess. Hopefully long enough to get the job done.

The two-lane road reveals the farmhouse ahead, so I ride the dirt driveway up until I reach the parking area. The place appears empty; however, I see someone step out of a trailer and walk over. "Morning."

"Mr. Coleman?"

I don't know much about the young woman, except that she's the makeup artist. "It's Lucy, right?"

"Yes. What are you doing here?"

I shrug before thrusting my hands into my pockets, "I was wondering if Mason might need me today."

"You didn't hear?" she asks, raising a brow. "We're packing up to leave. With everything that's happened, no one wants to stay. Caroline will be here soon, as well as the rest of the crew, to finish packing up. I came early to clear out my things, so I can get back to the hotel and help the others."

"I see. I hadn't heard any of this." I scan the grounds. "Is Kylie here, or back at the hotel?"

"She's at the hotel. It's just me out here for now, but like I said—"

"Caroline and a few others will be here," I cut in. "Okay. Well, do you need any help?"

Lucy glances back at the trailer. "Actually, yeah, I'd love some. Come on." She waves me over as she opens the door to her trailer. "I could use some help packing my lighted mirrors. They're a little heavy."

"Sure. Anything I can do to help."

CHAPTER 12

Kylie

Part of me felt relief when Jesse told me we were moving the production. I was still embarrassed by what happened in the elevator last night and even dreamed about it. According to Jesse, when the doors parted, I was balled up, fetal position, screaming my head off.

It had been years since I'd had an episode like that. The trigger was obvious. Jesse didn't pry, though. I'd told him long ago that I suffered from claustrophobia, never having explained the reason why.

"Kylie?"

Sitting up in bed, I look over my shoulder. "Go back to sleep. It's early." Normally, we'd already be at the shoot, but there was no shoot today. We were leaving, and I couldn't be happier.

I stand up and walk into the bathroom, hopping into the shower. As the warm water runs down me, I can't stop thinking about the elevator. Why had it jammed up the way it did? We'd been here a week, and not once had that happened to anyone else.

Stop. I rinse my hair and turn off the water.

Distrust and suspicion are second nature to me. Everything that went wrong in my life, whether it was car trouble, a job I didn't get, stubbing my damn toe, it was because of my past. I realize how stupid that sounds, but it's just the way my mind works now. So . . . the elevator? You guessed it: my past caught up to me again.

I get dressed and step out of the bathroom, looking over to see Jesse still sleeping. He'll be up soon, so I'd better make this fast. Slipping on my shoes, I grab the key card and step out into the hall, carefully closing the door so it doesn't slam shut. I walk to the stairwell because I'm not getting in that elevator again, and jog down the three flights of stairs. The sound of my footsteps bounces off the masonry walls. The metal railing clatters until I reach the bottom. Even being in here freaks me out a little, but I know it's only because I've already been set off, thinking everything is connected.

The attendant is behind the desk when I approach. "Good morning."

"Good morning, Ms. Forbes," he says. "We just set out the breakfast buffet if you're interested."

I glance toward the dining area. "Maybe later. Listen," I lean over the counter. "Who did you have working maintenance last night?"

"When the elevator jammed?" he asks.

"Yes."

He looks at his computer screen. "Again, I can't tell you how sorry I am that happened to you. But let me just take a look, because I think the last maintenance shift ended at five p.m. And, of course, it jammed later than that."

I wait for him to find the name. Is the person a local resident? Someone from the next town over? I don't know why I have to know, but I do.

"Ah, here we go." He squints at the screen. "I can tell you that the elevator was serviced yesterday, by the look of it. I wasn't on shift, but it appears it was scheduled for its monthly inspection."

Now, I'm curious. "That's interesting. I wonder if they broke something. Can you tell me who it was who inspected it?"

"Uh, I don't have a name, Ms. Forbes. But I do have a company. You're more than welcome to contact them and ask about it. Though, to be honest, this would fall under the liability of the hotel."

"Just a name, please," I ask. "I don't intend to sue, if that's what you're wondering. Please . . . it's important."

He hesitates, until finally grabbing a pen and sticky note. "Of course. This is the name of the company. Feel free to tell them what happened. We did file a report, just so you're aware."

I take the slip of paper. "I understand. Thank you." As I turn to walk away, I look at the name. It means nothing to me, but I can't let it go. Being back here . . . seeing the signs, the symbol. Someone knows me. Knows I didn't die that night. And I have to find out who.

As I walk away from the front desk, I see Caroline. "Hi."

"Good morning." She lays her hand on my shoulder. "How you feeling?"

I know she's referring to last night's incident. "Fine, yeah. Thanks for asking. And sorry if I freaked out anyone. It's just a phobia."

"No one was freaked out. We all just want to make sure you're okay," she replies. "I was getting ready to head out to the farmhouse. Make sure we clear out of there in the next few hours. You want to ride out with me?"

"Yeah, I can do that," I say. "I'll text Jesse and let him know."

"Great. Let's head out now."

I glance back at the front desk. The man behind it smiles at me, but then it fades. His face changes.

"Kylie?"

I turn back around. "Yeah, sorry. I'm coming." I follow Caroline out the door. Christ, my paranoia is getting the better of me. I need to pull my shit together or people will start asking questions.

We get inside Caroline's rental car. She drives out of the hotel parking lot and down the two-lane road. Neither of us wants to speak about what happened to Brandon. The whole notion of someone we know being murdered . . . it's a strange concept for most people. Not for me.

"What time are we heading out of here today?" I ask, trying to sound casual.

Caroline doesn't look at me, instead, she pinches her lips like she wants to say more than she's about to. "As soon as we can. The studio is freaking out. Monty and the other producers . . . they're all freaking out."

Now, she turns to me. "Have you heard anything more from the police? I keep calling that detective, but he keeps telling me they're working on it. I mean, what the hell, right?" She scoffs. "It's a town of, like, fifty, and they can't find a killer?"

I want to say something to offer comfort, but how can I, when I'm not comforted either? But what's more important is what I'm leaving out. Like the fact that I've seen something like this before. "I can't imagine it would be anyone who actually lives around here," I say. "It seems more likely that it was some transient, right?"

Caroline shrugs. "I guess so. Not that it makes me feel any better."

"No, me either." I look out through the passenger window. Guilt weighs on me. If I say something to Detective Burns, what will happen? I've been living the life of someone else for a long time. Will that change? What if it gets out, who I really am, and then the killer finds me? Because I have to think that's what all this is about. Tracking me down. Eliminating me. So how many people am I willing to watch die because I refuse to say something?

I see the farmhouse ahead when Caroline turns onto the driveway. "Where is everyone?"

She shakes her head, keeping her eyes on the house. "I don't know. There's still a lot to do here, so I'm wondering that myself."

I look at my dad, who's driving us. Mom is next to me. Kyle is in the backseat with me. Ahead, I see the house. Our new house. I already hate it, and I want to go back home. Back to Des Moines to be with my friends. I hate him for dragging us here.

This house looks super creepy. Other houses are nearby that look just as creepy. "Who are those people? Why are they dressed like that?"

Dad looks back at me, and smiles. The lines on his cheeks deepen. "Those people are going to be our new neighbors. And they're wearing dresses probably because they like dresses."

My mom glances back. "Not all girls are tomboys like you, Kayla."

"I'm not a tomboy," I reply.

"Yes, you are," Kyle says. "You always play sports with the boys. You don't have any dolls. You're always watching scary movies and action shows. You're such a tomboy."

I punch him in the arm. "Shut up."

"Ouch!" He rubs it. "Mom, Kayla hit me!"

"Don't hit your brother," Mom says.

I roll my eyes as Dad parks in front of the house.

"This is it, kids. Come on. Let's go check it out." He walks up the porch steps to unlock the door.

I survey the immediate area, shaking my head. "It looks like a farm or something here."

"That's because you're seeing everyone's vegetable gardens." Mom places her arm around me and ushers me to the door. "They're all self-sufficient. You'll come to love it here. I promise."

I hardly think so. Our dad drags us out here in the middle of nowhere. To what? Garden?

"Come on, Kayla. Get inside," Dad says. "Have a look around."

I'm standing in front of the farmhouse, and I hear Caroline call out to me. She's on the porch with the door open.

"Kylie? What are you doing?"

I shake out of my thoughts and walk up to meet her. "Nothing. Sorry. So, is anyone else here?"

"The door was locked, so I'm thinking . . . no."

I look back at the two trailers that remain. "When are they coming to take those?"

"By noon, is what I heard." She looks out toward them. "Would you mind checking that they're both empty, and unlocked?"

"Sure." I walk back down and head over to the trailers. One of them is for the actors. The other is Lucy's. I reach the first trailer and check to see that the door is unlocked. I knock. "Hello?" No answer, so I open it. It's pretty dark inside. Only a couple of windows, and the curtains are drawn on them. But it's clear that no one is here.

I continue inside, setting my hands on my hips. "They haven't bothered boxing up anything. Great."

I walk out again and make my way to Lucy's trailer. It's unlocked, and I enter, not bothering to knock this time. I see lights are on, but no one is inside. Some of Lucy's things are gone. Her makeup cases. The lighted mirror is wrapped in bubble wrap.

Come to think of it, I haven't heard from her since last night. It's only seven now, but I know Lucy. She'd be here to protect her things. I grab my phone and press her contact. The line rings, but voicemail answers. I don't bother leaving a message. Instead, I send her a text.

In your trailer. Some of your things are still here. When are you coming by?

I wait a few moments, but get no reply. Maybe she's still asleep. I turn around, heading back outside when I see Caroline approaching. "Actors' trailer still has stuff in it. So does the makeup trailer. I called Lucy, but got her voicemail."

Caroline presses her lips together. "Damn it. Everything's got to be cleared out. Come on. Let's get back to the house. I just talked to Mason. He and a few others are heading our way now."

I feel a pebble in my shoe, so I grip the metal stairs of the trailer and slip it off my right foot. That's when I see it. My shoe drops to the ground, and I bend down to pick it up, getting a better look to confirm my suspicion. *Oh my God. Is that blood?*

I hear Caroline call my name again, asking me to hurry, but I'm frozen, staring at the blood. *Jesus, where are you, Luce?* Some of her things are gone, so I know she's been here, but when? And where is she now?

"Kylie? What's the holdup?" she yells again.

I hear the rumbling of a car and look out toward the road. I see the plume of dust from the approaching vehicle.

I look down at the blood again, then jog back to see Caroline. *Someone's coming.* The words hang on my tongue. Blood. Lucy's blood? Do I say something? But before I can, Caroline starts walking down the steps.

"Good. It's Mason. Hopefully, he's not alone. We have a lot to do and need a few hands to get it done." Caroline glances over her shoulder at me. "Take a quick inventory, would you, Kylie? Note everything that belongs to us. Props. Equipment. All of it. Then when everyone else arrives, we can make sure it's all accounted for."

I nod as she walks away and stare at Lucy's trailer. I didn't see blood inside. Maybe I'm overreacting. Maybe she cut herself on the makeup mirror.

But why isn't she answering her phone?

I meander inside the farmhouse, but I'm not really here anymore. I'm back at the compound. I'm cleaning my shoes. I'm in the elevator of the hotel. I'm inside Lucy's trailer. I'm pulled in too many directions, knowing I can't keep this up. If only Lucy would just call me back. Text me. Anything to let me know she's okay.

My phone buzzes in my pocket. I snatch it, but disappointment surges when I see the name on the screen. "Hey, Jesse."

"Kylie, you're at the farmhouse?"

"I am." I crease my brow. "Aren't you coming here soon?"

"I'm on my way, yes. But I was at the front desk and the guy there . . ."

He stops mid-sentence, like I'm supposed to know what he's talking about. "And?" All I hear are his breaths now. "Jesse, what's going on?"

"He, uh, he asked me where you were and that he needed to talk to you. Something about how you were going to call the elevator maintenance people or something."

"Yeah, I was . . . I am, soon. Why? Jesse, you gotta tell me what's going on, because you're starting to worry me."

"Sorry, it's just that, well, he said he went back and looked at the security video, and uh . . ."

I run my fingers through my hair, waiting for him to spit it out already.

"He says it shows you pressing the emergency stop button inside the elevator."

I step back in surprise. "What? What are you talking about? It stopped on its own."

"Babe, he showed it to me. I saw you push the button. And when we went to get help after hearing you scream, the man on shift did something to override it, and that was when it restarted."

"So you're telling me I stopped the elevator myself?" I ask. "There's no way. You say you saw me, but there's no way, Jesse. Come on."

"I know what I saw, Kylie. Look, why don't I talk to Caroline and just have you come back here and finish packing your things? There's plenty of crew who can get ready to move out. I think you should be here. This whole Brandon situation . . ."

I close my eyes, trying to recall whether I actually did what he says I did. But it doesn't make sense. It's getting to me now. All of this. "Yeah, okay. I can't explain whatever happened in the elevator, but maybe I just need to get back and take care of things there." I look outside to see Mason and Caroline walking toward the house. "Mason's here now with his people. I'll talk to Caroline and take one of the other cars out here. She'll understand."

"Good. I still need to get out there, so just come back, and I'll see you later here at the hotel."

"Okay, yeah. Bye." I pocket my phone and watch Caroline and Mason make their way toward me. What Jesse said . . . it doesn't make sense. But I know I have to leave. I have to find Lucy.

CHAPTER 13

The Manning police station is almost twenty miles away from the farmhouse. I know I should've gone back to the hotel, just like I told Jesse I would. But something's changed. I feel stuck between two worlds. A painful past no one except Aunt Grace knows about, and a present where one of my co-workers was murdered and maybe another might be missing. And only I know the connection between the two.

I'm in the car, sitting in the station's parking lot, telling myself go inside. But not yet. I have to talk to Aunt Grace. It's early in L.A., but I know she'll answer. She always does. "Hi, it's me. I'm sorry it's so early."

"It's okay, sweetheart. What's going on? I haven't heard from you since that poor young man . . ."

"I know. The police are still investigating. But we're moving out of here. The director and producer realize that it's too much to make us all stay and finish the shoot."

"Oh, thank God," she says, clearly relieved. "Does that mean you're coming home soon?"

"Not home. Not yet. Sounds like there's a place in Montana. We're leaving here later today. I thought you'd want to know." I clench my jaw, holding back my need to ask her the question, but I can't avoid it any longer. After another moment's pause, I continue, "Aunt Grace, have you heard anything about anyone from New Hope?"

She's quiet for a moment, the topic seemingly expected, but not wanted. "What do you mean?"

"Has anyone contacted you about the ones in prison, or anything like that?" I press. Aunt Grace knows all about the members who are still serving time. She's kept track of everything related to them since it all happened. Since her sister was killed.

"No, of course not. Kylie, you know most of them are dead now, right? And the ones who are in prison are never getting out. Honey, you're safe from them."

I feel my eyes sting, because I don't know that. I don't feel safe at all. She doesn't know about the signs, the sticker, all the little things I've been seeing that make me think someone's out there taunting me.

"I'm not so sure, Aunt Grace." I hadn't told her exactly what happened to Brandon, knowing she would've insisted I come home immediately. But I don't think I can keep it from her anymore. I need to tell someone. I have to know if what I'm about to do is the right thing, even if I already know the answer.

"Have you ever heard the name Dale Coleman?" I ask, still keeping my sights on the station's entrance.

"Doesn't sound familiar. Why?"

I wipe away a stray tear and close my eyes, trying to keep my composure. Last thing I want is for her to worry even more. Though I don't think that's avoidable at this point. "I feel like maybe he knows something . . . something about me or about Dad."

"Why on God's green earth would you think that?"

I've plucked a nerve. She always gets dramatic when I'm getting at a truth she doesn't want to talk about. "Aunt Grace, please . . . I feel like . . . I feel like they're watching me," I say in a whisper. "They know I'm here. I've seen signs."

"What signs?" she shoots back. "What are you talking about? Are you in danger? That's it. You're coming home right now . . ."

I raise my hand as if she's standing before me. "Please, stop. Look, I . . . you know more about all of this than I do. And I've always respected the fact that you preferred not to talk about it."

"Because she was my sister," she whispers.

"I know. That's why I don't push. In fact, I'd prefer not to be having this conversation at all right now . . . but I think, if there's more, now's the time to let me in on it."

The doors of the station open and I see Dale Coleman. I sit up, gazing intently through the windshield. "I'm sorry, Aunt Grace, but I need to go."

"What? Why? Kylie, wait . . ."

I end the call and open the door to step out. "Mr. Coleman?" I call out to him, but he doesn't hear me. "Mr. Coleman?"

He stops on a dime when we make eye contact. "Kylie, what are you doing here?"

I could ask him the same thing, but I need to play this right. "I remembered some details that the detective should probably know, so I came here. I was just about to go inside."

"I see." He looks back at the building, shoving his hands in his pockets, and finally turns back to me. "Detective Burns needed some information from me. I came here to deliver it."

"What kind of information?" I tilt my head. Am I ready to believe him? That depends on his next words.

"My fingerprints. The size of my feet, if you can believe that. Said he needed all that to rule out what they'd found on the scene at the time," he replied.

Interesting, because I wasn't asked to submit prints, shoe or otherwise. The image of my dirty sneakers flashes through my mind. I shake it off. In fact, I don't know if anyone else had been asked. Does that mean Burns considers Coleman a suspect? "I haven't heard whether he's making any progress on the case. But we're all leaving here today, so I guess there's not much left for us to do."

"So Mason tells me," he replies. "I'm so sorry that you all are heading back to L.A., but of course, who can blame you?"

I don't bother correcting him, telling him where we're really going. Just as a matter of precaution because now, I'm not sure whether I can trust him. "Yeah, well, I guess I should get inside. Take care of yourself, Mr. Coleman." I head toward the door.

"Goodbye, Kylie," he calls out. "Safe travels. Oh, and say goodbye to Lucy for me."

I halt in my tracks and spin around. "Excuse me?"

"Your friend, Lucy. I saw her this morning. She was at the farmhouse. Well, in the trailer, actually. In fact, I helped her wrap up her vanity mirrors."

I march back toward him. "You saw Lucy earlier?"

He shrugs. "Yes. That's what I just said."

"When was that, exactly, Mr. Coleman?" I press.

"I don't know. Early. The sun was barely up. She was the only one out there at the time, which kind of surprised me, all things considered."

I feel a lump catch in my throat, because he's right. Lucy never should've been out there alone. She wouldn't have been, had I known. I don't know where she is, but something tells me she's not okay, and he's the reason why.

"Kylie, are you all right?"

"No, I'm not. Where is she?"

"Where's who?" he asks, as if we haven't been talking about Lucy at all.

"Oh my God. Lucy! Where is she? She's not answering her phone. No one's seen her — besides you. What did you to do her?"

His brows raise high, and his eyes are huge white orbs. "Me? I didn't do anything to her. Why would you say that?" He steps back, raising a pre-emptive hand. "Look, Kylie, I can see you're under a great deal of stress, but if you have concerns, by all means, go inside and tell Detective Burns. I assure you, I'm fully cooperating with this investigation. And I'm sorry to say that I don't know where your friend is. She was fine when I saw her a few hours ago. Goodbye."

I watch him walk back to his truck and drive away. What the hell is happening to me? I feel like I'm going crazy. Returning to my car, I slip inside, my head pressing against the steering wheel.

I've got Jesse telling me I stopped that elevator. There's blood at Lucy's trailer, and I can't find her anywhere, so I accuse Dale of hurting her without so much as an ounce of proof. I mean, if the guy did something to her, why would he come here? Taking a long, deep breath, I sit up again, wiping the tears from my eyes.

What am I even doing here?

It's this town. The farmhouse. The compound. I key the ignition and peel out of the parking lot, too afraid to say anything to Burns. Brandon deserves better. So does Lucy. But at this point, what if it *is* all in my head? Aunt Grace says they're all in prison. "But she doesn't know what happened to Brandon. You didn't tell her."

As I drive down the road at break-neck speed, the sun shines down on the hood of the car. Heat rises ahead of me, like a mirage of water. If I can figure out what Dale Coleman is hiding, why all this started the moment he arrived on set . . . but Lucy . . . I can't divert my focus . . . I'd remember Dale, wouldn't I?

"I'll be thirteen in a few months," I remind my dad while we sit at the dinner table.

Dad's face darkens as I mention my upcoming birthday. He sets down his fork and clasps his hands together tightly.

"Thirteen . . ." he murmurs. "Practically a woman."

Mom reaches over and puts her hand on Dad's arm. "Now, Clarence, thirteen isn't so old. Kayla's still Daddy's little girl."

Dad shakes off Mom's touch, his voice rising. "Don't tell me how to feel, Evie. She's growing up too fast, getting ideas in her head. I won't have it!"

I shrink down in my seat, tears pricking at my eyes. Dad has been so moody lately, quick to anger over the smallest thing. I thought he'd be happy about my birthday, but now I've just upset him again.

"Clarence, honey, just calm down," Mom pleads.

He slams his fist on the table, making the dishes rattle. "No daughter of mine will be cavorting around with boys at thirteen! If you even think about it, Kayla, you'll be grounded till you're thirty. You hear me?"

"For goodness' sake, she's not cavorting with anyone," Mom says.

I nod meekly, hot tears spilling down my cheeks now. Dad's face softens. "I'm sorry, Kayla. I didn't mean to scare you." I see his eyes redden, but I still don't understand why he's so angry. Then he continues, "Your birthday is something to celebrate."

I blink away the painful memory, returning to what has become a painful present. Dad had always been overprotective, but in those last months, he became obsessive. If only we'd realized what he was capable of then, maybe things would have ended differently.

I shake out of my thoughts and refocus on the road ahead. Refocus on finding Lucy. The scenery flashes by in a blur — cornfields, silos, farmhouses.

This rural landscape looks so wholesome on the surface, but I know that darkness lurks underneath. Isolated communities provide fertile ground for men like Lucas Shaw to plant their twisted ideologies.

I grab my phone and try Lucy again. And again, I get her voicemail. "Jesus! Where are you? Where the fuck are you?" I scream at the top of my lungs, pounding my palm on the steering wheel.

If she's dead, I know it'll be my fault. It's my job to protect her. I should've gone into the station. I should've told them what I know.

I take a breath, trying to slow my racing pulse, the trembling in my hands. *Think, Kylie.* I've been Kylie for so long, I never call myself by my real name anymore. Kayla Skinner died back at that house, right along with the rest of her family.

"Fuck Dale Coleman. I need to find my friend and get the hell out of here." But something in the back of my mind calls out to me. It's telling me to go back there. That Lucy is there. But I don't believe it. I can't. She's not there, because that would mean someone from New Hope took her and is using her to get back at me. Using Brandon. And who else is next? Jesse? Is that where I draw the line?

No, I won't go back there. Not again. I'm done with that place.

I spin the car around, and drive back from where I came. I have to get back to the hotel. Someone there has probably seen her. If Lucy is truly missing, I would've heard from one of the crew by now. No one's called. No one's said a word.

She's okay. She'll be at the hotel. Just go back there and you'll see for yourself.

Soon, the hotel emerges in the distance. The parking lot, nearly empty. I assume everyone is back at the farmhouse, packing up the set. Surely, someone would've seen Lucy by now. This whole thing is just my imagination running wild. It's the fear of Brandon's murder and what it might mean that fuels my muddled thoughts.

I get out of the car and make my way into the hotel lobby. The cool air feels good on my skin. I'd become overheated driving back here, not realizing the air conditioning wasn't on. Never mind that now. I walk to the front desk. It's the same man as before. "Hello."

"Ms. Forbes, isn't it?" he asks.

"Yeah, that's me. Look, I know what you told my boyfriend. The whole elevator situation."

"Uh, yes, ma'am. I'm sorry, that must've been confusing for you," he replies.

"You have no idea." I look around. "Hey, can you tell me if Lucy Marks is here? She's in room 235."

He eyes his computer screen, then presses a few keys on the keyboard. As he continues to look at it, I see his face frown. He shakes his head. "Is everything all right?" I ask.

"Well, I see that Ms. Marks used her keycard this morning. But I don't see here that she's returned." He looks at me. "I'm sure she's with another member of your team."

I nod, feeling a rising panic in my chest. "You're probably right. Thank you for checking." I start away when he calls my name.

"Ms. Forbes?"

I look back at him.

"Again, about the elevator . . ."

I raise my hand to stop him. "Don't worry about it. Clearly, it's my mistake." I head back to the stairwell because I don't give a shit what he just said, I'm not taking the elevator again. I open the door, and I feel a hand on my back as I'm about to enter.

I spin around. "Holy shit!" The sight of her douses the fear burning in my chest. "Lucy, there you are." I grab her by the shoulders. "Where the hell have you been? I called twice. Texted. For God's sake . . . I've been worried sick."

"I'm fine, Kylie. See?" She pats herself down. "I'm right here and I'm fine." She grabs her phone and stares at the screen. "I didn't get a notification. I'm sorry. We've been so busy clearing out everything. And there's not much of a signal around here."

"No, I'm sorry . . . I thought . . ." I wave my hand. "Never mind what I thought. I'm just happy to see you."

CHAPTER 14

Detective Burns

Inside the diner, I see him. The detective involved with the original investigation into the massacre at New Hope. I finally managed to track down the old man. He's in a booth, sipping on a cup of coffee, and when he raises his gaze, he sees me too.

I approach him and offer him a greeting. "Detective Graves. I'm Detective Burns. I appreciate you meeting with me on short notice. Must've been quite a drive for you."

"Not at all." Graves gestures to the bench across from him.

I slide onto the black vinyl booth, sucking in my gut a little to clear the table. "I'd like to pick your brain, if I could, regarding what happened at the New Hope compound back in 2004."

"I figured." Graves, a slim man, in his late sixties, with a full head of gray hair, nods — slight disappointment masking his face, as if the event still haunts him. "What's happened that's brought that shitshow to the surface again?"

I take out a manila folder from my laptop bag and set it on the table. "There's a film shoot going on at a nearby farmhouse. One of their crew was murdered."

Graves pulls the file toward him and opens the folder, slipping on his reading glasses.

"As you'll see there," I continue. "The victim is a young man killed in a similar fashion as Lucas Shaw."

"Lucas Shaw." Graves shakes his head. "I haven't heard that name in a long time." He flips through the files, landing on the crime scene photo of Shaw after he was killed. "All those folks . . . they had either been arrested or had committed suicide. And the family of the man who murdered Shaw, well, they were slaughtered that night."

"That was my understanding," I say. "However, the film's crewmember, he — uh — his throat was slit. Eyes gouged out with a fork."

"His arm?" Graves asks. "Did it have a marking on it?"

I shake my head. "No. That's the one detail that doesn't match. But I have to think, given the location, that these murders are somehow connected."

"Did this victim have a connection to the area? Family, friends? Anything like that?" he asks.

"None that I've found," I reply. "But considering the killing happened a few miles from the former New Hope compound, well . . . I'm just trying to figure out if there's cause for concern. Maybe a re-emergence of the cult? Taking it into a far darker direction?"

I hesitate a moment to let my words settle around him. I can see the thought had occurred to him before . . . that the cult might return. Does he know more? Like, who would be its leader, if that was the case?

"And we've got a local man — Dale Coleman — who came onboard the film crew as a contractor a few days before it happened," I say. "Could be something there. I'm working on that."

Graves sips on his coffee again. "So, what is it you think I can do for you, Detective Burns? I've been retired since then. Moved north up to Sioux City. I have no ties to this place anymore. Good riddance, you know?"

"Oh, yeah. I hear you." I nod, running my finger around the rim of my water glass. "Suppose it goes back to this

Coleman character." I set my gaze on him. "Seems he went by another name prior to 2004. And I'm wondering . . . why? He gave me what I thought was some bullshit story and I had another look this morning after he stopped by to offer up more details. What he says does seem true."

"But you don't believe him?" Graves asks.

I pinch my lips. "Not particularly. The timing of his hiring strikes me as too coincidental. So, I'm here to ask if you've heard of Dale Reese. That was his name before he changed it to Coleman. And that just so happened to have been right around the time the compound burned to the ground."

Graves raises his mug to his lips and finishes the last sip of coffee. He sets it back down again and peers through the window overlooking the parking lot. "Everything about that place . . . the people . . . Lucas Shaw . . . we'd tried for years to take them down. We knew what Shaw was doing with the young girls. But every time we'd get close to bringing charges, the feds would shut us down."

I lean back in surprise. "Why the hell they do that?"

He looks at me, dead in the eyes. "Ruby Ridge. Waco. The feds didn't want to get burned again. And because the compound was on federal land, all we could do was sit back and watch." He shakes his head, looking disgusted. "Turns out, the followers brought themselves down."

I slip on my reading glasses and pull the folder back toward me. "I read that Shaw's closest confidant was the one who killed him."

"Yep," Graves replies. "When we managed to snag a few of them, we were told the same story. Clarence Skinner murdered Shaw. Slit his throat. Took out his eyes. Carved out the tattoo he had on his right arm. It was their symbol."

I flip through the file again until I get to the picture of the symbol. "This one, here?"

He looks at it. "That's the one. From witness accounts, Shaw was planning on marrying Clarence Skinner's daughter on her thirteenth birthday."

"Jesus."

"Oh yeah." Graves shakes his head. "Shaw was the worst kind of pedophile. Got the parents to go right along with it. Anyway, Skinner wasn't having any of it, so he killed Shaw. Well, as you can imagine, Shaw's followers were pretty pissed off. They came after Skinner's family. Took 'em all. Burned down everything."

I rub my hand over the top of my head. "Goddam. So you never heard of Dale Coleman, or Reese?"

"No, sir," Graves replies. "You probably got all the information I had in that file of yours there. We made a few arrests. The remainder, they're dead, either from the fire or by suicide. So if you got a murder that looks a lot like what happened to Shaw . . ." He pauses a moment. "Well, it wouldn't be hard to get those details off the internet, for a start. So, you could be dealing with someone who's looking to avenge Shaw."

I nod. "Any idea if Shaw has family? Seems like something I could follow up on."

Graves reaches for his wallet and sets down a fiver. "A lot of folks, kids, died in that fire. Not much left in the way of remains. Shaw's wives did have young children, but they all perished. So if he had other family, it's no one I ever heard of."

* * *

Progress is happening, but it's happening too slowly. I have to find a way to jump start this thing or it's going to go cold. While Graves offered some insight, he fell a little short, in my opinion. Either he knows more than he was willing to say, or he'd forgotten. But it's not really something you forget. So, I'm thinking he didn't want me dredging up the past.

It's not my first choice, but it's out of my hands. I go where the leads take me, and that's all there is to it. So could Dale Coleman/Reese be related to Shaw? It's a possibility I can't ignore. Now, I'll have to find a way to prove it. How? By going back to the crime scene, finding his DNA. I'm guessing he won't willingly offer it up to me. He did offer prints, which turned up nothing. And his feet were larger than the shoe prints left in the mud on the side of the road. Strike two. But one of the sets of shoeprints don't match the victim, so someone else was out there. Damn if I know who. Regardless, first things first. Get Coleman out of my head so I can move on or make an arrest.

When I see the farmhouse ahead, it looks different. The trailers are gone. A few cars scatter the parking area. I knew they were leaving, but they cleared out fast. Can't blame them.

I get out and walk toward the house. A few people move around, carrying boxes, packing up things. I look for the lady in charge. We've talked before, of course, her being the main contact regarding the death of her crewman.

"Excuse me," I say to a young gentleman.

"Yes?"

He notices right away I'm a cop, seeing my badge on my hip. Although I can't say he remembers I'm the one who's investigating this thing. "Where can I find the woman who runs things around here? Caroline, I believe." I knew her name, just wanted to come off casual.

"She's inside." He thumbs back to the house and walks on.

I walk up the porch steps and stand in the doorway. Cool air hits me. The air conditioner is running and the door's wide open. What is wrong with these people? Never mind that now. I have to find Caroline.

Inside, there are only a couple of folks. Most of the stuff's gone. Just some heavy furniture. Can't tell whether it was here before they arrived or not. I never came out here. Had no need. This house is owned by some company, along with the farmland. Everything around here is getting bought up by folks looking to change the way we farm. It's all bullshit, but I imagine the lawyers were salivating when Hollywood came knocking on their doors about this place.

"Where can I find Caroline?" I ask to the room. All eyes turn to me. They all got a damn sorrowful look on their faces.

"In the kitchen," one of them says.

"Thank you." I carry on, heading straight into the kitchen. This is where it happened. A pinkish stain is still visible on the old linoleum floor. I see the kid in my mind's eye, like he was still laying here. I haven't seen a lot of murder, but they stick with you, the dead ones.

I see Caroline near the refrigerator. "Hello, Caroline?"

She turns around, her face looking a lot like the rest of them. "Detective Burns, what are you doing here?"

"Well," I say, my hands in my pockets. "I'm following up on a potential lead."

A gleam of hope sparks in her eyes. "You know who did it?"

"No, ma'am. I don't mean to raise expectations. I'm just working on something. A hunch, I guess you'd call it."

"Oh, I see." All hope drains from her face. "My team and I . . . we've told you everything we know about Brandon."

"No, I get that, ma'am. I'm actually here to ask you a few questions about Dale Coleman."

"Coleman?" She raises her gaze, like the name's sparked her memory.

"I believe he's the local man you all brought in to help with set construction?" I tell her, hoping to prod her along.

"Oh, yeah. Sure. I know who you're talking about. He's not here. Our lead set designer didn't need him anymore, so we got him paid up and that's it, I believe."

"You mind telling me what he did for you? What area he was working?" I ask.

"Mason?" she calls out, louder than I expect.

"Yeah?"

I hear a man's voice down the hall.

"The detective is here. You have a minute?" she adds, her voice still loud. Guess that's what makes her good at her job. She can get folks' attention, no doubt about it.

Footsteps sound on the wood floor, echoing through the hall. I wait until I see him. "Mason." I extend my hand.

"Detective, what can I do for you?" He glances at Caroline, then returns his attention to me.

"Mr. Dale Coleman. The local you all hired," I reply. "Can you tell me where you had him working?"

"Where?" Mason looks around, hands on his hips.

"Yes, sir. He was helping with set construction, as I understand it. Whereabouts was that? I'd like to have a wander 'round if I could."

He looks at Caroline again. She nods and he turns back to me. "I can take you out there. Follow me."

So I do. I keep up with the man, who walks outside like he's in a hurry. The sun's getting hotter by the minute, and I have to wipe the bead of sweat from my forehead with a handkerchief. "When you all think you'll be rolling out of here?"

"Got pushed back a little. It's scheduled for tomorrow morning now, but most everything will be out of here today," he replies.

"Well, I'm sure you folks want to put all this in the rearview. I know I do."

He glances at me, a half-smile on his face. "What's your interest in Mr. Coleman?"

"I'll be honest with you, Mason. I'm not sure yet," I reply. "But nothing's coming easy for me on this one, and so it's time to cast a wider net. See what I can catch."

We stop at a small outbuilding. Looks new and I figure it was built specially for the film.

"Dale did most of the work out here," Mason says. "My guys helped, of course, but I can't fault the man . . . he's a good carpenter."

I take a good long look at the building. More like a shed. "What'd you use this for?"

"There's a scene where a woman is kept in here against her will."

"I wonder . . . would folks be so interested in movies like this, where girls are always getting hurt or murdered . . . I wonder if they'd still be interested if they ever saw it in real life." I turn to him. "Cause I'll tell you, nothing hurts more than seeing innocent blood spilled. I'm not sure people get that."

"I think it's just a form of entertainment, Detective," Mason replies. "People like a good story. And in this story, the girl is a survivor."

"I suppose that makes me feel better." I take in a deep breath. "Listen, I'd like to walk around here, but don't feel like you need to babysit me."

"No, yeah, sure." He nods. "I'll leave you to it. And hey, I'll be in the house if you need anything else."

"Appreciate it, son."

"Thank you, Detective." He pauses a moment. "I hope you find the fucker who did this."

I smile. "That makes two of us." I wait until he leaves, then open the door to the shed. It's got a window. A florescent light above. Looks like they tried to make it appear old and creepy. I suppose they succeeded. I never was much for horror-type or thriller movies. I like to watch detective shows so I can laugh my ass off when they get the most basic of police procedures wrong. Still, to each their own. I'm here to find anything Coleman left behind.

My best shot is for Coleman to have scraped up something. Cut himself. Something that might've left a little bit of blood behind. I don't need much. Even if it's dried up on a piece of wood. It'll do.

The shed's only about ten by twelve, so I look around. A few shelves sit on the back wall. They got some old-looking wood flooring down here. A small rocking chair in the corner. I have no idea the plot of this movie, but I don't like it already.

I narrow my gaze, sharpening my old eyes for any sign of a mishap. Any hint of blood on the wood. *Something, please God, give me something to work with here, cause I am running out of ideas.*

I stop cold.

Now, I'm not a big believer in a higher power, but I'm fairly confident there's something greater than myself. No sooner did I ask for help, than help seemed to have arrived. I need my readers for this, so I slip them on and lean in for a closer look.

"Well, I'll be damned." I could use a flathead screwdriver. Maybe a utility knife. Yeah, that would be better. I walk out again in search of Mason. Instead, I find a man loading a piece of equipment onto a truck. "Excuse me, sir."

He stops to look at me. "Yes, sir. You're the detective."

"I am that. Listen, uh, you got a box cutter on you or something I could borrow a minute?"

"Sure." He reaches into his back pocket. "Will this do? It's just a Swiss Army knife, but it's sharp."

"This'll do just fine. I'll bring it right back."

"No problem."

I return to the shed, which clearly has no air conditioning in it. Lord knows how any actor could stay in here for long in the heat of the day. Never mind. I'm only here for one thing. And I'm about to get it.

Carefully, I carve away the section of the two-by-four with a smudge of blood on it. Lucky me, it's got a partial print embedded in it too. Can't hurt to get as much evidence as I can scrape up. Literally.

It takes a few moments of carefully carving it out of the beam, but I got it. I now hold in my hands someone's DNA. I sure do hope it belongs to Dale Coleman.

CHAPTER 15

Kylie

Jesse and I have been in our room for the past hour, packing, looking over the plan for the new location, which is out in Montana now. It's about as far away as I can get from here, and I couldn't be happier.

We aren't saying much to each other. The elevator situation . . . I know damn well I didn't press that button, but Jesse said he saw the video. I don't argue with him. No point, and I refuse to watch the video myself. Mostly out of fear he's right.

And then this thing . . . Brandon's murder. It sits between us. A third wheel that spins around our grief, neither of us knowing how to get rid of it. Jesse senses I'm keeping something from him, but doesn't press me about it. It's as if we're hovering over all the bad things that've happened over the course of a week, praying it'll all disappear. If we can just leave, this will all go away.

It's a selfish thought, I know. I've only been thinking about me and the impact this has had on me. But it's Brandon who's paid the price. A debt he didn't owe. A debt, I think, that whoever killed him wanted me to pay instead.

That should be enough reason for me to go to the police. At least, tell them what I know. What I remember of those dark days. Could it make a difference in the case? I have to assume it would, but then I try to talk myself out of it again. Insisting to myself that the police will find evidence and that will lead them to the killer.

Jesse walks over to me as I peer through the hotel room window at the setting sun. "Kylie, hey."

I turn to him. "Yeah?"

"I just got a text. Looks like they're all packed up. The trucks move out in the morning."

I breath out my relief. "Thank God."

"Listen, I feel like . . ." He hesitates, licking his lips and running a hand through his thick blond hair. "Do you want to talk about what happened in the elevator?"

I look down, closing my eyes, unprepared for this conversation. "No. I already told you what happened. I didn't push the button, Jesse, I didn't."

He raises his hands. "Okay. Okay, I hear you. But since we got here, I don't know . . . you seem different. Preoccupied or something. I really wish you'd talk to me."

"It's nothing, really." My lie comes out easier than I expect. Of course, I've lied about this particular issue plenty of times over the course of the past twenty years. "I suppose just being back here, back in Iowa, it reminds me of my parents."

"Right. Sure. That accident must've been so hard for you. And your Aunt Grace, she's a godsend."

"Yes, she is," I reply. "Back to tonight, uh, I assume we'll all head down to the restaurant for dinner and an update?"

"I believe that's the plan," Jesse replies. "You up for that?"

"I am. But I'm taking the stairs."

He smiles at me. "Fair enough."

* * *

We head toward the lobby, both of us taking the stairs and not the elevator. Jesse is nothing if not supportive. And on our arrival, most of the crew are there. The actors, too. Still, everyone wears their hearts on their sleeves. All of them, knowing we're leaving without Brandon.

"Why don't you sit down?" I say to Jesse. "I need to powder my nose."

"Why didn't you do that upstairs? We just left . . ." He stops himself. "Never mind. I'll be over there." He aims a finger toward the others.

"Okay." I head toward the restrooms. As I pass the elevators, I can't resist taking another look. Stepping closer, I inspect the brushed metal doors, running my fingers along the seams, looking for any sign of something that might've made it stop.

And when I still see nothing, I'm anything but convinced I actually stopped it myself. Now, I walk down the hall, toward the rear exit. I see only one camera mounted on the ceiling, but Jesse said another one was inside the elevator. I don't recall it. I don't recall anything of those minutes that ticked by while I screamed, scaring the shit out of everyone.

Footfalls sound behind me as I stand in the corridor. It's a soft patter, almost drowned out by the hum of the nearby ice machine. But on spinning around, I see only an empty hall before me. Just red and gold carpet stretching out into the lobby. Then I hear the soft scuff of a shoe against the carpet ahead. I turn forward again, straining my eyes into the dimly lit hall, searching for any sign of movement.

"Hello?" My voice comes out soft, bouncing off the walls and returning to me as a hollow echo. "Is someone there?"

Only silence answers, a suffocating blanket that seems to swallow up my words and everything else around me. I don't even hear the crew in the hotel bar anymore. The footsteps have stopped, replaced by an unsettling stillness that sets my nerves on end. I can't shake off the prickling sense that hidden eyes are watching me, tracking my every move.

The air around me feels thin. I need to go outside, clear my head. With trembling hands, I fumble with the metal handle of the exit door, desperate to escape the oppressive hush of the hallway.

The door swings open, and I step out into the still-warm evening air. I try to steady my fraying nerves, inhaling deeply. Just stressed and on edge after everything that's happened.

As I walk around the side of the hotel, the parking lot comes into view. The sight of the cars parked under flickering streetlamps is familiar and reassuring; it's an anchor in this sea of unease. It helps to settle my nerves.

"Kayla?" a voice calls out from behind me.

I freeze on the spot, my breath hitching in my throat. No one here knows that name. I'm stuck in place as I wait for the voice to call out again, but there's only more silence. "Who are you?" I say into the darkness, my voice barely a whisper. I'm speaking to no one, and the fear grips me tighter than ever. "Why are you here?"

I'm answered with silence once again. My eyes sting as I try to keep from collapsing into a heap on the ground. *Don't do this. Don't give in. It's just your imagination.*

But Brandon's death isn't my imagination.

I take a deep, shaky breath and turn back, heading toward the rear hotel entrance again. Stepping inside, everything appears as it was. Even the sound of chatter drifts back toward me. I need to pull myself together before facing the others.

As I re-enter the lobby, I spot Jesse waving me over to the group gathered near the restaurant. I force a smile and head their way, pushing aside my unease.

"There you are," Jesse says, draping an arm around my shoulders. "I thought you got lost on the way to the bathrooms."

I smile, forgetting the reason I'd gone into the hall in the first place. I never even used the restroom. "Sorry about that."

Caroline stands and garners everyone's attention. "All right, guys. I know this has been an extremely difficult day for all of us. Brandon was . . ." Her voice cracks. "Brandon was at the heart of this production. His passion for his work was clear to anyone who knew him."

Murmurs of agreement ripple through the crew. I study their faces, wondering if his killer is among us. If any of them know who I am.

"We've decided to continue filming as a tribute to Brandon's memory," Caroline adds. "It's what he would have wanted. So tomorrow we head to the next location as planned. You have the flight schedules in your email. It won't be easy, but we'll get through this together."

Everyone voices their support, their tones filled with determination and resilience. Even I start to feel a little more at ease, reaching for Jesse's hand. He smiles at me. Then it comes . . .

A blood-curdling scream arises from the hall, cutting through the chatter. Voices immediately silence and movement stops, like someone hit pause on a movie scene. Is this in my head or is it really happening? No. This is real. Everyone heard it.

Someone shrieks again — louder, more desperate. "Jesus." I push back my chair, the metallic screech of it toppling over echoes. Panic blankets the room as everyone jumps up, but I run. Run toward the source of the scream. And then I see her.

One of the assistants looms over, screaming. "Lucy!"

She's slumped against the wall, her legs splayed out, her arms hanging down, hands resting in her own blood. She gurgles, blood spilling from her neck. I push the other woman aside, kneel before her, cupping her neck. "No, no, no. Please . . . Lucy, can you hear me?"

She's alive; she knows I'm here with her. He didn't get her eyes. The assistant must've interrupted him before he could finish . . . whoever 'he' is.

"Who did this to you, Luce? Please, answer me . . ." I beg, still trying to slow the bleeding from her neck. My hands are covered in her warm blood. Her mouth hangs open, trying to form words.

Jesse clutches my shoulders. "Kylie . . ."

"Call 911!" I yell. "Lucy?" My plea hangs in the air. "Please don't die. Please." I feel his hands squeeze this time.

"Kylie, step back. Come on."

I shrug him off. "No! I won't let her die."

From the corner of my eye, I see the manager rushing toward us, holding what looks like a first aid kit. I think we all know nothing in that case will help her.

"Babe, you gotta get back," he says, pulling me away. "Let him try. We've called the police. They're coming."

I look at Lucy; her eyes are sleepy now. The gurgling has stopped, though blood still pours from her neck.

"Let me try," the manager says, kneeling beside me, flipping open the case of bandages and ice packs.

Jesse helps me up. I look around to see everyone crying and screaming. "It's my fault."

"What?" Jesse demands. "What are you talking about?"

"I was just outside. I heard something. Someone . . ."

"You did? When?"

"Outside, the parking lot." He lets me go and darts into the hall, toward the door at the back. He disappears outside. "Jesse, don't go out there. Please!"

* * *

The police are here. They've surrounded the hotel, searching the perimeter. But they won't find the killer. He's gone. I know it's a he because he called my name. My real name. All the signs . . . her blood. The symbol. Brandon. Now, Lucy is gone, too. She was my responsibility. My best friend, and I could've stopped it. I could've told the detective that I was there that day. The day New Hope burned to the ground. The day my family was slaughtered. But I didn't. So yes, Brandon and Lucy are dead because of me. The man who called my name proved as much.

I see Detective Burns walk into the lobby. Most of us are huddled in the restaurant. More than a few of us have had drinks. Not me. I refuse to drown my misery in booze. I need to feel this pain I caused.

"Ms. Forbes, I'd like a word with you," Burns says to me. And only me.

"You want me to come with you?" Jesse asks.

"No. I'll be okay." I extract myself from Jesse's embrace and follow Burns out to the courtyard. He wants to speak in private. He knows who I am.

"You told them you heard someone outside. That you went out there only minutes before Ms. Marks was discovered," he says.

"Yes. I'd gone to use the restroom. Felt like I needed some air, so I went outside." The words lie on the tip of my tongue, begging to be spoken. It's me they're after. Whoever 'they' are. But I say nothing more.

"Did anyone see you out there?"

"No. I was alone." I see him jot down something in his notebook.

"So, no one at all saw you outside?" He squints at me. "Only when you returned to the group?"

What's he getting at? I rack my brain, thinking of every moment leading up to when I heard the scream. Then I think back to what happened in the hardware store. My shoes. The elevator. *Oh my God . . .*

"Tell me what happened when you heard the scream," Burns says, keeping a steely gaze on me.

"I–I ran back into the hallway to help. When I got there, Lucy was on the ground. There was so much blood." I do my best to steady my tone.

Burns jots down words again in his notebook. "And before that, before Lucy was killed, was the voice you supposedly heard male or female? What did he or she say to you?"

Supposedly? I hesitate, the words sticking in my throat. What should I say? That it was a man's voice, calling me by my real name, the one I've tried so hard to bury? The name that links me to the tragedy of the past, that marks me as a target now in the present?

"I'm not sure. It was dark. I didn't see anyone. The voice was faint, just a whisper. I couldn't make out any words." The lie burns my tongue, but I hold the detective's gaze, willing myself not to waver.

He regards me steadily, as if trying to see through to my core. "Nothing at all? No name? You didn't go looking for the source of the voice?"

I shake my head. "No. I was . . . startled. I thought I imagined it at first. When I didn't hear anything else, I went back inside."

After a tense moment, he glances down and scribbles in his notebook again. "And you didn't see anyone? No shadows moving, anything like that?"

"Like I said, Detective, it was just the voice and then silence."

He presses his lips together, raking his eyes over me. Examining every inch of my body. My heart hammers in my chest as it becomes clear he suspects me.

"Okay, Ms. Forbes," he finally says. "I think that's all for now." Burns nods, glancing around the courtyard bathed in darkness. "You should get back inside with the others. We've swept the premises, but until we have a suspect in custody, no one should be out here alone."

I follow him inside as we return to the lobby. The manager approaches him as I make my way back to Jesse.

"I need the name of every employee clocked in right now," Burns says to the man.

I see him eye the bar.

"Where's he at?"

"Who, sir?" the manager asks.

Burns must've felt my gaze as he glances at me. I continue on my way but hear him reply.

"Your bartender."

CHAPTER 16

It's me he's after. I see that now. Can I really sit back and watch another friend and co-worker die such a brutal death? The fear in this hotel is palpable. The only reason most of us are still here is because the cops haven't finished clearing the scene.

First thing in the morning, everyone will be gone. But what if the killer is among us? What if he is one of us? Why not come for me, then? Why hurt others to get to me? It's a question I can't seem to shake from my thoughts. But the one I haven't asked myself is, what if it's me? What if *I'm* the killer? Can I continue to ignore all the signs?

I look over at Jesse, who's only just managed to nod off. It's two in the morning. I won't sleep. Maybe not ever again. But can I leave without disturbing him? I can't stay here. I have to go back because I think he's there, waiting for me. Is it Lucas? No. I saw his body. He didn't survive my father's attack.

Maybe someone had been released from prison, and they figured out I'm alive. God knows how. The only person who knows I survived the massacre is Aunt Grace. If it is someone from New Hope, they're close. They're watching me. So, the time's come for me to end this. *I'll find you. I know where you are, and you can't hide there forever.*

And if it *is* me? No. It can't be. It's not possible.

I get out of bed and slip on my clothes. With my phone and car keys in hand, I step out into the hall. The door clicks shut.

Jesse can't know where I'm going, so I turn off the app that tracks my location. We both use it, so we know if one of us is in trouble. It was my idea, and he didn't balk at the suggestion. But for now, this is on me. This is my problem to fix.

Long ago, my father taught me how to use a gun. I wish I had one now. I'm a decent shot, or at least I was.

I carry on into the stairwell and walk outside. The air is still warm and muggy. I should be afraid. Afraid he's out here waiting for me. And I suppose I am. But if I leave with everyone in the morning, will he follow? I can't risk it, even if I have no idea whether this is going to work. I've lived this moment before. Escaping a killer. Those people don't have any hold on me now. I was only a kid then.

I get inside the car. The engine purrs as I press the ignition. I'm careful not to turn on the headlights. Driving out, I know that I'll find this person, and I'll end them. I have a knife with me. Jesse keeps one in his toolkit. He has no idea I took it, or what I intend to do with it. But if I don't survive, at least my friends will still be safe. I'm not going to lie . . . I really don't want it to come to that.

As I drive down the darkened road, the yellow dashes in the center of it keeping me focused, a light on the dash illuminates. Damn it. I need gas. I could push it, but hey, I'm not that crazy. No point in getting stranded out here. I have to at least give myself a fighting chance for survival.

Are there any gas stations around? I recall one. A 24-hour station on the right side of the road, before the turn that takes you to the freeway. "Perfect."

I see it ahead. The lights are on, so I pull in. As I step out, I see a set of headlights appear in the distance. They weren't there before. I'm being followed.

The store is closed, and only the pumps are running. Oh, God. Do I get back in the car and floor it? I'll run out of gas within twenty miles, maybe less. I'd better decide, because that vehicle is getting closer. And as I keep my gaze on it, its shape comes into focus.

"What the hell?" It's a truck. And I recognize it. "Dale?"

Of course it's him. I don't know how he knows who I am, but it's clear that he does, and now he's coming for me. Visions of Lucy fill my head. Her last moments of life as she stared at me, spilling blood from her neck. I force myself to see her, reminding myself that I have to be strong. Reminding myself I would've never hurt her, or anyone, but especially her. Lucy and I were close, like sisters. She was the age Katie would've been now. Part of the reason I was drawn to her was because she reminded me of Katie. Tears sting the back of my eyes. He's the one — Dale Coleman — and he's turning in now.

I slip back behind the wheel, as if somehow I'm better protected, when he pulls to a stop in front of me. I peer over my shoulder, figuring the only way out is to reverse. But then I see the pump's dispenser hanging from the car's tank. "Goddam it." Screw the damage. I have to get out of here.

I slam the gearshift into reverse and the pounding on my window makes me jump. I see him, staring at me, his fists still clenched.

"Kayla. Kayla, I won't hurt you. I swear it."

"Get away from me!" I scream. Then I realize he called me *Kayla*.

"Grace Forbes. I know her," he says.

Confusion pulls me in its grip. "What?" My voice is only a whisper, because I'm not sure I heard clearly.

"Your aunt. Please, Kayla, let me explain. It's not safe for you here."

"Yeah, no shit," I say.

He steps back, raising his hands in surrender. "I was there. I know what happened."

My lips part as I draw deeper and deeper breaths. I stare at him. Is he lying? How would he know about Aunt Grace? I don't understand.

"I know what your father did," he continues. "And I know why he did it."

Do I trust him? Do I dare step out of this car? And then he raises the sleeve on his right arm. I thrust my hand over my mouth. The symbol. He's one of them.

Dale steps away from the door. His eyes plead with mine. I grip the handle, fear pressing down on me so hard I can barely breathe. I'd been alone with him enough times that if he'd wanted to kill me, he'd already had plenty of opportunity to do it, so I take my chances. Maybe he has answers.

I open the driver's door, snatching the knife and my phone from the passenger seat. Can't afford to blindly trust him.

"Kayla Skinner," he says, in a hushed tone. As I step out of the car, he continues, "I'd like to formally introduce myself. Retired FBI Special Agent Dale Coleman."

"FBI?" I say, as confusion swirls. "How do you know me, then?"

"Like I said, I was there. I'm not surprised you don't remember me." He smiles. "I was a lot younger, my hair was long and dark. Not this short, graying, thinning hair I have now." He pats his stomach. "I was several pounds lighter. And you were young, with no reason to notice me. I didn't make myself stand out too much, and that was on purpose."

"I don't understand," I reply. "After it all happened, no one ever said anything about the FBI."

He tucks his hands into the pockets of his jeans. "I was undercover. After it all went down, my cover died along with everyone else in the compound." He hesitates a moment. "Now, it looks like history is repeating itself, and I'm here to help you."

In an instant, I hear a whizzing sound slice through the air, then the echo of a pop from the gunshot. Dale jerks back, his eyes on me, startled. He stumbles and falls to the ground before me.

"No!" I scream, whipping around in search of the shooter. A vehicle races up toward us.

Dale grips my ankle and I look down at him. "Kayla, go."

I stagger toward the car, my head dizzy with fear. The echoes of more gunshots reverberate around me as I hurry to seek shelter in the car. Every nerve in my body screams for escape; I know I can't stay here. But Dale . . .

Tires screech behind me on the concrete forecourt of the gas station. The threat, racing up behind me. I press the ignition, desperate to escape and prepare to shift into drive. Dale's truck is parked in front me. "Goddam it!" I press on the gas, pushing into it, hoping to move the ancient, heavy truck, but this damn rental car is small and lightweight. The tires spin beneath me, and I struggle to control the wheel. Nothing I do is making the truck move. "Fuck!" If I turn left, I'll run Dale over. I'm stuck.

I hear the rev of an engine behind me, then the clash of metal. I'm propelled forward, a sudden jolt that sends me crashing into the steering wheel, the airbag exploding in my face.

My head spins. My face stings from the blow. I realize I'm trapped, the other vehicle pinning me in place. Panic seizes me as I lock eyes with the figure emerging from the truck behind me. His features slowly come into focus. Thin, tall, but I don't recognize him.

Frantically, I push against the driver's door, only to feel it stick under a collapsed frame. With no means of escape on this side, I scramble toward the passenger door, but it remains obstinately shut as well. My gaze darts back to see the man now brandishing a knife. Why not the gun? Why not shoot me now, just like he did Dale?

"Who are you?" I manage to choke out.

"You know who I am," he replies, his voice muffled as I sit in the car.

I turn around and kick the passenger window until it shatters. Glass claws across my stomach and arms as I climb through. Blood spills down my body, but I don't care, because if I let him get me, I'm dead.

Tumbling out onto the ground, I have only seconds to get up and run. I hear him grunting nearby, and I scramble up onto unsteady legs. I do what Dale told me. I run. Into the darkness, my breaths shallow. My footsteps on the asphalt thump in my ears. He has a gun. All he has to do is point and shoot, so I run faster and faster.

There's nothing out here. No one around for miles. It's the dead of night, and the only person who could've helped me is lying in a pool of blood next to my car. Dale. Jesus. He was FBI. I don't understand. How did he know me? Grace?

Questions for another time, because I'm running for my life, and I need to find a place to hide. I hear an engine behind me, and I'm caught in the headlights. It's him.

I dart into the cornfield, the stalks slashing my arms as I push through them. My lungs burn and my legs ache, but I can't stop. The sound of the engine grows louder, the light bouncing around as he pursues me through the field. I scramble and slip on the uneven ground, mud sucking at my feet. But I keep moving, kept alive by raw adrenaline.

I chance a look back and see the glow of headlights cutting through the corn. He's right behind me. I push harder, my breath coming in ragged gasps. The stalks thin ahead and I burst from the field onto a dirt road. No cover here. I spot a house just ahead. The farmhouse? Am I back at the farmhouse?

I don't hear the car anymore, but I still see lights. I can only pray he got stuck in the muck of the cornfield. But then, he could be on foot. No time to waste. I need a place to hide.

I race up the porch steps and try the handle. Locked. Of course it is. We've moved everything out. I look behind me, squinting to see any shadows moving in the darkness, but I don't see a thing.

With my elbow, I crash through the side window. The shattering glass echoes inside. I crawl in, causing more and more cuts along my body. I'm soaked in my own blood.

Inside, I don't dare turn on a light. Instead, I run toward the back of the house. There's a sunroom back here. I can get out that way if necessary.

I crouch down behind a reclining chair, struggling to quiet my frantic breaths. The picture of a landscape on the wall in front of me blurs as tears fill my eyes. But I quickly blink them back, knowing I can't afford to lose control. Not now.

The cuts covering my body sting, and my clothes are damp with blood, but I push the pain from my mind. Survival is all that matters now. I strain to listen past the hammering of my pulse. The creak of floorboards. The rustle of corn stalks outside. Is he here? Has he found me?

I peer around the edge of the recliner. The room is cloaked in shadow, moonlight filtering faintly through the windows. Movement catches my eye. A curtain fluttering from the breeze of the window I just smashed.

I think of Dale lying on the concrete. Who was he? He says he was there, but I don't remember. FBI? How? Did Grace really know all this?

In the darkness, every creak and groan of the old house puts me on edge. I strain to hear any sounds of pursuit over the thunderous pounding of my heart. The silence almost seems louder than any noise.

After what feels like an eternity, I hear the crunch of footsteps on gravel outside. Holding my breath, I edge closer to the front window and peer out. A dark figure stalks toward the porch, knife glinting in the moonlight. He means to not just kill me, but to hurt me in the process.

Panic balls tighter in my gut. The footsteps reach the porch and stop outside the front door. I hear the handle rattle as he tests it. But he doesn't bother climbing through the broken window. Instead, the door gives way, and the splintering of wood scatters everywhere.

CHAPTER 17

2003 — FBI Special Agent Dale Coleman

The world is different now. It's been three years since 9/11, and as a federal agent, nothing is the same. Even my latest posting. A radical cult-like group in southwestern Iowa led by a man named Lucas Shaw. I was recently assigned to work undercover as Dale Reese, and Shaw has finally accepted me. I'm in.

Today, I made up an excuse to leave. Blaming family obligations, though I am fairly certain Shaw held some suspicions. So, I had to take care not to be followed. It's part of the job.

I'm here now, in Des Moines, to report to my boss, Assistant Special Agent in Charge Lockridge. I alter my appearance so as to look professional. On the compound, it's a come-as-you-are type of place. My hair hasn't been this long since high school. I haven't worn a suit since the day I was assigned this case. I have to be honest, I feel human again.

"Morning, sir," I say, walking into the ASAC's office.

"Agent Coleman, take a seat." The old man gestures to the chair across from him.

I unbutton my suit jacket and sit. "Sir."

"How are things going over at New Hope?" Lockridge asks. "You've been there two months. Are you getting close to Shaw?"

"In a manner of speaking, sir," I reply, knowing how hard it's been for me to get within arm's length of the man. "He's got a lot of people around him, including Clarence Skinner. A man I believe has ulterior motives."

"How do you mean?"

I lean back in the chair. "I've sensed a change in him. He seems short, on edge. At first, I believed him to be somewhat of a reasonable guy, but as the weeks have gone by, I've sensed a more extreme belief in him. I don't know what that means. And to be honest, I'm not sure what to do about it, so I'm keeping my eye on him." I shift my weight in the uncomfortable chair. "The people Shaw surrounds himself with are careful who they let get close to him. This hasn't been easy, but I'm carving out a place for myself there."

I hand over a file. "You'll see my notes inside and the most recent report." I wait a moment for him to peruse the information. "Shaw is admired by them. Loved. And there are rumors he intends on taking another wife. Soon."

"Rumors?" Lockridge asks.

"For now, but I'm working on that, too. I understand he waits until the girls are thirteen, then takes them as brides."

"Jesus H."

"It gets worse from there, sir," I add. "If they don't produce a child within a year, they're cast out of the group. However, I'm not sure that's ever happened. I haven't seen this take place, so I can only assume it's a rumor until I do."

"Why isn't this enough to bring charges?" he asks. "Age of consent is sixteen here. And that's only if the partner is within four years of that. We can't let these kids . . ."

"Because all his current wives are at least eighteen now, sir. Well, they say they're eighteen."

Lockridge closes the file and studies me. "Your job was to infiltrate the group. Get close to Lucas Shaw and determine whether they're stockpiling weapons."

"I'm aware of that, sir. I know we're on the lookout for domestic terrorist groups. But I don't think Shaw is interested so much in attacking us as he is in controlling his followers." I pull to the edge of my seat, resting my elbows on the metal arms of the chair. "And going back to Clarence Skinner, well, I think his daughter might be next. I think Lucas has his sights on her to be his wife. That could explain the change in behavior I'm seeing in Skinner himself."

Lockridge tilts his head, narrowing his gaze. "Go on."

"Kayla Skinner. She's about to turn thirteen. And what I do know about Clarence and his family is that his wife had been a member of New Hope years ago, long before Lucas Shaw led the group. In fact, he'd been a follower at that time. Then by some circumstance, I'm not aware of yet, Clarence Skinner meets her — Evie Forbes. She leaves the cult, only to return five years ago with her husband and children. Including the oldest, Kayla."

"The wife?" Lockridge asks. "She's got deep ties to the group."

"Deeper than Clarence Skinner, yes, sir," I reply. "We have a lot of moving parts. I need to see how they connect. I'm asking for more time because I have a feeling something's about to go down."

* * *

Present Day

My vision is fuzzy, but I see light above me. It takes a minute to focus on it. Fluorescents, flickering in the night. I'm still under the awning at the gas station. Pain sears through my back, a harsh reminder of my reality — I've been shot. Hard to forget when I'm lying in a pool of my own blood. Each breath is a struggle, and my strength is waning.

The coward shot me in the chest. Missed my heart, but I'm pretty sure at least one lung was hit. I don't know, but it hurts like hell. Each breath I take is a struggle. I blink as the car before me comes into view. "Kayla." My voice rasps out. "Kayla? Where are you? Are you hurt?"

Fear grips me when I get no reply. If she's dead . . . "Kayla?" Still nothing. She needs help, and so do I. I look back toward the road where a hint of gray light emerges through the trees — dawn is breaking. Must be four or four-thirty in the morning. That means I've been here for at least two hours — two hours too long. I have to get help.

I attempt to push myself off the ground, aiming for my truck parked a few feet away. But I see it. Kayla's car must've been pushed into it. Her front end is crumpled. My truck . . . I doubt it will even start now.

"Anyone here? I need help. Hello?" The echo of my own voice is the only response I get.

The pain is excruciating as I drag myself along the ground, each movement sending fresh waves of agony through me. Shattered glass shimmers on the concrete under the lights, catching my eye — it's from the passenger side of the car she was driving. *That's how you got her.*

My truck seems miles away, but I know it's my only hope. Inside is my lifeline — my phone. I can call for help, alert Detective Burns. I'll have to tell him everything. How I barely escaped from New Hope in the nick of time, how the fire had consumed everything, but I managed to survive. And so did Kayla.

I've been living on borrowed time since then, ever since the night I helped Grace Forbes with her niece. I've been waiting, fearing they would return. And it seems, after all this time, someone did.

The truck is close now, just a few feet away. *Move, goddam it!* I command myself. But I'm older now. Not the young federal agent I used to be. On a good day, moving is hard enough. Let alone when you've been shot.

Still, I try. Each pull forward is a battle against my own body, each movement punctuated by a groan of agony. My head grows light and my vision blurs at the edges — signs of blood loss and impending unconsciousness. I can't pass out now — not when help is so close within reach.

My hand stretches out toward the truck door, but falls short. The door is too high up — an insurmountable obstacle in my current state. Tears of frustration blur my vision as I realize the futility of my efforts — if I don't stand up, I'm not going to make it.

Gritting my teeth against the pain, I pull myself onto my knees. *That's it. You can do it, old man.* My kneecaps feel like they'll shatter under my weight, but I push through and manage to get one foot under me for balance.

Almost there now.

I grip the sideboard, using it as leverage to pull myself to my feet. I press down, screaming in agony now.

I can't. I just can't. I'm sorry, Kayla. I'm sorry, Grace.

CHAPTER 18

Kylie

The door from the sunroom . . . that's my only shot at getting out now. He's inside the house, and he will find me. Rushing back outside into the darkness, I see a hint of dawn emerge. I don't know how long I have before he realizes I've made it out. I just need enough time to lose him. Can I make it back to the hotel?

I think about Dale. Is he still alive? Did he go and get help? No one knows where I am. My phone is still in the car. And I turned off the location so Jesse wouldn't know where I'd gone. Now, he'll never find me.

But I can't think about that now. I have to survive, so I run. Back into the cornfields. Glancing over my shoulder, I still see the farmhouse cast in shadow. I know the road isn't far. Maybe I can make it back to the gas station? Maybe it'll be open, and they'll see what happened. They'll help Dale.

I feel sick from the adrenaline. From the fear. From the cuts all over me. But I keep running, sprinting through the cornfields, my lungs burning, my legs throbbing. The stalks whip against my arms, leaving thin red welts alongside the deeper gashes. My mind conjures shadowy visions of the shooter emerging from the farmhouse, his face still obscured by darkness. *Who the hell are you?*

Up ahead, I can see the road, a gray ribbon cutting through the endless sea of corn. The gas station sits just off the shoulder, its fluorescent lights piercing the pre-dawn gloom. I push myself harder, nearly stumbling over the uneven ground. Just a little farther.

My car. Dale's truck. I seem them both. He's still here. Oh God. Does that mean he's dead?

As I burst from the fields onto the cracked asphalt, I scan the gas station, hoping to see someone there. I slow to a jog, then stop, hands on knees as I gasp.

An engine sounds in the distance. I stand upright again, looking back. It's him. He's coming, and I know he'll come here first. Out of steam, I jog ahead.

"Dale?" I see him leaning against the passenger door of his truck, an arm hanging over the sideboards. "Dale? Oh my God." I run to him and crouch low. "Dale, wake up." I slap his cheek but get no response. "Please be alive. Please be alive." I press my ear against his lips. A faint sound of breath. I take in his fragile state. He's barely hanging on. I can see it. "Dale, I'm going to get help. Just hang on and don't die."

I run back to my car and see my phone on the floorboard of the passenger seat. Running around to the other side, I reach over the shards of glass clinging to the door frame, but I'm unable to reach it. Climbing inside is my only shot at getting it.

The sound of the looming engine grows louder. Lights appear far off in the distance. I have only seconds, so I climb in, tumbling onto the passenger seat, and reaching down for the phone. I have it. It's in my hands.

With shaking fingers, I dial emergency. The dispatcher answers. "Hello? Hello, I need help. Someone's been shot. I'm being chased. Please, send help."

"Ma'am. Tell me where you're at," she says.

I look around, shrugging. "At a gas station. I–I don't know where exactly. I'm outside Carroll. About fifteen minutes west." I look out toward the road. "Please, send help. He's coming."

"Okay, ma'am, I need you to stay on the line, all right? Don't hang up. I need you to tell me when you hear the sirens, all right? I'm sending them now."

"You don't understand . . ." I hear a voice. "Dale."

"Ma'am?"

I scramble out of the car and run back to him, still holding the phone. "Dale? Jesus, are you okay? Oh my God. Can you stand? He's coming. We have to leave right now."

He's groggy. Strange noises come from him. "Dale, please." I pocket my phone, careful not to end the call and hook my arms under him. "Please, get up. Please!"

He tries to speak but isn't making any sense. "Where are your keys? We have to get out of here." I do my best to control my sobs, but I'm growing weaker by the moment. "The cops are coming. They're sending them here." I have no idea if they'll find us, but I have to give him hope.

I yank his under arms and he moans in pain. The blood on his back mixes with the blood on my shirt, but I try again. "Get up!" I yell. "I don't want to leave you here. Please . . ."

Time's up. He's too close. The lights grow brighter and brighter. I can hear the 911 operator calling out to me. I set Dale back on the ground and pick up the phone. "Are they coming? Please, they have to get here fast. He's dying."

"Who's dying? Ma'am, are you hurt?"

"I'm fine." I'm not, but I'm in better shape than Dale. "Dale Coleman. He tried to help me. He's been shot. He's dying."

I look to the road. "I have to go. The man in the truck. He's coming back and he'll kill us both." I pocket the phone again and look at Dale. Tears spill down my face. "I'm so sorry." I run around to the driver's side of his truck, stepping inside.

Frantically, I search for his keys, praying they aren't on him somewhere. But then, I see them in the console. "Thank you. Thank you, Dale."

I turn the engine, slamming the gearshift into reverse. I have no fucking clue how to drive a stick. I'm going to die because I never learned.

My foot presses on the gas pedal, harder than I expect. The tires squeal. I see him. He's driving up here. I have to go. Now.

"Please don't die, Dale. I'll send help. I promise."

I peel away, and in the rearview, I see him. Still on the ground, not moving. But I have to keep my focus ahead. I grind the gears, the engine sputters. I press on the clutch. "Come on!" I push it into what I think is first gear, and finally, it moves. I only know about clutches from what I've seen in movies. How far will that get me?

The two of us . . . we're coming up on each other fast. Like a game of chicken. I shift again, increasing my speed, but the truck nearly stalls. Soon, I see that the short, narrow road to the gas station isn't wide enough to pass together. I spin the steering wheel, veering off onto the softened earth. The wheel shakes in my hand and I struggle to control the old truck.

There he is. We lock eyes, but only for a moment because he's pointing a gun out the window. A round is fired off and I instinctively duck. It clinks against the front fender of the truck as I speed by.

I look through the rearview and see his brake lights. He's turning around. "Shit." I press harder on the gas, the engine revs. The RPMs, near the red. I know that's bad, so I shift again. Finally, I make it to the road, speeding away as fast as this old truck will go. And when I look back again, I don't see him. Relief washes over me. Until I realize . . . *Dale*. He's going after Dale.

I don't look back again, but I see the call is still connected and I pick up my phone. "Hello? Are you still there?"

"I'm here. I thought you were gone," the operator says, with relief in her tone. "Are you okay? I heard a gunshot."

"I'm okay. But he'll kill Dale. Are they close? I don't hear them."

"Where are you, ma'am? Are you driving?"

"Yes, it was my only way of escape."

"Then where are you going? I'll send a unit," she replies.

"Please help Dale first. I'm begging you. Please help him." I hurry down the road, refusing to slow at all. The truck is hard to steer. I'm not sure I'm doing this right, but it still runs. I feel like I'm barely able to stay on the road.

"I don't know if they'll find your friend in time. Tell me where you're going."

"The Radisson on Berkshire. I'm ten minutes away."

"They'll be there soon."

I end the call, gasping for breath. Shit. Jesse. What if he woke up? I hurry to call him. The line rings. He must have it on silent because it goes to his voicemail. I hang up, setting down the phone on the bench seat.

As the adrenaline subsides, the pain grows. I'm covered in blood. It's all over my hands now, too. But I'm sure that belongs to Dale. Oh, God. I left him. I left him to die.

The road ahead starts to blend with the still-dark sky. Though behind me, I see a hint of a rising sun. I check the time on my phone. Somehow, I made it through the night. I escaped a madman. Twice. But who is he? I thought I wanted to know. I thought I was done being a coward, but I was wrong. And now, someone else is dying.

But you're not a killer.

Buildings appear in the distance. I'm almost there. The town passes by my window and I realize I have to slow down. I'm no longer in danger. Soon, the hotel looms ahead. I turn into the parking lot and stop the truck.

The tears flow harder now and I'm not sure I can stop them. Every ounce of my body hurts. But I try to stem the emotions that rush to the surface. I have to go inside where it's safe. The police will be here soon. They'll find the man who came after me. The man I'm certain has killed Dale Coleman.

Finally, I gather the strength to open the heavy truck door and climb down. My legs are weak and almost give way under the pressure. I nearly collapse, leaning against the door for support. It's quiet out here. No birds, no traffic.

I take a step, testing my strength. Then another. Finally, I let go of the door, closing it behind me as I walk toward the hotel's entrance. I can only imagine what they'll all think. For God's sake, I look like I walked through a field of razor blades. But I press on, finally reaching the door, grabbing the handle to open it. That's when I hear the sirens. I close my eyes, a slight smile on my lips. The police are almost here.

The lobby is empty. No one at the front desk. The lights are off in the restaurant. I look at the elevator. *Nope.* I decide on the stairs, even though I'm not sure I'll make it up three floors. But Jesse is waiting for me. I have to see him.

It takes painfully long for me to reach the top, but I do and carry on down the hall. My feet dragging on top of the carpet, I use the walls to keep myself from falling over. The door is ahead. I pat down my pockets and realize I don't have the keycard anymore. It must've fallen out, so I knock. Nothing. I knock again. "Jesse?" Keeping my voice low, I call out to him again. "Jesse, open the door. Please."

Finally, I hear rustling around, and then, there he is. I gasp at the sight of him. Something I wasn't sure I'd ever get the chance to see again.

"Kylie? Holy shit, what happened to you?" He grabs me harder than I expect, and I wince.

He loosens his grip. "Oh, babe."

I see his eyes redden and I can't help but sob in his arms. We stand in the corridor for what feels like forever until he pulls me inside.

"My God, Kylie." He studies my appearance. "We need to get you to a hospital."

I expect him to demand answers from me. What happened? Where did I go? *Why* did I go? Instead, his only concern is how badly I'm injured. "The police are coming now. I'll be okay. I know I don't look it, but I will."

A tear falls down his cheek. "Then please . . . tell me what happened to you."

***

Jesse got me cleaned up as best he could. We didn't have long before the police arrived. We're downstairs now. Several of the crew have come down. They see how I look. They see the cops. And it's Caroline who steps in to protect me. "She'll talk to you soon. Give her a minute." She turns back to me. "Let's just go and get some coffee."

"Is Dale okay? Did you find him?" I ask the officer before Caroline ushers me away.

He looks at his partner when both of them turn to me. I see it in their faces. "Oh God. No." I sob into my hands and feel Jesse's arm around me.

"I'm sorry, ma'am. He'd already passed by the time we arrived."

The lobby doors open, and Detective Burns enters. He walks toward us, compassion written on his face. "Kylie, Jesse." He sets his hand on the officer's shoulder. "I'll take it from here, guys. Thanks."

"Yes, sir, Detective." The officer nods for his partner to join him.

After they fall out of earshot, Burns sits down across from us. I look at Caroline, who steps away too.

"I'm sorry about Dale Coleman. There's a few things you should know about him."

"He was a federal agent."

Burns creases his brow. "He told you?"

"Just before he was shot by the man who came after me."

Burns takes out his notebook. "It took me a while, but I got his DNA and found out who he really is . . . was. And then I wondered. Why would a retired federal agent ask for work on a movie set? He had a good pension. So that made me question his motives. I have to admit, I thought he might've been responsible for the murder of your friends."

"He tried to help me last night," I say. "It's my fault. And I know why he was here, working on this movie."

Burns leans back, folding his arms over his broad chest. "Care to fill me in?"

I look at Jesse, knowing this is going to change everything between us. But what choice do I have? Three people are dead. I'm the missing puzzle piece. And I have to be the one to finish this. "My father murdered Lucas Shaw from the New Hope community twenty years ago."

I feel Jesse's eyes on me. I feel his breath on my cheek, but I keep my gaze on Burns.

Burns tilts his head. "You're Clarence Skinner's daughter?"

"Yes, sir. The oldest. Everyone thought I died," I say, placing my hand on Jesse's knee. "Just like the rest of my family."

CHAPTER 19

It doesn't take long for the whispers to start. Burns is coordinating with the other officers in the hunt for the man who killed retired federal agent Dale Coleman. And two others. People who were my friends.

They know it's my fault. Brandon and Lucy. They're dead because I didn't come forward. I see Jesse standing at the bar. Confusion masks his face. We have much more to say on the matter, but right now, I have to talk to Caroline.

I see her near the elevator and walk over. "Caroline, do you have a minute?"

She looks down, like she's thinking whether talking to me is a good idea right now. I don't blame her. But when she glances up at me, her eyes fill with tears.

"You should've told me about your past, Kylie. I would've changed the location. I would've done anything to protect you and the people I call my friends and colleagues."

Guilt weighs on me, but I see truth in her words. "Please understand that I've had to protect my identity. I've done it for years, and I thought all of this was behind me." My voice catches. "I'm so sorry, Caroline. I hope you can forgive me."

She places her hand on my arm. "Despite what you think, this isn't on you, Kylie. You're not responsible for what a crazed killer does. No one here blames you."

"I'm not so sure about that," I say, looking around at everyone. "You have to get them all out of here. The sooner, the better."

She raises her brow. "And you? You're coming with us, yes?"

I glance over at Jesse, then set my sights on Burns and his officers. "No. I have to stay here and put an end to this. Someone figured out who I am, who I was, and tracked me down. No one is safe around me, Caroline. Not anymore."

From the corner of my eye, I see Jesse heading our way. Caroline notices and holds my gaze for a moment. "I understand why you think that, Kylie, but remember that it's the job of the police to find this person. Not you." Her eyes dart to Jesse as he arrives. "Regardless, we'll all respect your decision."

"Thank you," I reply. "Please, just get everyone away from here. As fast as you can."

Jesse nods at Caroline as she walks away. "Everything okay?"

I turn to him. "Depends on your definition of okay. Sorry. I know that's not what you mean. But Jesse, I do think you should leave with the rest of the crew. Everyone's moving out in the next couple of hours."

His brow creases. "Do you really think I'm going to leave you here? First of all, you're coming with us, Kylie. You have to. Staying here is the worst thing you can do."

"If I go, he'll find me again." I press my lips and close my eyes a moment. "I can't let that happen. I'm staying here, Jesse."

"Then so am I."

My emotions rise to the surface. "You must have a million more questions for me . . . about who I was. Who my family was . . ."

"No," he cuts in. "I don't care about any of that. Because whatever happened only happened because of your family.

Your parents. You were a kid. None of this is on you. I need you to understand that."

Burns makes his way over to us, but the look on his face doesn't fill me with hope. "Kylie, we haven't been able to track down the vehicle you described. It's entirely possible he left town. Maybe even left the state."

Jesse takes a step forward. "What does that mean? Is Kylie safe?"

Burns raises a reassuring hand. "It means, we're looking. We've issued a statewide 'be on the lookout.' Meaning, every jurisdiction in the state is looking for a suspect and vehicle matching the description Kylie gave us."

"What can I do in the meantime?" I ask.

He takes a moment, darting his gaze between Jesse and me. "Pack your things and leave with everyone else."

"What? No. I can't do that." I feel heat rise under my collar and aim my finger toward the exit. "He'll follow me. No one's safe while they're around me. No, I'm staying here until he's captured."

Jesse slips his arm around my waist. "And I'm staying with her." He looks at me. "You won't change my mind, Kylie."

Burns sets his hands on his hips. "I'm afraid I can't let either of you stay here. This person, whoever he is, knows you're here. That much is certain, given what happened to Ms. Marks. I've already instructed the hotel manager that this entire place is an active crime scene. Everyone is being asked to leave."

"Come on, babe," Jesse says. "Let's just go back to L.A. Forget about the rest of the shoot. I'll bet, after what happened to Lucy, Caroline will suspend production anyway. No one wants to work on this film now. Let's go home."

Burns eyes Jesse for a moment then sets his hand on my shoulder. "Can I have a brief word with you in private?"

I look at Jesse, who nods. "Yeah, okay."

I follow the detective outside. The late morning sun beats down on my face. Warm air envelops me. My cuts are bandaged; some had to be stitched by a paramedic. And as the heat rises, and sweat forms, it trickles down my neck, soaking my bandages and stinging my skin.

"Listen," Burns says, wiping his index finger under his nose. "The person you saw, you said he was a young man."

"Well, not young exactly, but the brief moment I saw him, he looked . . . I don't know . . . thirty-five, maybe forty. It was dark, and I didn't get a good look at him because I was too busy trying not to run myself off the road."

"Got it. But you have no idea who this man is?" he presses on.

"No." I shrug. "I would've told you. All I know is that he has to have been at New Hope when we were. When my dad destroyed it. And then, they destroyed us."

"Is it possible he's a relative of Shaw's?" Burns asks.

"I mean, yeah, it's possible. I was only thirteen. I couldn't tell you anything about any other family Lucas Shaw might've had, except he had multiple wives, if I recall. They weren't much older than me and I think they had very young children, but I understood they'd all died in the fire."

I study him for a moment, and I can see wheels spinning. "What is it, Detective?"

He cocks his head. "I want to catch this guy just as much as you do. And if you leave with everyone else, you're not wrong. He could come after you again. Clearly, he knew you were here. It's possible he's been tracking you for some time. I don't know enough yet to draw any sort of connection as to how he found you, but he did. And if he found you here, he'll find you back in L.A."

"I have family there," I say. "The woman who raised me. If he comes after her, too—"

"My point exactly," he replies. "Look, I'm heading over to Coleman's house now."

"What for?"

"Files. I've put in a couple of calls to his former bosses. He has no family, unfortunately. They're on board with me taking a look at any files he has regarding whether he suspected this could happen."

"That someone would come back here?" I ask.

"Yeah. I'm guessing he stayed here for that reason. I don't know if he knew a survivor, or . . ."

"He knew I survived," I cut in. "He said he knew my Aunt Grace. She came to get me the day after the rest of my family was killed. So he knew all about me." I glance away. "I guess he figured this wasn't over yet."

Burns shakes his head. "Listen, stay here. I'll keep two patrolmen stationed at each exit. Your co-workers are leaving, but if you want to put an end to this nightmare once and for all, I can help you do that. I'm confident Coleman has more information. I just need to find it."

I raise my brow. "You're telling me I can stay?"

Burns casts out his gaze over the parking lot and toward the street. "For the time being, until I know more. I'll have the place fully covered, so don't you worry about that."

"And Jesse?" I ask. "I'm not sure I want him here for this."

"I'll leave that up to you, but by him being here, he's a target, too." He pats me on the shoulder. "He needs to know that."

CHAPTER 20

Detective Burns

Searching a dead man's home feels like a violation. Especially when the man was former law enforcement. It's not the first time I've done it, but it doesn't change the fact that I don't want to be here. Then again, I suspect Dale didn't want to die. So, I'm going to do everything in my power to find his killer.

According to his boss, Dale retired fairly recently. Before that, he'd been assigned to work at the Des Moines FBI field office and made the commute, about 90 minutes or so each way, since he left the undercover assignment at the New Hope compound.

I'd heard about all that, of course. But at the time, I was living in Des Moines, working for PD. We'd had enough on our plates than worrying about what was going on a hundred miles away. No one ever thought those folks would come back, least of all me. I wonder, though, if Dale did?

So, now I have to find out who it was who killed Agent Coleman, and two other innocent people. And I have to do it before he gets to the one he's really after . . . Kylie Forbes. Now known to me as Kayla Skinner.

One of my officers accompanies me as we enter Dale's home. He seemed to live a modest life. And he lived alone. Funny how my view has changed, now that I know the truth about him.

Public records showed he was never married, and he has no children. It seemed his entire reason for living hinged on keeping that girl safe and the New Hope folks from re-emerging. He'd kept her safe, that much was true — for a while.

"He's got an office down the hall," I say. "I just need you to keep eyes out for me."

"You got it, boss," the officer replies.

I carry on into the short hallway. The first door on the right is a bathroom. Past that is another door on the left. Looks like his bedroom. And at the end of the hall, I flip on the lights since the curtains are drawn. "Here we go."

First place to start is his desk, so I sit down in the chair. Nothing quite like the feeling of sitting down in a dead man's chair, but I push on. Opening his desk drawers, I see a few files. But in the top right drawer, I see several notebooks. "Bingo."

It doesn't take me long to see that they're in chronological order and I wonder if he'd pulled them out when he realized Kylie Forbes had come back home.

I grab the first notebook, dated nearly twenty years prior, and begin skimming through the pages. The handwriting is neat and precise. These appear to be his notes from his time undercover with the New Hope cult.

The early pages describe his unease infiltrating the isolated community, mostly cut off from the outside world. He writes about Lucas Shaw, the charismatic leader who entranced his followers with talk of achieving purity and salvation. Dale seems skeptical of Shaw from the start, disturbed by the absolute control and devotion he demands.

As I read on, the notes become more alarming. Dale recounts episodes of punishment for perceived sins, public shaming, and physical abuse. Food and sleep are restricted, physical labor and prayer mandated for hours on end. Dale's writing reflects his frustration at gathering evidence while maintaining his cover, and his growing concern for the children subject to Shaw's abuse.

One section describes how Coleman had slowly gained Shaw's trust and is invited into the inner circle. It seemed Shaw had taken a liking to him.

Coleman wrote about long discussions with Shaw, gaining insight into how his distorted mind worked. There are also notes on Coleman's efforts to collect evidence of illegal activities at New Hope.

In the meeting room, I watched a storm brew inside Clarence Skinner. He took his seat next to Lucas, as usual. But his expression no longer reveals admiration, but what I swear is contempt. There was heavy tension in the air today — a palpable shift from the usual harmony between leader and follower.

And then, something unexpected happened. A new presence disrupted the established dynamics when Clarence's wife, Evie, took her place on the other side of Shaw. Her arrival seemed to unravel something within Clarence; a ripple effect that hinted at feelings of inadequacy or maybe betrayal. They engaged in hushed conversation, and I wasn't the only one to notice.

When Lucas began the meeting, all eyes gravitated toward him, as usual, except for one pair that seemed fixed on an invisible fracture in the carefully constructed facade. Every glance exchanged between Clarence and his wife seemed to teeter on the edge of rage and disgust.

I close the notebook and gather up the remainder. There's more here about this cult and I have to know why Dale believed it was still a threat. He wouldn't have retired here if he didn't have a reason. So what did he know that I don't?

This would've been so much easier had he told me the truth about who he was. Why the secret? Was it simply to protect the girl? But why did she need protecting from me?

Getting up from the desk, I push the chair in, like no one was ever here. I scoop up the notebooks and walk out to see the officer still at the front door. "Any sign of the truck?"

He turns back to me. "No, sir. No one's driven by at all."

* * *

By the time I return to the hotel, I see that the parking lot is almost empty. My heart sinks. A shame, what happened to these folks just trying to do their jobs. Bringing much-needed money into town. And I can't imagine what that girl must be going through. The guilt she bears. None of this is her fault, but it's hard to convince someone who is hell-bent on taking it on the chin, regardless.

I walk inside to an empty lobby. Just the attendant behind the desk. As I approach him, I ask, "Excuse me, are all those Hollywood people gone?"

"Yes, sir. The last of them left about thirty minutes ago. Just the woman and her boyfriend are still here." He leans closer. "Detective, can I ask why they're hanging back?"

I raise my hand. "It's only temporary. They'll be under police protection. Don't you worry about that. We'll be getting them somewhere else that's safe very soon. You won't be closed but a few days while we get all the evidence we can find."

"Sure. Okay," he says.

I lean in. "Uh, would you mind calling their room for me? Ask them to come down?"

"Of course."

He makes the call and I step back, checking the emails on my phone. Nothing new on the BOLO. The description Kylie offered was fairly general, but the fact she could even recall his features shows her tenacity.

I shake my head. Simply can't imagine what she went through back in those New Hope days.

"They're coming, Detective," he says.

"Appreciate it, sir." I tuck my hands in my pockets and meander toward the lobby. "Oh, hey, uh, I asked the manager to get me a list of employees on shift yesterday. You have any idea where he's at? I need that information ASAP."

"I'll call and ask him right now, Detective."

"Thanks." Glancing back into the hall, I see where the young woman, Lucy Marks, was killed. And what's worse is that they have but one security camera in that hall. And guess what? It doesn't work. Hasn't for months. In fact, only a few of the cameras here do function. I already sent the footage to the station for the computer guys to take a look. Haven't heard anything back yet.

I hear the stairwell door open and see the couple emerge. Her eyes are still red. I can only imagine the conversation they had today.

Kylie greets me with, "They're all gone, Detective. We're the only ones here."

I notice Jesse take her hand. "Well, then, let's talk about getting you both out of here."

Kylie turns to her boyfriend. "The sooner, the better."

My phone buzzes in my pocket, so I grab it. "Detective Burns, here."

"We have a sighting."

It's my dispatcher. I raise my index finger and step away from the couple. "Where? When?"

"About thirty minutes ago. Dark, two-door, older model Chevy pickup. Male, dark hair, approximately thirty to thirty-five years old. Last seen coming out of a McDonald's in Carroll."

I nod, running various scenarios through my head as to how to handle this. It could mean these folks' nightmare might be over. "Send me the location, and have a unit meet me on scene, along with local authorities. They gotta have security cameras there. It's our best shot at getting a better look at this guy . . . and where he might be going."

I end the call, pocketing my phone and returning to the couple. "Like I said earlier, I'll have two teams here, guarding the entrances. Another laying low out front. I need you two to stay put. There's been a sighting up north in Carroll. I'm going there now to see if we can get a look at this guy."

I start heading out, but turn back. "Do not leave this hotel."

CHAPTER 21

Kylie

Fear and uncertainty consume me. At least I have Jesse at my side, but what danger am I putting him in? We'd cleared the air earlier. Talking about all the things that had happened at New Hope. As much as I had the nerve to tell him, anyway. He still doesn't know the whole story. Dale Coleman somehow played a role in my survival in those early years, and again now. However, I have a feeling only one person knows the extent of his involvement — Aunt Grace.

I see the afternoon sun cutting through the trees, shining into the hotel lobby. We're sitting on the gold-colored sofa. Quiet. Both of us absorbing, doing our best to understand our current situation.

Glancing into the hall, I see a tinge of red lingers deep in the carpet fibers where Lucy was murdered. How did he get in? Who is he?

"There's more to this than I know, Jesse," I say to him, pressing my hand on his thigh. "It's like this man's been watching me since that night. Waiting for me to return."

"He couldn't possibly have known you'd come back here, Kylie," he replies, using the only name he knows me by.

"Dale must've believed I would, or else why stick around this place?"

"Maybe to keep an eye on those who might try to resurrect New Hope," he says. "From what we know, he spent a long time working to bring them down."

"And ultimately, it was my father who did."

Jesse turns to me with an inquisitive stare. "He never said a word to you before all of it happened?"

I rack my brain, as I had so many times before. How it all went so wrong.

I look older than my age. Everyone tells me so. Of course, I'm painfully aware of the fact as my bra size is already a B cup. I'm embarrassed by it and usually keep my arms folded over my chest to hide it.

I'm supposed to see Lucas today. He talks to all the kids when they reach thirteen. Something about how we're grown-ups now and that it's time we take on more responsibility for the good of the community. I feel like I already do a lot, since my parents are always so involved in the council. Neither are around much, so I'm left to take care of my younger brother and sister.

As I make my way to Lucas's office, I see my mom in the hallway.

"Good morning, sweetheart," she says. Her beautiful chestnut brown hair hangs over her shoulders in soft waves. Her face is thin with high cheekbones and a narrow jaw. Compared to the other moms, she's the most beautiful to me.

"Hi, Mom. I'm on my way to talk to Lucas."

"Of course. The meeting." She tilts her head and shifts her weight under the long dress. "I don't need to remind you to be respectful and do as he says."

"I know. I won't disappoint you, Mom."

She leans in to kiss my cheek. "Good. I love you. Be sure to come find me when it's over and tell me how it went."

I nod before carrying on through the hall, eventually reaching Lucas' office. My mom loves Lucas. Maybe more than she loves my dad. Then again, everyone's drawn to him. Even me, I admit.

"Hello?" I say, peeking into his office.

He looks up at me from behind his desk. Blue eyes. Dark hair that goes to his shoulders. It's kind of messy, but in a cool way. "Kayla, come on in, kiddo. Have a seat."

My nerves bundle up in my stomach, and I sit down across from him. "Hi, Mr. Shaw."

He closes the lid on his laptop. "Oh, now, Kayla. It's just Lucas, remember? We don't do formal around here. That's for those on the outside who don't understand what community truly means."

"Sorry, Lucas," I say, feeling weird about calling him by his first name.

"Okay, then." He leans back in his chair and rests his arms on it. "Do you know why you're here, Kayla?"

"Because all of us kids meet with you when it's our thirteenth birthday?" I say, more as a question than answer.

"That's right. And I do this to let you know that there'll be expectations placed on you." He leans forward. "You, in particular, Kayla. Do you understand?"

"Not really, no."

"Well, only the very special girls who turn thirteen are asked to give of themselves more so than others. For the good of our community."

I stay silent for a moment, still not understanding what he's talking about, but then he finally continues.

"I've spoken to your parents about this. And they're both on board." He smiles. It's not like the kind of smile I've seen on him before. "Kayla, after your birthday, you and I will become closer. You'll be at my side. And with your father's permission, you'll come to stay with me for a while."

I've been here since I was eight, so I knew that some of the girls, when they got older, moved in with Lucas. They seemed happy enough, I guess. I don't really know for sure, because they stopped going to class with the rest of us. In fact, we didn't see much of them, and I wonder if that will happen to me too. "So, I won't stay in my house anymore?"

"No. I'm going to teach you things, Kayla. Things you won't learn in school."

It starts to dawn on me, the meaning of his words. I'm not a child, but I suddenly feel like I want my mom. "Mom and Dad say it's okay?"

He smiles again, leaning back in the chair. "Of course. It's all part of our special bond. The bond each and every one of us here at New Hope share. A bond I know you'll come to appreciate."

I regard Jesse, feeling my eyes sting. "It was only when I was older that I realized the kind of man Lucas Shaw really was. I have to assume Dad knew all along. And I guess he wasn't 'on board' with it after all."

"But who was the man who came after your family?" he asks.

I think about that awful night and try to shake away the images burned in my head. "I never saw his face. I got out of the house and eventually made it to a pay phone."

"And that's where your Aunt Grace came in," he adds.

"Yes. Neither of us knows who killed my parents, my brother and sister. But according to Aunt Grace . . . she was the one the police called because my dad didn't have any extended family. Just Mom. She said they told her the man who killed my family shot himself in the head not long after. They couldn't ID him because he didn't legally exist, I guess. Had no prints in the system. No dental records. No DNA traced back to any relatives. The guy was a ghost. Most of them were, though. It was part of what they stood for . . . staying off-grid."

"Sounds like they were pretty good at it," Jesse says. "I'm so sorry, Kylie. I–I just can't imagine." He squeezes my leg. "We'll get through this, okay? I won't let those people hurt you again."

Jesse doesn't know this is out of his hands. But it's not out of mine. I've seen the killer's face now. If Detective Burns doesn't find him in Carroll, I believe he'll come back here to try and finish the job.

I stare through the lobby window for another moment before facing him again. "He's coming back, Jesse. He's waited for me for this long, and he won't give up now. We have patrolmen out front and at the back entrance. I have no doubt they're smart men, but this man . . . this is a man who got to Brandon, who got to Lucy, practically under our noses."

"What are you saying?"

I take in a long, slow breath. "I'm saying he'll find a way to get to me, because he sees me as the one responsible for killing the Prophet. So that means, I have to be the one to get to him first." I get up from the lobby couch.

Jesse stands up to meet me. "What are you doing? Detective Burns said to stay put."

I grasp his shoulders. "Please go. Go with the rest of the crew. It's not too late. He's not here for you, and I don't know what I would do if I lost you. Please, Jesse. I'm begging you to leave so I can end something that should've ended years ago."

"Are you serious?" he scoffs. "If you think I'm leaving you to deal with a psycho killer, then you're the crazy one. Look, whatever happened when you were a kid wasn't your fault. It was the fault of your parents. I'm sorry they're dead, and your brother and sister, but none of it is on you. And neither is what's happening now."

"They all blame me, Jesse. You saw in their eyes as much as I did," I say. "I have to do this for Brandon and for Lucy."

He sits back down, folding his arms like a petulant child. "I'm not going anywhere."

I can't help but chuckle at the sight of him. It's the last feeling I expect to have, but there it is, nonetheless. I squat to meet him and take his hand. "I don't want to lose you. I can't. I've lost too much already."

His gaze pierces me. "You won't lose me. Not now. Not ever." He raises his chin. "So, if you want to get this son of a bitch out into the open, then we do it together."

I give in and sit back down next to him. We're quiet again, both staring outside like we're waiting for the world to come crashing down around us. We'd already agreed not to go up to our room, feeling safer here in the hotel lobby until Burns gets back with news.

The moments tick by. Our phones are quiet. No production emails. No text messages. I close my eyes and think about Lucy, feeling a fresh wave of emotion rise to the surface. I rest my head on Jesse's shoulder.

And when I open my eyes again, dusk has settled. Now, the faint glow of headlights appears through the window. "What time is it?"

"Almost seven," he says. "You dozed off."

I get up and walk to the exit, gazing through the door to see who's coming. The officer outside raises his palm, insisting I stay put while he places his other hand on the butt of his gun.

It doesn't take long, however, for the figure to emerge from a now-recognizable vehicle. I turn to Jesse. "It's Detective Burns. He's back."

His face lightens with relief. "Thank God."

He joins me at the doors, and I feel his hand on my back as we wait for Burns to approach. I see the look on his face. "Oh no."

"We don't know anything yet, Kylie," Jesse says, trying to keep me calm.

I step back, Jesse follows, and we wait until Burns enters. And when he does, he locks eyes with me. The truth is written all over his face. "You didn't find him."

He pinches his lips, glancing down for a moment. "No. I'm sorry, we didn't."

I push back the tears that threaten to spill. Not tears of sadness or even fear, but of anger. I'm pissed, and I won't let this asshole get away with what he's done. I feel Jesse's arm around me, and I shrug it away. "No, don't tell me everything's going to be fine, Jesse, because it isn't." I fix my gaze onto Burns. "Detective, what are we supposed to do now, huh? We can't stay here. First of all, he knows we're here. Secondly, I feel defenseless in this place. It's too big. No offense, but that man got in before we knew who he was. I have no doubt he's scoped it out to find the vulnerabilities. And—"

"I agree."

I stop in my tracks. "What's that?"

Burns nods. "I agree with you, Kylie. In fact, I want you both to go get your things and hurry back down here. I'm getting you both the hell out of this town."

CHAPTER 22

We hurry upstairs to our room, eager to gather our belongings and leave this place behind. My hands shake as I shove clothes and toiletries haphazardly into my suitcase. Jesse does the same, his anxiety evident in the way he's packing.

In ten minutes, we're back in the lobby with our bags. Detective Burns is waiting by the front entrance, checking his watch impatiently. When he sees us, he takes our things and leads us outside to his car.

As we follow him into the darkening sky, I grip Jesse's hand tightly. The air is heavy and damp, matching the mood that hangs over us. Burns loads our bags into the trunk while we slide into the backseat.

As we drive away from the hotel, I glance back at its shrinking silhouette. I wonder if the killer is inside, watching us leave.

Jesse puts his arm around me, sensing my unease. I lean into him, finding comfort in his solid presence. At least we're getting away from this place.

"I'm sorry I didn't find him, Kylie," Burns says, his hands gripping the wheel. "We were too late. And what security video we did see of him, didn't leave us with much of a direction."

"But he was there?"

"It seems so, based on your description."

I consider why this man, who's haunted me since our arrival, would choose to simply leave, knowing I was still here. It doesn't make sense. Is his plan to wait it out? Wait for me to return home? Does he know where my home is? If so, then why wait this long to come for me?

"Detective, before Dale was killed, he told me that he'd been working undercover at New Hope."

"That was my understanding, too," he says, glancing at me through the rearview mirror. "And he'd stayed here to keep an ear to the ground on any rumblings of the—"

Bright lights appear out my window, speeding toward us. In an instant, my shoulder slams into the rear passenger door as the car is pushed sideways. Screeching metal, shattering glass, engines revving . . . the sounds collide along with the vehicle that hit us.

I look over at Jesse. His eyes are full of fear as the car tips on its side. I outstretch my arms, prepared to fall on him, but the seatbelt holds me in place. We roll over and over. My limbs move as though devoid of bones. We're all ragdolls, the way our arms and legs flail.

My head spins as the car rolls over twice, three times before coming to a stop on its roof. We slide down into a ditch on the side of the road. I'm hanging upside down, the seatbelt cutting into my gut, blood dripping into my eyes.

For a moment, everything is still and quiet except for the hiss of steam escaping the crumpled engine compartment. We're all upside down, secured only by our seatbelts. A low groan escapes Jesse. Burns curses under his breath as he struggles to free himself from the driver's seat.

"Jesse?" I choke out. "Are you okay?"

"I'm — I'm okay, I think. You?"

"Yeah. Yeah, I'm okay." In the front seat, I see Burns. "Detective? Detective, are you okay?"

"Kylie! Jesse!" Detective Burns' voice cuts through the ringing in my ears.

"We're okay," Jesse calls back, already unbuckling himself.

He falls as soon as his belt gives way, a heavy thud on the interior roof of the car.

With a grunt of effort, Burns kicks open his door above us. The dome light flickers on, casting an eerie glow across the smoke-filled interior. I blink hard, orienting myself, as Jesse's face appears below me, eyes still brimming with fear. He helps me undo my seatbelt. I fall hard on my shoulder next to him.

"Jesus, Kylie. I'm sorry. You all right?"

"Yeah. We have to get out."

Jesse crawls out first, then reaches inside for me. My legs are shaky, and I have to cling to him for support as I tumble outside. Detective Burns is out and shines a flashlight behind us. We see what hit us.

"Oh my God. It's him." But before I can do anything, Burns hobbles toward the vehicle, his flashlight shining all around.

The truck sits askew across the road, its front end crumpled from the impact. One headlight shines brightly into the night while the other sits dark and shattered.

Burns peers inside the truck's cab, sweeping his flashlight back and forth. He turns back to us, brow furrowed. "There's no one—"

A gunshot rings out. I see Burns' eyes widen as he spins and fires off two rounds. But it's too late. He's hit. He staggers toward us, the gun slipping from his hand and falling to the ground.

"No!" I scream, ready to rush toward him, but Jesse grabs me. "Kylie, hide!"

Burns topples to the pavement several feet away.

Jesse pulls me along, throwing me behind the overturned car, using it as a shield.

"We can't stay here. We have to get away from him," he whispers.

I look out into the blackness. "How did he find us?"

"There's no time. We have to find a way out of here."

But I've already done this, and I only barely escaped. How the fuck is this happening? Then I see Burns' gun on the ground. "Jesse, look." I point to the road, the truck's headlight gleaming off the weapon. "If we can get out there, get the gun, we have a chance."

I look back at Jesse, then over to Burns. My God, how many people have to die?

Finally, I scramble out from behind the car, darting into the roadway, and snatching Burns' gun from ground. I can see he's still alive. His eyes capture mine, silently warning me to go. More gunshots ring out, tearing up asphalt as I scurry behind the car again.

Jesse looks at me. "For God's sake."

I check the weapon. "I'm going to kill him." The words tumble from my lips, a promise that hangs in the air. Just as I stand to fire the shot, my eyes scan the darkness, but find nothing. No sign of him. He's gone. Vanished. I look back at Jesse, who's clutching his side. "Shit, you're not okay, are you?"

"I'll be fine." His voice is strained, but there's an attempt at reassurance in it.

He flinches at my touch. "Where's my phone?" My voice is filled with urgency. I get down on my hands and knees and crawl back to the overturned car. "I have to call for help." In that moment, I see Burns' chest rise and fall as he lies in the middle of the road. Jesus, he's, still breathing. There's still a chance for him.

I search inside the wreckage, but it's too dark to see anything clearly, the cabin light, no longer burning. I use my hand to feel around for the phone. "Come on. Come on. Where are you?" My voice trembles with frustration and fear.

A rock shuffles past me, like it'd been kicked by an unseen foot. I freeze, staring through the rear passenger window into the impenetrable darkness outside. I look back to check on Jesse, and I see I've left the gun behind, then a hand clamps down on my wrist.

I scream. Adrenaline surges through me as I struggle to break free from the vice-like grip. Out of the darkness, a face emerges. Cold, emotionless eyes bore into mine as I try to wrench myself away.

"Let go of me!" I yell in desperation, panic rising in me like a tidal wave. My screams echo through the air, carrying out into the fields of grass and corn.

The man's mouth twitches into a smile. "Not a chance. I won't let you get away again." His voice is deep and cold. His free hand grabs a fistful of my hair and with a brutal yank, he drags me from the wreckage.

Through the corner of my eye, I catch a glimpse of Jesse struggling to get to his feet, the gun just out of his reach. Our eyes lock for a brief moment before my attacker hurls me to the ground.

"Kylie!" Jesse yells. He tries to move but crumples, clutching his wounded side.

The man looms above me, blocking out the moonlight.

"Why?" I gasp out between sobs. "Why are you doing this?"

He looks at me with loathing in his gaze. He pulls me up, dragging me along the asphalt. I struggle against him, my skin scraping and bleeding along the rough surface, but he keeps pulling.

"Kylie!" Jesse screams again, his voice filled with raw terror.

The man tightens his grip on me. "He can't help you now, Kayla."

CHAPTER 23

Detective Burns

Sirens surround me. I hear people talking and finally manage to open my eyes.

"Detective, can you hear me?"

A man looks down on me, his face etched with concern. It hurts to breathe. It hurts to move. Then I remember what happened. How I ended up here.

"Detective Burns?" the man asks again. "Do you know where you are? Sir, please talk to me."

"Kylie," I breathe out. "Jesse."

"Jesse's being loaded onto an ambulance right now," the man replies. "He's going to be okay. He says someone took Kylie."

"No." I close my eyes.

"I'm sorry, Detective, but we need to get you to the hospital. You were shot near your shoulder blade. It exited out the front, near your clavicle. Can you walk, sir?"

I concentrate, all my energy focused on my legs. "Are they moving?"

"Yes." He smiles. "Yes, you're moving." He peers over his shoulder. "Let's get him out of here, now!"

Two more paramedics arrive carrying a backboard and I see a uniformed officer. "Hey," I call out to him. "Hey, over here."

"Sir, I'm going to need you to stay still a minute, all right?"

The paramedic works to move my fat ass onto the board. The officer approaches.

"Detective Burns," he says, looming over me. "Thank God you're awake."

"You have to find her." I reach out for him, wincing in pain, but manage to clutch his pant leg. "He'll kill her."

"Copy that. We've already sent out units. We'll find her, Detective."

I close my eyes again, feeling weaker by the moment, doubting whether his words will come true. Thank God the kid is still alive. Jesse.

They raise me up; every single movement causes me pain. I'm just grateful I can still feel pain. I'm loaded onto the ambulance. I see the other ambulance and know Jesse's inside, but I can't see him. They've already closed the doors.

"The truck," I ask the paramedic. "The truck that hit me. Where is it?"

"Sorry, sir. There was no other vehicle here when we arrived. The young man who called for help said the other vehicle took off with his girlfriend inside."

"Goddam it. How the hell did that thing even run after what happened?" I close my eyes, knowing I let the girl down. All I had to do was get them someplace safe. I peer out a final time and see an officer holding a weapon, barrel facing down. "Hey, you."

He turns his attention to me. "Yes, sir?"

"Is that my gun?"

He nods. "Found it near the vehicle."

"Christ. Then she's out there completely defenseless." The door slams shut. I feel helpless to do anything for Kylie now. Everything I read in Coleman's files, it all leads to an idea that seems to have come true: someone from New Hope survived. But how did they know about Kylie? Who told them? There's more to this, and I have to find out.

I pat down my clothes in search of my phone.

The paramedic lays his hand on my arm. "Sir, please, I need you to keep still, all right? It's going to take us a while. The nearest hospital is fifteen miles away."

"I need to make a call."

"Not right now, Detective. You've suffered a serious gunshot wound. The more agitated you get, the more movement you make, the worse off you're going to be. You understand what I'm telling you, Detective?"

I nod, almost imperceptibly. "She's probably already dead anyway."

* * *

The heaviness of my eyelids makes it a struggle to open them. But when I do, I only see haze. A blur all around me, but I hear beeps and hushed voices.

It's still dark outside. Still night, at least, from what I can see through the slats of the window blinds.

"Mr. Burns?"

A slight voice, soft and caring calls out to me. I look up to see a woman's face. Indistinct features through my foggy eyes. "Detective," I say, my voice hoarse and burning.

She smiles. "Detective Burns. Sorry. You've come through the surgery, sir. How are you feeling?"

"Like I've been shot," I say, always the smart ass.

"Well, you were. But the good news is the bullet missed anything major."

It takes a moment to register her words. "Missed?"

"Yes, sir, Detective. You were shot in the back. Came out through your chest. You don't remember?"

"No, I do. I remember now." I turn away from her and it all floods back to me. "Jesse?"

"Jesse Cooper? He came in with you. Yes, sir. He's doing fine. Some broken ribs, but otherwise, he'll be fine." She thumbs back. "The doctor should be in shortly."

"Did they find her yet?" I ask, fixing my gaze on her.

"Sorry?"

"Kylie. Did they find her?"

"Um, I'm afraid I don't know." She lays her hand on my arm. "I'll go get the doctor for you."

I hear the door open and close. The nurse is gone. I look around, searching for my things. "Where's my phone?" If I can just call the station. Someone must know something.

Aunt Grace. Kylie's aunt. I bet she has no idea what's going on. And, maybe, she has answers. Is it possible she knows who came after Kylie? Who killed the others?

I try to sit up, searching for my things. "Goddam it. Where the hell is my phone?" I look over at the door. "Hey! Can you hear me? I need my phone, goddam it!"

The door opens and I see a white coat enter. "Doc, I need my phone. It's a matter of life and death."

"Detective Burns. Please, lie back down. You've just come out of surgery. We can't risk your wound reopening."

"You don't understand. This is really and truly a life-and-death situation. Please. I need to contact my captain. Now."

"Okay, okay." He reaches out, pushing gently on my shoulder. "Relax. I'll find your phone."

He steps out again. Every moment that passes could mean Kylie's life. I have to talk to her aunt. She's the only one who can help Kylie now.

Minutes pass, and I'm getting pissed now. I grab the call button and press it over and over. "Someone better get the hell in here."

The door bursts open. "Detective Burns, are you all right?" The nurse rushes to my side. The same nurse as before.

"I need my phone. Hell, I need *a* phone. Please. It has to be now."

Steps sound behind her and I soon see the doctor return, holding something.

"Is this what you're looking for, Detective?" He hands me the phone.

"Yes, sir. Thank you. Thank you." I don't bother waiting for them to leave, instead, I call the station. "Yeah, it's Burns. I need to talk to Captain Lyons. Now." I look at the doctor and nurse. "Thank you. I got it from here. Sorry to cause a fuss. Actually, no, I'm not sorry. I'm trying to save someone's life."

The line picks up. "Captain, it's Burns."

"Jesus, you're in the hospital. What are you doing?" he shouts at me.

"Never mind all that. Listen, I need help. I need a phone number." I stop cold. "Hang on." I look back at the nurse, who's checking my chart. The doctor's long gone. "Is Jesse Cooper awake? Can I talk to him?"

"I'm afraid he's been given a sedative after trying to get out of his bed."

I can't help but smile, knowing the kid is only trying to find his girl. I turn back to the call. "Sorry, Captain. Look, I need the phone number of a Grace Forbes. Garden Grove, California. It's urgent."

"If this is about Kylie Forbes, we've got every unit out there looking for her. You're gonna have to let us do the job, all right?"

I close my eyes, taking a calming breath, realizing I can't talk to the captain the way I might like to. "Sir, please. Can you just ask someone to run it down? I might be able to get it from the boyfriend, but he's out cold right now. I have no idea how long before he awakens again. But however long it is, I can tell you, Kylie Forbes doesn't have that kind of time."

CHAPTER 24

Kylie

The odds he would bring me back here were exactly one hundred percent. His mistake, because this place isn't a secret. Everyone knows what was here. I don't say a word, because either he doesn't intend to keep me alive long enough for anyone to find me, or he wants them to find me, and then make a giant spectacle out of my death.

Either way, I'm not feeling great about my likelihood of survival. As we sit in his busted-up truck outside what was the New Hope compound, I wonder if Jesse's okay. Is Detective Burns alive?

He hasn't told me his name. I have no idea who he is, but I sit in silence, not wanting to give him the satisfaction of knowing just how afraid I am. His eyes are on me now. I look ahead at the darkness, with its reminders of a past I've tried hard to forget.

"I'm surprised you stuck around after everyone left." His voice is deep and monotone.

"I don't know who you are or who you think I am." My words come out fractured. "But you're making a mistake."

"A mistake?" he asks, aiming his index finger ahead. "The mistake was yours. Yours and your father's. That, out there, was the mistake. And I'm here to rectify it."

"I don't know what you're talking about," I insist.

"Really, Kayla? You're going to keep playing this game?" He rams his shoulder into the driver's side door, forcing it open. "You fucked up my truck, too." He climbs down and hurries to the passenger side. This is it. He's going to kill me now, and I didn't get a chance to tell Jesse how much I love him. Assuming he's still alive. I can't be sure of anything right now.

He opens my door and snatches my arm. "Let's go, princess."

I tumble out onto the soft ground. My shirt is torn to shreds where he dragged me along the asphalt, and blood has soaked through the once-bandaged cuts from the broken glass. It's hard to walk, but he pulls me anyway.

Looking around, I see nothing but blackness. No headlights from approaching cars. Nothing. Why aren't they coming for me? They must know I'm here. Unless Burns is dead. Maybe Jesse, too. There would be no one left who knows anything about me or this man. No one except Aunt Grace.

"What is it you want me to see, because there's nothing here," I say. When he stops and turns to me, his eyes are slightly familiar. Do I know him? He looks a few years older than me. Clearly, he's someone who knows about this place. Maybe he'd even lived here for a while. "Who are you?"

He smirks. "I was wondering when you might ask that question." He starts on again, dragging me through the burned remains.

I stumble on large pieces of concrete. Do my best to avoid the many shards of glass that I can see in his flashlight beam. But he still hasn't answered me. "Did your family die here?"

Still, he says nothing, only pulls me along. "Where are we going? If you're going to kill me, then just fucking do it."

He comes to a halt, whipping back around to me. "You think . . . after what your father did . . . that you're going to get off that easily? Think again."

"So it's revenge you're after," I shoot back. "My father's long dead, you asshole. I had nothing to do with any of it."

Finally, we stop, and I realize where we are. "The community center." It was where the kids went to school and where the adults held their meetings. And it was the last place I'd seen Lucas Shaw before my father killed him. I only recognize it because of the garden patch out front. It's not there anymore, but I see the railroad ties that used to surround it.

"I wasn't sure you'd remember," he says.

"You still haven't told me who you are. Look, I was here, but it wasn't a choice. My father—"

"Your father never wanted to be here. It was your mother," he cuts in.

"What?"

He tilts his head, a slight smirk on his lips. "You have no idea, do you?"

I stay quiet, waiting for him to continue.

"Your mom was here long before your dad. It was Clarence who convinced her to leave New Hope, only to come back a few years later."

"Stop. You have no idea what you're taking about," I say. "How do you know anything? You won't even tell me who you are."

He starts to walk, tightening a circle around me. I can feel blood trickling down from my stomach and onto my bare legs.

"Clarence knew he would lose your mom if he didn't uproot you and your brother. Coming back here was the last thing he wanted. And then your mother had your little sister. This was where she wanted to be."

"Why?"

That's when he stops, squaring up to me.

"She wanted to come back because of me." He steps closer, inches from my face. "I'm your brother, Kayla. Evie was my mom, too."

My head grows light as his words echo in my ears. "No. I don't understand. How is that possible? Who's your father, then?"

The look on his face says it all.

My legs weaken and my chest pounds. "No."

"Lucas," he says flatly. "My name is Scott. Lucas Shaw was my father, and Clarence Skinner murdered him. You're the only Skinner left, Kayla." He stares into my eyes. "You know, I didn't see Lucas the day he was killed, but I know what happened to him. The way his eyes were carved out of his head. Your father thought he could steal Lucas's power by taking them."

"What the hell are you talking about?" I'd heard the man who murdered my dad talk about what'd happened to Lucas' eyes, but I never understood why, or what it meant. "Power? What kind of power?"

"The power Lucas had over our believers. He wanted it for himself."

"You're lying," I shoot back. "So it was you who murdered my family? Your own mother?"

He shakes his head. "No. I don't know who came after Clarence or the rest of you. I only know what Clarence did to my father. And I know that Lucas had planned to marry you. Well, as you might guess, my half-sister couldn't also be my stepmom. I imagine that was why Clarence did what he did."

My stomach turns at the thought. All of this. My entire life, I believed it had been my father who brought us here. But he tried to get us out. Tried to save my mom, too. It was her fault. I thought about Aunt Grace. She and Dad must've hatched this plan to burn it all down and get me and my siblings away from here.

"You understand now," he says, studying my face.

"I was just a kid," I whisper. "I couldn't have stopped it if I'd tried. Why go after my friends? They did nothing to you. I did nothing to you." He doesn't care. He wants revenge, and I'm the only path for him to achieve it. And now, I see that if I don't find a way out of here, I'm dead.

I see his gun still gripped tightly in his hand and I know I need to make a move soon or I'll never get out of here alive.

As he turns to pull me along again, I spot a chunk of concrete near my feet. I pretend to stumble, dropping down and grabbing the heavy piece.

In one swift motion, I swing with all my might, striking his wrist. He cries out in pain and surprise, his grip on the gun loosening. I lurch forward, grappling for the weapon.

We struggle, and I feel the metal scrape my fingertips. With a deep growl, I wrench it from his hand, immediately scrambling back and pointing it at him.

He swipes at me, my hands gripping the gun for dear life. It's all that stands between me and death. I try to push him back so I can get a clear shot. I lurch toward him, shoving him. He stumbles with a grunt of pain and rage. I have only a moment to release the safety. But he comes at me again, this time clamping onto the short barrel.

"Let it go!" I scream, my nails digging into his skin. He swings a fist at me, but I duck under it. My fingers finally close around the butt of the gun. I yank at it with all my might.

He roars and smashes an elbow into my ribs. The breath leaves my body in a painful whoosh, but I don't let go. I bring my knee up sharply, connecting with his groin. He howls and loosens his grip just enough for me to rip the gun from his hand.

I swing it toward him, my hands shaking. He freezes, eyes wide. "Don't move," I warn. Blood drips from his injured wrist, but the look of anger in his eyes is unchanged.

He lunges at me, ignoring the gun pointed at his chest. I squeeze the trigger in a panic, but nothing happens — the safety is still on. *Fuck*. He grabs my wrist, twisting it hard, and I cry out as the gun clatters to the ground. I try to break free, but his grip is like iron.

In desperation, I rake my fingernails across his face, drawing blood. He roars in pain, momentarily loosening his hold. I wrench my arm away and dive for the gun, scooping it up. My hands shake so badly I can barely unlock the safety.

Just as I flip the switch, his foot connects with my stomach in a brutal kick. I go sprawling across the dusty ground, gasping for air. The gun . . . lost to me. I had my chance. Through watery eyes, I see him stalking toward me, murderous intent etched on his face.

I scramble to my feet and run into the burned remains of the compound, desperate to find a place to hide. I duck through a crumbled doorway, the charred walls closing in around me. It's pitch-black inside, and the air is choked with ashes that swirl up with every step. I struggle to muffle my coughs as I feel along the walls, searching for somewhere, anywhere to conceal myself.

My heart pounds wildly in my chest, and the adrenaline coursing through my veins is the only thing keeping me on my feet. I can hear him trailing through the ruins, his heavy footsteps crunching on the debris. He calls my name, his voice echoing through the skeletal rooms.

"Come out, come out, wherever you are," he taunts.

I duck behind a crumbling wall, struggling to control my ragged breathing. The ashes still swirl around me, and even after all these years, the acrid smell burns my throat.

A burned floorboard creaks nearby, and I clench my jaw to keep from crying out. He's just on the other side of the wall. I can hear him breathing.

I fight down panic. I can't let him find me. Up ahead, I see a doorway, the door hanging crookedly from one hinge. I rush toward it, my shoes crunching on shards of glass. Slipping through the opening, I find myself in a small interior room. The far wall has partially collapsed, breaching another area.

I creep toward the gap in the wall, peering through into the next room. It's lighter in there, moonlight filtering in through empty window frames. My eyes scan the debris — a few charred chairs, piles of rubble . . . and in the far corner, darkness.

Hardly daring to breathe, I squeeze through the hole in the wall and scramble over the debris. I reach the corner, crouching down into the darkness.

I think of Jesse. I think of Aunt Grace. Will anyone find me, or is anyone left who can?

Changing the past is beyond me, yet this psycho believes I'm responsible for what happened. I think back, desperate to see him here in this place before it all went up in flames. I don't remember him. Was he kept from me? Was he the reason Dad was angry?

And no matter what, I never would've married Lucas. Never. And my father . . . he tried to stop it. None of this makes sense, because Dale was there. He was FBI. Why couldn't he arrest Shaw for what he was doing to the girls?

I silence the thoughts in my head when I hear him again.

"Kayla, you're better off coming out because if I find you, I won't be in a forgiving mood."

I hold my breath, willing my pounding heart to quiet as Scott Shaw's footsteps draw nearer. Still low, my knees begin to ache. The burned wood in front of me barely conceals me in the darkness. I clench my fists, steeling myself. If he finds me, I will not go down without a fight.

The footsteps stop, and I squeeze my eyes shut only for a moment, praying he will move on. But then, I see him. I lunge forward, my fist connecting with Scott's jaw. He staggers back with a grunt of surprise. Not waiting for him to recover, I barrel past him, sprinting for the doorway.

I make it back out into the open. The ruins of New Hope are just shadows around me as I race toward the road, having no idea where I might go. I just know it's not here. My feet pound against the earth, my lungs burning. Scott's enraged shouts echo behind me. *Why doesn't he shoot?*

The nearby fields close around me as I dart inside. These corn stalks are brown, dying, but still thick enough to embrace me. I could attempt to get to the truck, but there's no way he left his keys inside. The road. That's my only shot. Stick to the thin tree line and pray for the best.

The Chevy pickup is just visible behind me now. I risk a glance back and see him closing the distance between us. I hear the crack of a gunshot split the night air. I instinctively crouch low as a bullet whizzes past me.

The truck's headlight cast a long shadow from behind, capturing me in its path. Another shot rings out, but hits farther away. I stop. The truck comes to a halt. I won't outrun him. We both know that. His door opens and he takes aim at me, trudging ahead. "You're ruining everything, Kayla."

"Fuck off."

"You're so tough, aren't you?" He continues toward me, the truck still running in the background. Both of us are now captured in the single headlight that burns.

I stand firm, but my hands shake. I realize this is the end. "Go ahead. Kill me."

He smiles, moving close to me. So close I feel his breath on my cheek. "I don't want to kill you. Now, get back in the truck."

I don't move. Not until he shoves me, and I nearly fall to the ground. He yanks me up. "Let's try this again, shall we? I don't *want* to kill you, but I will if I have to."

I follow him to the truck. He reaches around me to open the door, offering me a momentary opportunity. So I take it.

I ram my elbow into his gut, knocking the wind from him. He doubles over, and the gun falls from his hand. I snatch it up without hesitation and step away from him.

He catches his breath and pulls upright again. "Don't stop now, Kayla. I can see the murder in your eyes. Just like your father." He lurches ahead. I squeeze but the trigger clicks. I double-check the safety's off and try again. Nothing. It's empty. *Shit.*

He's in front of me now and I swing, the butt of the gun slamming into his temple. It's enough that he stumbles back, dazed from the blow.

No time to waste, I run to the driver's side and jump in before he returns to his feet. I stomp on the gas pedal and the tires spin, spewing gravel. He reaches for the door, but I swerve away. The truck fishtails onto the road as I floor it. I look into the rearview. There's my brother. Now, I know who he is, but if I don't find a way to end him, he will end me.

CHAPTER 25

Detective Burns

It's taking too long, goddam it. I've been sitting in this hospital bed for an hour waiting for the captain to call me back with that number. I'm out of time. Kylie's out of time.

I hoist my legs over the edge of the bed, my feet barely touching the floor. It's quiet out there in the hall. Light spills in from outside the door to my room that's been left cracked open. Is Jesse awake? He's the only other person who might have that phone number.

The IV pole is next to me, so I clutch it and use it to steady me as I put my weight onto my legs. They're wobbly, and I grip the bed for stability. *Come on now, old man. Fucking get your shit together.* I soon get a jolt of pain, reminding me that I'd been shot. I'm lucky to even be standing. I could've ended up like Dale Coleman.

Can I make it to hall? Can I make it to Jesse's room? A wheelchair would be handy right about now. Instead, I take my chances, releasing the bed, but clinging to the IV pole, using its wheels to help me reach the door.

I crane my neck, peering into the sterile corridor. No one is in sight, so I step out into the hallway. I have no idea what room this kid is in. Only one thing left to do. "Jesse?" I call out. "Jesse Cooper?"

It only takes a moment for a nurse with furrowing brows to head toward me like she's a seasoned mall walker. "Sir, what are you doing out of bed?"

"I need to know what room Jesse Cooper is in. It's a matter of life and death. Please, can you help me?" I don the most sympathetic gaze I can muster, wondering if she sees through it. Then her look softens.

"He's down three doors." She links arms with me. "Come on. I'll help you."

We walk slowly, and I feel as though I could move quicker, but I decide not to push my luck with this nurse. She has the ability to drug me up, knocking me on my ass, so I let her set the pace.

"This is it." She gently pushes open the door. "Mr. Cooper? Are you awake, Mr. Cooper?"

I hear a moan inside the room.

"The kid's up. Thank God."

The nurse side-eyes me, pursing her lips, before stepping inside. "Mr. Cooper. I have Mr. Burns here for you."

"Detective," I say.

"Detective Burns." I get another side-eye, but I don't care. Inside, the kid's looking worse for wear, but he's still a young man. Younger than me. He'll be fine.

"Jesse, I have to contact Kylie's aunt, Grace Forbes. Please tell me you have her phone number."

He shifts his weight, moaning. "Where's my phone? I have it."

I look at the nurse. "Please, can you help us find it?"

She walks to his bed and bends over, peering under the side table. When she stands up again, she's holding a plastic bag. "Here are your things, Mr. Cooper. Your phone should be inside."

She hands the bag to Jesse, and he rummages through it. Slowly. Too slowly. So I walk over. "You need me to take a look?"

"No. I got it. It's in here." He retrieves it. "Where is Kylie?"

I look down. "I don't know, son. But, fingers crossed, Grace Forbes has some idea who the hell is behind all this."

Jesse opens the screen and searches for her number, then offers me the phone.

I glance at it a moment. "Probably best if you make the call, son. I can talk to her once you set the stage."

He checks the time. "It's pretty late, even in L.A. I don't know if she'll answer."

"Please, just try," I say. "Neither one of us has any idea what that girl has gone through or continues to go through. Grace Forbes could be our only chance at finding Kylie."

Jesse's eyes well as he makes the call. With the phone at his ear, he waits. All I can do is wait too, praying this woman answers.

He perks up. She's answered. "Hello, Grace, it's Jesse."

I cross my arms, listening only to his end of the conversation.

"I know it's late, and I'm so sorry, but it's Kylie." He closes his eyes a moment, forcing the tears to spill over. "Grace, I'm going to hand you to Detective Burns. Yes, ma'am. Detective. Please." He winces, pressing his hand against his side.

"Give me the phone," I reach out for it, and he hands it to me. "Ms. Forbes, I'm Detective Burns. Ma'am, there's a lot to unpack here, and I will tell you everything soon. However, right now, we're looking for Kylie. Ma'am, she's been taken."

"No. Oh God, no. Is it them? Did one of them come for her? I knew she shouldn't have gone back there."

Her voice is fractured, and she begins to sob. I don't want to be an asshole, but we don't have time for this. "Ms. Forbes, please . . . the description Kylie offered was of a man, dark-haired, around her age, maybe a little older. Does this sound at all familiar to you? I have to know who you think could be after her."

The line goes quiet for a moment.

"Ma'am?"

"They're all supposed to be dead or in jail. I don't understand," she says.

"Yes, ma'am, but someone's taken her. Please, do you have any idea who it could be? I don't mean to scare you, but we are running out of time."

"Uh huh." Her breaths sound in short gasps.

"Please, just take a breath and think about it. I need names. Anyone. I'll put all my officers on digging into anyone you think could have done this."

"Scott Shaw."

"Shaw?" I immediately recognize the last name. "Who is Scott Shaw, Ms. Forbes?"

"Kylie's half-brother. He's a few years older than her. She never knew about him. None of the kids knew. Only Lucas Shaw, Clarence, and obviously, my sister, Evie, Scott's mother . . . And me. But I thought — I'd hoped — he was dead."

"Holy shit." I rub my forehead, trying to absorb her words. "Lucas Shaw had a son with Kylie's mother?" I look at Jesse, whose expression mirrors my own. "Okay, okay, look. Do you have any idea where he lives, or how to contact him?"

"No, sir. Like I said, I wasn't sure he was still alive, but I received no information otherwise. With my sister gone . . . well, everyone scattered to the wind."

The news knocks me on my ass, and I'm not sure what to tell her. "All right. Listen, I know you're terrified right now, but we will find Kylie. I promise you. I'll keep you posted. Goodbye, Ms. Forbes. And thank you." Pocketing my phone, I look at Jesse. Christ, I have no idea what to do next. Why didn't Dale Coleman have this information in any of his files? How could he have not been aware?

"She has a half-brother?" Jesse asks, still wincing with each word.

"Yeah, that's how it seems," I reply, shaking my head in disbelief. "Grace didn't know whether he was alive, but given the description Kylie provided, the person she saw in that truck was similar in age to her."

Jesse blinks hard. His face scrunches up like he's about to unleash a torrent of emotion. "I can't believe this."

"It's a hell of a lot to take in, son. I'll admit that. But Kylie has no idea, all right? She was never told, from what her aunt said." I reach out to offer some comfort, which isn't easy for me. But I see this kid is in pain, mentally and physically. "Kylie kept a lot from you, but you have to understand that she believed it was the only way to protect herself, her aunt, and you, too."

"What do we do?" Jesse asks, his eyes pleading. "How do we find her?"

I raise my sights as if it might help me think of a plan. "Grace Forbes thinks it's this Scott Shaw, so that's where I'll start. I need to get back to the station and run a background. See what I can churn up." I start toward the door but turn back. "I'll find this guy, Jesse. And he'll lead me to Kylie." As soon as I step back into the hallway, the nurse marches toward me.

"That's it. You're going back to bed now. You need to rest."

I'm quickly reminded, once again, that I've been shot. I feel the wound burn as the nurse takes hold of me by the arm. "I don't think you understand, ma'am. I have to find this girl."

"Then I'm afraid you'll have to get someone else to do it, sir. I can't let you leave."

I'm still wearing a hospital gown and have an IV sticking out of my arm. And I'm pretty sure my ass is hanging out for all to see. "Yeah, okay." I agree with her, knowing full well I won't be heeding her orders. She presses her hand against my back and ushers me through the corridor and into my room.

"Careful now," she says, helping me back into the bed. "You need rest."

"Sure," I say, taking caution with each step. It takes another minute or two for her to get me settled in. Patiently,

I wait for her to leave. And when the door closes, I throw off the covers. "Screw this."

Maybe I can't do this alone, but I won't wait until morning, so I reach for my phone. "Captain, it's Burns again. Listen, I have a lead on who has Kylie Forbes, but as you know, I'm somewhat incapacitated at the moment."

"What can I do?" he asks.

"Scott Shaw. I need to know everything there is to know about this guy. Where he lives. Where he works. If he has an alias. Anything we can find." The line goes quiet for a moment, and I wonder if he's still there.

"You think he's the one who has this girl?" the captain finally replies.

"Yes, sir." I nod. "Absolutely."

CHAPTER 26

Kylie

The only light ahead of me is coming from the headlight of the truck. I glance into the rearview mirror, but no one is behind me. Did I make it? Am I free of him? For now, maybe, but I know this isn't over. I have to get to Jesse. I have to see that he's okay.

Far off in the blackness, I see dots of light. Red and blue. "Thank God. The police." Tears fill my eyes as relief settles over me. We drive closer to each other. They're out looking for me, which means Jesse's okay. And maybe Burns, too.

My foot lifts off the gas. The truck slows as the swirling lights become clearer. I almost forget how much pain I'm in until I begin to laugh — a kind of relieved laughter — but it tenses my stomach muscles. Fresh blood spills from my wounds. I can feel it trickling down my legs again. I glance down at the streaks of blood across my thighs, staining my shorts and T-shirt.

Finally, I drift to the side of the road and come to a full stop, shutting off the engine. The truck sputters and chokes for a moment before quitting. The police car slows, too. So I push on the driver's door, but it doesn't budge. "Come on." I slam my shoulder into it, and when it still refuses to give, I let out a frustrated moan, or a sob. I'm not sure which, because ramming into it hurt like hell.

I can't get out, but the windows — it's an older truck with a window crank. I grip it and turn. It's stiff, but with some effort, it rolls down. The outside air fills my lungs. I'm free and I'm going to be okay.

The officer's car stops dead in the middle of the two-lane road. I look around and see no other vehicles. Good thing, because he's blocking the lanes. He steps out and heads toward me. "Officer, I need help. Someone's after me. I was kidnapped and—"

He raises a palm at me. "Calm down, ma'am. What's your name?"

Hang on. I know him. He was one of the officers at the hotel. "Kylie Forbes. Please, you have to help me. Others are hurt, too. I can show you—"

"Step out of the car, please," he says.

I look at the door. I look at him. He must remember me. Something's wrong here. "Sir, I can't. It's stuck. I'm trying to tell you what's happened. I'm injured. Others are hurt, including Detective Burns. Can you help us?"

He yanks on the door, grunting and tugging away. I lean back, thinking, O*kay, calm down. He's trying to get you out.* I see his badge on his belt, the gun in his holster. He looks like a cop. The car's a dead giveaway, too. And I'm sure he was the one at the hotel.

While he continues to yank on the door, I look at him. "Officer . . . what's your name again? Weren't you at the Radisson before?"

He stops, letting go of the door, and sets his hand on his gun. It's the look on his face that raises my hackles. *Oh, shit. I'm in trouble.* I key the ignition. The engine clicks and clicks. Finally, it turns over.

"Ma'am, turn off the truck. I'm trying to get you out of this thing," he says with a dead stare, letting go of the weapon.

He knows he fucked up and revealed his true self to me, and now he's trying to act like a cop again. I glance into the rearview mirror. Still, I see no one. I'm out here alone with this man who has a gun. This seems to be a running theme, like a goddam nightmare I can't wake up from.

If I don't floor it right now, I won't get another chance. "Get the hell away from me." I slam my foot on the gas. The tires spin in the soft shoulder. Smoke rises from the exhaust. The engine coughs, threatening to die on me. *Don't you fucking die.*

He's reaching for his gun. I yank the wheel left and the tires are freed. The truck wobbles and shakes, but I keep my foot glued to the floor.

The officer steps back, raising his weapon. The tires reach the road, spinning smoke into the air. I nearly lose control as it lurches forward. "Come on, you piece of shit. Go!" My foot feels like it's going through the floorboard. I manage to gain control of the truck and peer through sideview mirror. "Shit."

He's got his gun aimed at me. Shots ring out, pinging the truck. I see sparks from where they hit. Within moments, I get far enough away; he can't hit me. The lights on his patrol car shrink in the distance. He won't be far behind, I know it. Can the truck stay ahead? My hands tremble as the scope of this becomes clearer. This is how they found us.

How many of you want me dead?

I speed down the road, back toward town, and I'm damn sure not going to stop for anyone else. Will he follow me back here? I suppose that depends on how many police officers are involved in this, or if it's just a few guys under Scott Shaw's control.

Detective Burns? He can't be one of them. He would've killed me already, not tried to save me. I still can't be sure, then, if he and Jesse are alive, or safe. Scott must've called his people, told them what direction I was headed.

It takes me a minute to gain my bearings, and when I do, I hear sirens again. *He's coming.* I'm only minutes from town. I just need to make it to the police station. They can't all be like that guy back there. Right?

The truck chugs along as parts of the front fender whip against the tire. I'll be lucky if it doesn't puncture it. But I'm not stopping. Not until I reach my destination.

My mind still reels at what Scott said. My brother? I can't believe it. I won't. Because that would mean my mother lied to us, and my dad went along with it. Why? And how is he still alive? So many questions, but I have to stay focused. Get to the police. Get help for Jesse and Detective Burns.

Lights from town arise in the night sky. In the rearview, headlights draw near. "Please. Let me make it. Please." The truck is going full speed. Steam starts to rise from the engine. "Don't die on me now. Come on. Come on."

I drive past the hotel. I'm not going back there, so I press on. Streetlights burn on the sides of the road. Civilization is here. The police station is only a couple of miles from the diner and hardware store. I'm almost there, but he's gaining on me.

I begin to realize that they never left this place . . . the people of New Hope . . . existing just under the surface, until the time came for them to rise up again, taking down the last of the non-believers. And that's me.

The road splits off. I turn left, heading toward the edge of town. I have no idea of the time, other than it's still dark. Not a single light burns in any of the buildings. But police stations are always open, right? Even here in this small town? Christ, I hope so.

Will they believe me when I tell them one of their officers tried to shoot me? I pull into the station, cutting the headlight. I beat him by a minute, at best, but will he risk coming here? Whoever he is? I have to get inside.

The door is still jammed, so I don't bother trying to open it. Instead, I climb over to the passenger door. It's stuck, but this time, I lay on my back and use my legs to kick it, ramming again and again. The door opens, and I practically spill out.

My gut still bleeds, and I clutch it with my left arm, hobbling toward the police station. Lights are on inside. Is the door unlocked? I grab the handle and pull. It doesn't open. I try again. Still nothing. For God's sake.

Then I see an officer inside hurrying to the door. He reaches for the other side, and it opens with ease. I quickly realize the one I'd tried was locked. "I need help. Someone's after me."

His gaze rakes over me, studying my appearance. "My God. You need a hospital." He carefully takes my elbow and with his other hand, helps me inside. "What's your name?"

"Kylie Forbes. An officer, he came after me. He's right behind me."

The man stops and leans back toward the doors again, trying to get a look. "I don't see anyone there, ma'am. You say it was an officer? Are you sure?"

"Yes, I'm sure. He was going to return me to him."

"Okay. You're going to have to back up." He helps me onto a lobby chair. "Tell me, from the beginning, what's happened."

"Sir, it's a long story. I need to know if Detective Burns is all right. He was hurt. So was my boyfriend."

"Wait." He eyes me. "Burns? You know what happened to him?"

"Yes, sir. That's what I'm trying to tell you. He was helping us, but Scott Shaw, he took me. He shot Burns, attacked my boyfriend, Jesse Cooper, and then took me." I'm out of breath, trying to relay the story quickly in case the bad cop has the balls to come in here. But something in this man's eyes makes me want to trust him. I pray I'm not wrong. "I escaped and an officer I thought was there to help . . ." I glance through the lobby doors again. "He shot at me. Please . . ." I can't stop the tidal wave of tears running down my cheeks. I'm scared, in pain, and . . . "I have to know if Jesse is alive."

"Come with me." He helps me off the chair and guides me into a long corridor. We enter a room that looks like, well, sort of a nurses' office, like at school. "Sit down. Don't move. I'm going to get help."

A small mirror is mounted near the door, and I see my reflection. My face is smeared with blood. Hair, nothing more than a matted brown mass. My eyes, puffy and red. The sight of me makes my chin quiver. What's happening? How is any of this real? I left that nightmare so long ago, and now, it's here and so many people have died. *Jesse, I need you. Please be okay. Please be safe.*

"Ms. Forbes." The officer returns with another man. He's older and looks like he's in charge. "This is Captain Lyons."

"We've been looking for you, miss," Lyons says.

I straighten my shoulders, eyes wide. "You know me?"

"Yes, ma'am," the captain replies. "Detective Burns told me all about you."

I drop my head into my hands, sobbing. "He's okay? He's alive?"

The captain walks inside, laying his hand gently on my shoulder. "Burns is hurt, but yes, he's alive. And he's looking for you."

I gaze up at the tall, older man with deep lines in his forehead. "Is Jesse okay, too? Jesse Cooper. Did Burns mention him?"

"Yes, he did. It seems Mr. Cooper is doing fine. I don't know the extent of his injuries, but he and Burns are in the hospital."

The news sets my emotions into overdrive. Relief swells in me. Tears spill uncontrollably.

"Ms. Forbes, we know about Scott Shaw. In fact, we're learning as much as we can about him now. You say he took you?"

He hands me a tissue and I blot my eyes. "Yes. I–I grew up in the compound. New Hope. My dad—"

"I'm familiar," Lyons says. "I was here then. But I didn't know about Scott Shaw."

"That makes two of us," I say. "You have to find him. He took me out to the compound, or what's left of it. He's fucking crazy."

"How did you get away?" he asks.

"Honestly . . ." I wipe my eyes again. "I have no idea."

The captain turns to the other officer. "Keep working on a location for this son of a bitch. Let me know when you have something. In the meantime, we'll get a unit out to the former compound and see if Shaw left anything behind that might give us an idea of where he's headed."

"Copy that, Captain."

The officer leaves. I compose myself and eye the captain. "Sir, another officer, I didn't get a name, he stopped me on the side of the road. He must know Shaw, because he tried to get me to go with him and I almost did, but I recognized him from the hotel." I shake away the image from my mind. "And then when I sped away, he shot at the truck."

He looks at me, suspicious of my accusation. "You're positive it was a police officer?"

"Yes, sir. In a police car and everything. Burns had posted him at the Radisson while we were there. But he acted like he'd never seen me before." I study him while he considers my words. "He followed me, but when I came here, he must've figured I'd tell you about him. He must still be out there somewhere. Maybe even working to get Shaw out of town."

The captain shoves his hands into his pockets. "I'll find out who's on patrol right now. We'll get you to the hospital, too. To see your boyfriend and have you looked at."

CHAPTER 27

Detective Burns

Why hasn't the captain called back? Surely, they found something on Scott Shaw by now. Sitting here in this hospital bed is starting to piss me off. I can see the sun peeking through the blinds. Soft gray light spills into my room. I've been here for too long. Shaw will have had plenty of opportunity to escape with Kylie . . . or to have killed her.

The meds have worn off, and the bullet wound sends bolts of pain through my shoulder and chest. But can I move? Yeah, I can move. But move where? I don't know where to find Shaw.

My phone rings on the table next to me. I reach over, grimacing as the pain shoots through me again. But it's worth it when I see the caller ID. "Burns, here."

"We have her. Kylie Forbes is here at the station."

Tension falls from my face. "Thank God. Is she okay?"

"She'll be heading your way soon," the captain says. "She's pretty banged up. Probably needs stitches, but otherwise, she seems all right."

"And Shaw? Do you know where he is? Anything pop up in the system?"

"The guy's a goddam ghost," he sighs. "He's not going by his real name, I can tell you that. So without DNA, prints, something . . . we're shooting in the dark. Listen, she claims one of ours shot at her. The man you posted watch at the Radisson."

"What?" I blink hard, trying to absorb his words. "Is she sure?"

"Oh yeah."

It dawns on me then and I close my eyes. "That's how he found us. He's got eyes on the inside."

"We know who he is and we will find him," Lyons continues. "In the meantime, I've sent two units out to the old compound. She says he took her there. God knows how she escaped."

"Can we trust them?"

"Hell if I know."

"At least here, she'll be safe." I look at the door. "I'm gonna do my best to get out of here. There's a shitload of secrets either Coleman was hiding, or our own files got wrong. She tell you who Shaw is?"

"Yeah, her half-brother. Couldn't believe it myself," the captain replies.

"Yeah." I shake my head. "Listen, I'll stick around here until she arrives. Make sure she's all right. No doubt, she'll want to see her boyfriend."

"He's there with you, right?"

"Yep. Some broken ribs. Not too bad," I reply. "Captain, if anyone gets any whiff of where this guy is . . ."

"Copy that. I'll keep only those I'm sure I can trust in the know, and I'll keep you posted. Don't leave there without the doc's sign-off. You got that, Burns?"

I wasn't gonna wait for the doctor to finish his early round of golf and then come into the hospital. But I also wasn't gonna tell that to my boss. "Yeah, I got it, sir. We'll be in touch." I end the call, stepping out of the bed.

The good news is that Kylie's safe. God knows how that woman survived, but it isn't the first time, so I guess I shouldn't be surprised. The problem now is finding the psychopath who's after her.

My clothes are in the bag under the table next to me. I reach down, wincing, but able to grab my things. Now, to dress before Nurse Ratched returns. I step into my black dress pants, every movement sending pain through my upper body. Pulling on my white button-down is excruciating, and it's covered in my own blood. *Never mind.*

I step into my shoes and walk toward the door. Once again, peeking out to see if the coast is clear. I have to go see Jesse again. Tell him the good news. Good for now, anyway. This is far from over.

Each step is painful, but I press on, soon arriving at Jesse's room again. I see him pulling on his shirt. The light of a new day shines through the window behind him. "You're up."

"Yes, sir," he says.

"I have news." I walk into his room. "Kylie's safe. She's on her way here. Captain says she's sustained some injuries, but is otherwise okay."

He covers his mouth with his hand, stifling his emotions. I feel for the kid. "We have a ways to go, but everyone knows who this guy is now. That was his advantage before. Not now. We will find him." I hope my words provide some comfort, though there's more he doesn't know. "It looks like Shaw has some of our people in his pocket."

"What?" Jesse asks. "How do you know?"

I'm hesitant, but the kid deserves to know the truth. "One of ours shot at Kylie as she made her escape." I see he's about to unleash his fury, so I raise my hands. "Captain Lyons, he's aware now, and only those he's sure he can trust will know anything about this, you got it?"

The redness in his cheeks fade. "Yeah, I got it."

"All right. I'm going to head down so I can see her coming." I make my way out to the lobby, each step sending stabs of pain through my chest. But I have to see Kylie for myself. I have to know she's truly all right.

As I push through the double doors, I scan the nearly empty waiting area. An older couple sits huddled together, the man patting the woman's hand. Nearby, a mother bounces a fussy toddler on her lap.

The morning light streams in through the large windows, casting everything in a soft glow. Nurses and doctors move briskly about their routines. And then I see her.

Off to the side, the elevator doors slide open and a young female officer steps out. I know the officer; she's a rookie. No way is she working for Shaw. She gently guides a fragile-looking woman along with her, and even from across the lobby, I immediately recognize her as Kylie.

Her face is pale and hollow with dark circles under her eyes. Kylie looks small, her slender frame swimming in an oversized police department T-shirt. An angry red gash mars her bruised cheek. She seems to fold into herself as the officer guides her to a chair.

I start toward her just as she breaks away from the officer, catching sight of me. "Detective Burns," she says breathlessly. "Have you seen Jesse? Is he . . ." Her voice trails off, anxiety creasing her brow.

"He's fine. A little banged up, but he's been asking for you since he got here," I assure her.

Her worry shifts to relief, fresh tears filling her eyes. "You have no idea how good it is to see you."

I gesture for her to follow me toward Jesse's room. As we walk, I take in the cuts and bruises marring her skin. She moves gingerly, as if nursing some hidden injury. But if she's in pain, her face tries hard not to show it.

I rap my knuckle on Jesse's door, and push it open without waiting for a response. "Hey, there's someone here to see you." I gesture for her to enter, but she blows past me, rushing to his side.

They cry in each other's arms, and I feel both happy and angry at the same time, because this isn't over. Someone is still after her, and that someone would have no problem taking out anyone in his way to get to her. I'm not going to let that happen.

I slink out into the lobby, leaving them to have their moment, and walk over to the officer. "What do you know about Scott Shaw?"

"Just that everyone's out there looking for him," she says. "Lyons sent a couple units to the old compound."

She looks beyond me a moment, toward the hall where Jesse's room is. "Listen, that woman, she says an officer tried to take her, tried to kill her, when she made her escape in Shaw's truck."

"So I heard. It was one of the guys I personally posted at the hotel."

"Right. Well, if someone on our side isn't who we think he is . . ."

I look away. "Yeah. Got it. Lyons suspects there could be more. Listen, I'll take care of her from here. She's going to need to see a doctor. Thanks for bringing her down. But do me a favor?"

"Anything."

"Anyone finds that asshole, or the ones helping him, you tell me, got it? He came at me, too. And killed a former fed. None of them will get away with it."

I make my way back to Jesse's room. The two are talking, holding hands. I clear my throat to make my presence known. "Excuse the interruption."

Kylie turns around and smiles. "It's okay, Detective. Come in."

I walk over to them, hands in my pockets, feeling sheepish for the intrusion, but we still have business to tend to. "I'm glad you're safe, Kylie, but you still need to get a doctor to take a look at your injuries."

"That's what I've been telling her," Jesse says, perched on the edge of the bed, his feet dangling.

I lick my lips, holding my tongue while I figure out what to say when Kylie sets her sights on me.

"Scott Shaw is still out there, and he has help," she says.

"I'm aware," I reply. "I need to get back out there and get working on finding him."

She gives me a once-over. "You're in no condition—"

I raise my palm. "I'll be fine. You two are safe here. I need to help my team find these people and put an end to this." Before she can say another word, I stop her. "Call your aunt. She's terrified and needs to know that you're okay."

As I make my way to the door, I stop again. "I'll keep an officer out here, all right? One I know I can trust."

Kylie nods.

"Thank you, Detective," Jesse says. "For everything."

CHAPTER 28

Kylie

The doctor who tends to me says Jesse will be discharged soon and can join me then. But I have to be here for the next few hours until they run some tests. What tests? I have no idea. Still, I don't refuse because I know it isn't safe out there for me. Or for Jesse. And I know Burns will come back with answers. I just hope they're the answers I'm looking for.

I did as he asked and called Aunt Grace, letting her know I was safe. So many questions burned in my mind. Like why she never told me the truth about my mother. Why I never knew about my half-brother. But I didn't have the energy to confront her on any of it. Not yet. She was just so grateful I was safe. And I didn't know when I'd get the chance to hear her voice again, so I let myself relish the moment. To be fair, Grace didn't know Scott Shaw was still alive. I couldn't fault her for that.

I wonder, though, if Burns tracked down that officer who was clearly helping Shaw. Why would he do that? Who was he? These are questions I don't know if I'll ever get answers to. With Dale gone, the only other person who was there, with me, is . . . I realize might never get to the truth. Because whatever Scott Shaw's truth is, it isn't the same as mine. He's a monster. Just like his father.

"That should do it," the doctor says, pressing down the bandage on my stomach. "You'll have to be careful. No heavy lifting. In fact, don't lift anything for a while, you understand? You'll pop those stitches."

"I understand. Thank you, Doctor."

"I'll need you to sit tight here for a while until all the blood work comes back," he continues. "I want to be sure you don't have an infection. Then you're free to leave."

I don't tell him that I'm not exactly keen on leaving. "Got it. Thanks."

When he walks out, Jesse enters. I smile, my emotions rising to the surface again. I'm just so grateful he's all right. I can't believe we made it through all of it. "Hi."

"Hey." He walks toward me, eyeing the doctor's handiwork. "You look better."

"I feel a little better. Doc gave me something mild for the pain, and with the bandages, yeah, I'm feeling okay."

He nods. I can see he wants to ask where we go from here, knowing what's out there waiting for me, for us.

A nurse enters, capturing our attention. "Mr. Cooper?"

Jesse turns around. "Yes?"

"If you don't mind, I'll need you to fill out some paperwork, and then you're free to leave."

He turns back to me, and I nod. "Go. I'll be here waiting for the blood tests a while."

Jesse squeezes my hand before heading out to follow the nurse. I see him clutch his side. He's still in pain.

When he disappears, I slowly rise and head to the bathroom. I haven't showered in almost two days and wouldn't mind a splash of water on my face. As I shuffle inside, I stop at the window. The sun's been up for a few hours now. Have they found him yet? As I peer through it, I glance down at the parking lot. It's a small hospital and I'm only on the second floor, so I have a pretty good view.

Another patrol car arrives. There's one parked at the entrance already. But when I see the person step out, my heart falls into my stomach. *Oh my God. He's here.*

I whip around to my door, which is partially open. I hurry toward it, and step out, craning left and then right. *Where the hell are you?* The officer stationed out here is gone. But I know there's still one at the entrance. Can I get there in time to warn her?

I don't have my phone; it was lost in the battle for my life. Jesse must've pocketed his. "Goddam it." I walk into the hall and see the officer returning to my door. "Officer, there's another policeman. He's in the parking lot. He's the one who shot at me."

The officer raises his hand. "It's all right, miss. You're safe. Just stay here, and I'll go check it out."

"Thank you." I watch the officer march quickly down the hallway, disappearing around the corner.

After what feels like an eternity, he reappears, yet he's wearing a strange, hardened look. As he gets closer, I see his hand slide down to the holster on his hip. My heart drops.

"Let's take a walk," he says in a calm voice.

No. No fucking way is this cop one of them, too. He can't be. Burns trusted him. How many of Shaw's people are on the police force? Is this how he's managed to stay off-grid for so long? These guys have been protecting him. Why?

"Don't make a sound," he warns. "We're just going to go for a little ride."

He grips my arm and leads me down the hallway. I want to scream, to fight, but I don't dare risk them taking it out on Jesse, wherever he is. We walk out a side entrance into the parking lot. He opens the back door of a nondescript sedan and shoves me inside. I'm sure I feel a few stitches pop.

As he slams the door shut, the sound reverberates through me. I sit paralyzed in the backseat as the officer drives away from the hospital. It's clear that New Hope is alive and well, with many new followers. And Lucas Shaw's son, my brother, wants them to hunt me down to make me pay for what happened.

"There's no place left for you to take me," I say, trying to sound firm. "They'll come looking, just like before. Shaw won't win this."

He doesn't say a word, just keeps driving.

"You're a cop. Why are you doing this?"

He peers at me through the rearview. "You have no idea how many of us there are. And it's all thanks to you."

"What?" I say in a whisper.

"All of this . . . it was all to get you back. Back where you belong."

I look around as he drives, realizing he's heading out of town. He won't be dumb enough to take me back to the old compound. Burns will know to look for me there. But now, I realize I can't let him take me anywhere. If I stay in this car, I'm as good as dead.

My door is locked, and the only way out is through him. And at this point, I'd rather die trying than die by Shaw's hand.

I wait until we arrive, and I immediately recognize the place as the farmhouse. How could I not? I'd escaped him once here already. "What are we doing here? Are you stupid? You think the cops won't look for me here?"

He rolls along the gravel until coming to a stop. "You don't get it, do you?" He peers at me through the rearview mirror. "Who do you think owns this place, huh? Your knights in shining armor won't come here. We've made sure of that."

I take in his words. The owner? Scott Shaw set this up from the beginning? I don't know how he found me. How he knew I'd be on this film, but he did. Word must've gotten around that Hollywood was knocking, and he answered. Why pull me back into this when I'd done nothing? Said nothing? No one even knew the truth about who I was.

"Come on. It's time to go inside." The officer steps out and walks to the rear passenger door. Can I do it? Can I make a run for it, or will he shoot me?

Defeat weighs on my shoulders, and I begin to doubt my ability to survive this time. The officer opens the door and reaches in for me. I scramble to the other side, trying the door, but it's still locked.

As he reaches deeper in, I ball up my fist and swing as hard as I can, connecting with the officer's jaw. He pulls away in surprise, and I seize the opportunity, launching myself out of the car. My feet hit the gravel and I break into a sprint.

The officer is shouting behind me, but I don't look back. I race toward the tall grasses and fields, praying I can make it to the cover. My breaths come short and fast, and my injuries scream in protest, but I push myself harder.

Just as the fields are within reach, I hear the crack of a gunshot and a bullet whizzing by my head. I glance back and see the officer lowering his pistol, his face a mask of rage.

I crash through the cornstalks, branches whipping against my skin. In the distance, I hear the officer cursing as he gives chase. I weave between the rows and his steps fade behind me. I stop to catch my breath, knowing I can't stay long. That's when I hear him. Scott Shaw calls out to me: "We will kill him."

Jesse. He's talking about Jesse. As I catch my breath, my lips tremble at the thought. If he was able to get to me, with the help of cops, then he'll get to Jesse, too.

"Think about it, Kayla. Don't be selfish," he says. "Come back, and you won't have to worry about his safety."

He's right. There are too many of them now. Maybe the only honest cop left in this town is Detective Burns. I hope I'm wrong, but they have me trapped now. I won't let Jesse get hurt because of me.

I close my eyes for a moment, standing tall. I've been living on borrowed time anyway, right? The rest of my family died long ago. I should've died with them. Brandon and Lucy would still be alive. Dale Coleman, too. "All right. I'm coming out."

Stepping through the field, I make my way back to the house, accepting my fate. I can't — I *won't* put anyone else's life at risk. It's my turn to pay for the sins of my father.

The farmhouse comes into view as I draw near, and I consider how it was Shaw found me. Figured out my work and how to get me here. He couldn't have acted alone. Was it possible Aunt Grace unwittingly aided in the effort? If so, then she could be in danger, too.

It's too much to think about and I'm weak, in pain, exhausted. I feel like giving up. I raise my hands and step out of the field. "Don't shoot."

I see two officers aiming guns at me. I glare at them. "You don't even know what you've done."

"Come on."

One of them yanks my arm, pulling me toward the house. Shaw's back inside, waiting for me again. I see him in the doorway, a triumphant smile on his face. "You should've killed me the first time you had the chance," I say.

"Oh, sister . . . I already told you, I don't want to kill you. I love you." He closes in on me, standing inches from my face. He takes in my scent, closing his eyes. "You're family. You're *my* family."

CHAPTER 29

Detective Burns

Embedded among my ranks are those willing to aid Scott Shaw. I see that now. I return to the station, casting a wary gaze at everyone. People I once trusted. Now, I trust no one, except maybe Captain Lyons. God, I hope I'm not wrong about him, too.

My phone buzzes in my pocket. I grab it, not recognizing the number, but answer anyway. "Detective Burns."

"It's Jesse, sir." He's breathless, fear instilled in his tone. "They got to her. I don't know how, but they did. She's gone."

I raise my eyes to the ceiling, defeat closing in on me. "Son of a bitch. Then they're in on it, too. Goddam it. Where are you?"

"At the hospital. I left to sign my discharge papers. Came back, and I couldn't find her anywhere. The officer you stationed outside her door, he's gone, too. You let them take her again."

His words echo in my ears. He's not wrong. "Jesse, listen to me. Stay where you are. I will find her." I pocket my phone, standing in the corridor, wondering who the hell I can trust right now. The captain? Another detective? I don't know. Maybe no one.

How could I have been so stupid? After Lyons and the rookie told me about one of the patrolmen, I didn't think there could be others? Sleepers. How many more are there?

My search so far has opened my eyes, but there's more. Retired Agent Coleman was living in this town to keep an eye out for a re-emergence of New Hope. Did he see this coming? Did he contact his former colleagues at the Bureau to alert them?

I rush outside, the pain in my shoulder still shooting through me like another bullet. But the only way I can hope for answers is to go back to Coleman's home. No one here can help me now. Coleman had to have known what was coming, which was why he went to work on the film. Now, I have to find out. Without a word to anyone, I return to my car, pulling out of the parking lot before anyone can ask me anything. I won't alert them. I don't know who to trust.

I head straight to Coleman's house. Pulling up out front, I run to the door. It's locked. No time to waste, so I bust the front window and climb inside. More cuts and scrapes on me, but I don't feel any of it right now. Shaw has her, and he won't risk her escaping again. All I can do is bust my ass to find her before he decides to kill her.

Coleman holds the key, but he's dead, so I'd better find it fast. I march through the hallway into his office, where I'd been before. It looks the same, meaning no one else has been in here. Good.

I pull out all the file cabinet drawers, tipping them onto the floor. Papers spill everywhere. On my hands and knees, my back screaming in pain, I search through them, praying something stands out. I've read his journals. Not one thing about Scott Shaw. Maybe he didn't know about him. But how could he not? He was there when it all happened.

I scan as much as possible, as quickly as I can. "Come on, goddam it. Show me something, man. Otherwise, you gave your life for nothing."

I sift through the piles of papers, medical reports, newspaper clippings, looking for anything that stands out. Then I see it — a stack of photos banded together, tucked under several files. I grab them and flip through quickly. Houses. Farmland. What the hell is all this? Then I recognize one of them. "Holy shit. That's the farmhouse where they were filming."

As I examine the images, I notice the same man in each of them. Some taken with others. Some, where he stands alone. And I can just make out his face. That's Scott Shaw, just as Kylie had described. It must be.

I feel the puzzle pieces fall into place, but not just yet. Not quite yet. What I do understand now is that Coleman knew about Lucas's son. That's a hell of a secret to keep. Unless he did bring it up to his former colleagues.

Soon, after sifting through more papers, I see deeds. Several of them. The name on these deeds? Scott Brooks. In the margins, I see Coleman's scribbles. I turn the documents to read them. *Scott Brooks = Shaw.* It dawns on me. These deeds . . . this land . . . it's all owned by Scott Shaw. And then, I recognize one of the addresses. "That's it. That's the farmhouse."

He set this up. All of it. But how? How did he get the money to buy all this? And why didn't Coleman tell any of this to Kylie? We could've protected her. Then again, who knows how many cops Shaw has in his pocket?

A thick manila envelope catches my eye. I pull it out — it's unmarked, sealed tightly. I tear it open. Inside are surveillance photos of Scott Shaw meeting with various people, their faces circled in red pen. I scan the images, recognizing some of the figures with a jolt.

It's Captain Michaels. Sergeant Powell. Even Officer Drake, one of the younger recruits. They're all pictured with Shaw at different locations, passing envelopes, appearing to converse in shadowy corners.

The truth hits me like a punch to the gut. Shaw's been working with these officers for God knows how long. They've been helping him rebuild his following in secret, aiding his pursuit of Kylie. My own team, my trusted colleagues — they betrayed us all.

CHAPTER 30

Kylie

As I sit in the kitchen, I see the faded red stain left behind by Brandon's murder. My half-brother, Scott, sits across from me, his henchmen close by. Officers, all of them. I wonder if Burns knows yet. Jesse must've called him. He must be terrified right now. The only thing that keeps me going is knowing he's safe so long as I'm here. I'm the one Scott wants. Just me.

"I keep wondering why it is you haven't killed me yet." A bold stance, I know, but I can't let this asshole see that he's scaring the shit out of me.

The look on his face, Christ, I'd seen that look on my mother's face countless times before. Only now do I recognize it.

Shaw pulls the chair closer. "Despite what you think, sister, this was never about ending your life."

"Yeah, sure," I scoff. "Because that's how it's coming off, right? Murdering my friends. Murdering Dale Coleman. Why am I here?"

"Because you're a survivor. You're one of us, whether you want to believe it or not." He leans back, tilting his head.

"My father was right about a lot of things. But he was also wrong, too. What he did to the young girls." He looks away as if disgusted. "It didn't have to be that way, and it was the reason we lost everything."

"Why couldn't you let me live my life?" I ask. "I live a thousand miles away, doing nothing to you. Speaking to no one about my past. Yet you brought me back, didn't you?"

He shrugs. "I suppose there's no harm in admitting now that I've always known where you lived, thanks to Dale Coleman. He's kept track of you and your aunt."

My eyes darken at the mention of Aunt Grace.

"Oh yeah, I know about her, too," he says. "Don't worry. She's safe . . . for now."

I thought Dale was on my side, but had he been feeding Shaw information about me and my family? "If Dale was helping you, why'd you kill him?"

"He wasn't helping me," Shaw replies. "I've been keeping track of him since your father murdered mine. It didn't take long to figure out he was a federal agent. And when he retired here, I had expanded the group enough to have people in law enforcement keeping tabs on him." He shakes his head. "Guess he couldn't leave well enough alone. But going back to why you're here now . . . I wanted to bring you home, Kayla. This is where you belong. Our mother knew that, and her death, well, I've taken care of the person responsible . . . don't you worry about that."

"You know who killed her? You know who killed my family? You said it was just some coward who took his own life."

"I've always known, Kayla," he says, leaning closer still. "And the story you heard is the one you were meant to hear."

He's inches from my face. I can smell his breath, coffee mixed with cigarettes, and it makes me want to vomit. I flinch when he reaches for me, tucking my hair behind my ear. "Where were you back then? I don't remember you there at all."

"Lucas kept me as far away from you and your family as possible. See, he wanted you, but if anyone else besides your parents knew you and I had the same mother?" He shakes his head, tsking. "I think that would've been a step too far, even for them."

"No one knew about you?"

"Just your folks. Lucas made a great many mistakes that I don't intend to replicate."

So my father knew about Scott. Maybe that was why he didn't want to go along with sending me off to marry Lucas. That was a line he couldn't cross either. Of course, I was only thirteen. That should've been reason enough.

I stare at Scott, trying to process this overload of revelations. My head spins as I think of the years of manipulation and lies that had shaped my life. I feel the room closing in on me, the weight of Scott's gaze making it hard to breathe.

"Why now?" I force out. "After all these years, why bring me here?"

Scott leans back, regarding me with those wanting eyes. "It's time for a new beginning, sister. Our numbers have grown; we've rebuilt much of what was lost. And now that Lucas is gone, I can finally bring you home where you belong."

I shudder at his words. The thought of being trapped here, forced into whatever twisted role Scott has envisioned for me, makes me feel ill.

"Jesse will come for me," I say firmly. "He won't stop until—"

"Until he's dead," Scott cuts in. "Just like your friend Brandon. And that pretty girl, Lucy." He looks away. "She was very pretty. I am sorry for that."

I feel my stomach lurch at the mention of my friends' murders. Brandon and Lucy . . . their lives cut short at the hands of this madman.

Scott continues, "You belong with us now, Kayla. With your family."

"You're not my family," I spit out. "You're a monster."

Scott's expression darkens. In an instant, his hand is around my throat, squeezing. I gasp for breath as stars twinkle before my eyes.

"You will learn respect," he whispers in my ear. "You will learn to love me, sister."

Finally, he releases me, and I double over, coughing and gulping air. The officers standing guard don't even flinch. They're loyal only to Scott.

I know I have to be smart if I'm going to survive this. As much as I want to fight back, I'm outnumbered and overpowered. "I'm sorry," I reply, keeping my eyes lowered. I think of Jesse, praying he stays far away. If he tries to rescue me, he'll be walking straight to his death. But what about Burns? He must know now that the people he thought he could trust, he no longer can.

My survival rests on my shoulders now. My only option is to submit. Will Scott buy into my sudden change of heart? That depends on just how arrogant and self-righteous he is. If he's anything like his father, then he'll buy it, so long as I feed into his hubris.

"Look, we both know that detective, maybe others, will come for me. And they will look here," I say.

Scott keeps his gaze on me but says nothing.

"You know we have to stay on the move."

"We?" he asks, a hint of hope in his tone.

"Yes. I'll do as you ask, but only if you promise not to hurt Jesse or Grace. Otherwise, I'd just as soon slit my wrists right now. And then what will your newfound followers think, knowing your own blood would rather be dead than follow you?"

Scott considers me for a long moment. I hold my breath, worried I've overplayed my hand. But then he nods slowly.

"You make a fair point, sister. It is best we relocate for now. Somewhere more private while you . . . adjust."

His agreement surprises me. I expected more resistance, more assertions of control. Either I'm a better actress than I realize, or Scott is more pragmatic than his zealot father.

The latter thought chills me. Lucas ruled by fear and retaliation. But Scott . . . Scott is patient, methodical. He'll use my love for Jesse and Grace as leverage; I'm certain of it. I shove down my dread. "I just need some time. This is all a lot to take in."

Scott smiles. "Of course." He turns to one of the armed men. "We'll go to the other property."

As the man scurries away, Scott places a hand on my cheek. I fight the urge to recoil at his touch.

"We'll go someplace where no one will find us."

I raise my lips slightly in acknowledgment, keeping my expression neutral as Scott leads me outside to a waiting SUV. I try to take in everything that's happened. Scott Shaw is my half-brother. He was kept secret from me, but has been watching me for years. And now he intends to draw me into this twisted cult he's rebuilt.

The revelations about my past leave me reeling, but I force myself to focus on the present. On surviving the next few hours and days.

Scott holds the door open for me as I climb gingerly into the backseat, my injuries still paining me. I'm sandwiched between one of the guards and Scott as he slides in on the other side. His hand finds my knee and I stiffen.

"It won't be long now, sister," he says. "Soon you'll understand everything."

I say nothing, staring straight ahead as the SUV pulls onto the road. The tinted windows make it impossible to see where we're headed. But I suspect it'll be a remote location. There's plenty around here to choose from.

CHAPTER 31

Detective Burns

Jesse needs to know what's happening, so I drive to the hospital, hoping he did as I asked and stayed there. When I step out of my car, I search for patrol units. God knows how many are in on this. How many helped Scott Shaw to murder three innocent people, even if he didn't do it directly.

All these years and it was Dale Coleman who'd kept the worst of it at bay, protecting that girl from the truth, for better or worse. But it's out now. And she's gone. The only people I know I can trust now are Jesse Cooper and Captain Lyons, until he proves otherwise.

Inside, I ride the elevator to the second floor, ignoring the throbbing pain in my back and chest. I reach around to try to feel the bandage, wondering if my stitches are intact, or if I have blood soaking through my shirt.

It feels dry, for now. The doors open and I glance left, then right, heading straight toward the nurse's station. *There he is.* "Jesse?"

The young man turns around, relief in his face. "Detective Burns, where is she? Do you know? Is she safe?"

I gently grip his arms. "Take a breath, son. You're in no condition. I don't know where she is, but I do know we can no longer trust the police."

"What?" His eyes crinkle. "Any of them?"

"I don't know who's with Shaw and who isn't. I think the captain is our only hope." I glance around to be sure we're alone. "So I don't plan on risking it. It's you and me, for now, all right? We have to be the ones to find her."

"Okay. Yeah." He takes a steadying breath. "Where do we start?"

I consider Jesse's question. Where do we even begin searching for Kylie when Shaw has corrupted the police force and has resources I can't fathom? I know we're working against the clock — the longer Kylie stays missing, the slimmer our chances are of finding her alive.

"I think we start with what we know," I say. "Scott Shaw has purchased property under the name Brooks, the managing member of an LLC that holds the deeds. I uncovered four locations when I looked into Dale Coleman's papers earlier. And . . ." I hesitate a moment, despising the fact I'm about to drop another shoe. "One of them is the farmhouse where you were filming."

"What?" Jesse asks, disbelief masking his face.

"It would make sense for Shaw to take her to one of the places he owns. No doubt they'll be isolated, much like the farmhouse. He'll want to keep her secluded while he . . ." I trail off, gritting my teeth at the thought of what he might do.

Jesse's face hardens with anger and determination. "So we're just going to take a shot in the dark and pick one?"

"I can almost guarantee, it won't be the farmhouse. I don't think he's that stupid. So that leaves us with three others," I say, hesitating a moment. "You got a better idea? There's only three. I'm positive he has her at one of those locations. So are you with me on this?"

Jesse looks around, then sets a steely gaze on me. "I will get her back."

"Then we need to move. Now." I scan the area again. "How are your ribs? Can you walk all right?"

He places his hand on his side. "I'll be fine. You're the one who got shot. I can manage."

"Good." I lead the way to the stairwell and open the door. "Go." Jesse makes his way down the steps, looking like he's in pain, but trying hard not to show it. "You're doing all right, son. Just keep going." I follow, and I'm slower than he is. Of course, I've been shot and I've got twenty years plus on the kid, but I do my best to keep up.

We reach the door that leads to the hospital lobby. I stand ready, my hand on the door. "Me first. I need to make sure we're clear." I push it open, leaning through to check the coast is clear. "We're good. Let's go."

I walk out, appearing calm, collected. I glance behind me at Jesse, making sure he's doing the same. I don't see any officers outside. We just might make it out of here.

The doors slide open, and we step out into the afternoon sun. Is it afternoon already? How long ago was she taken? I've lost track.

The sun beats down on us as we make our way across the parking lot. I scan the rows of cars, looking for anything suspicious. My hand hovers near my holster, ready to draw if needed.

We reach my sedan, and I usher Jesse into the passenger seat before sliding behind the wheel. As I start the ignition, Jesse speaks up. "Which property do we go to first?"

I consider that for a moment. "The one on Oak Street. It's remote, not that far away, and I suspect he'll think there's less chance of being spotted."

Jesse nods, his jaw set.

I pull out of the parking lot and head for the freeway. What will we find when we get there? Will Kylie even be there, or will this be yet another dead end? And if she is, what state will she be in? Who knows what Shaw will have put her through.

I glance at Jesse as I drive. He stares straight ahead, lost in thought. But there's an intensity to him that wasn't there before, a lethal determination that promises consequences for anyone who's hurt Kylie. I know that dark desire for vengeance all too well. And I pray it doesn't consume him as it once did me.

The house on Oak Street is set back from the road, nestled among overgrown trees and bushes. As we pull up, it looks dark and deserted, almost like it's been abandoned for years. I cut the engine, and we sit there in silence, scoping out the place.

"No vehicles around. No lights or movement inside that I can see," I say. "We need to be smart about this."

Stepping out of the car, we move stealthily, approaching the back of the house. The house is dark, no signs of life inside. Still, we approach with senses heightened for any indication of a threat. At the front door, Jesse stands guard. I break the nearest window without a second thought, and then climb through, walking around to open the front door. "Let's check it out."

We step into the dark foyer, the beam of my flashlight cutting a swath through the gloom. The air is musty and stale, with a lingering scent of mildew. This is one of Shaw's houses, but it doesn't look like anyone's been here for a while.

We sweep each room, confirming no one else is present. No sign of Kylie, either. My heart sinks, but I steel myself.

In what looks to be a den, a large corkboard on the wall catches my eye. Pinned to it are photos of the movie set, shots of the crew, even a few of Lucy and Brandon. Surveillance photos. "He was here."

Jesse moves in next to me. "Oh my God. These are all from the film shoot."

It doesn't take long for him to see the images of Kylie and him together. He covers his mouth for a moment, seemingly in shock.

"Look, we know he's been watching," I say, trying to reassure him of our goal. "Let's search for any indication of where he might've taken her."

I peer at the board again and see a photo of Lucas Shaw. With my index finger, I rest it on the photo. "This is him. I saw pictures of Lucas Shaw in Coleman's files. He was the leader."

Jesse leans closer. "I've never seen him before. I never knew any of this."

I regard him. "She was only trying to protect you." My eyes drift over the rest of the board. Most of it seems to be details about the movie — production schedules, staff rosters, location photos. He must've gotten hold of this information because of whatever contract he'd signed with the producers to use his farmhouse. Maybe they'd kept him updated, obviously not realizing who he truly was.

In the bottom right corner is a photograph that draws my interest. "This is him. Scott Shaw."

Jesse takes a closer look. "He looks like the man Kylie described. I didn't see him. I was already on the ground."

"Me too," I say. "But who's he standing next to?"

Jesse shakes his head. "I–I don't know."

"Neither do I." I rip the photo from the board. "But I know Kylie's not here, so we have to keep looking."

CHAPTER 32

Kylie

We'd been driving for forty minutes. I've had to feel Scott's leg next to me, touching mine. I swear he'd inched closer to make me more uncomfortable. Now, the SUV stops. I look out through the windshield, then around at the men beside me. I don't recognize the place at all. "Where are we?"

Scott pats my knee. "Your new home — for the time being." He steps out, offering me his hand. "Let's go."

I wonder how he's managed to brainwash these police officers. How could they fall in line with a madman spawned from another madman? And how did he have money to buy this place? The farmhouse, too?

"Get out. Now," Scott says, still holding out his hand for me.

I climb down, avoiding his touch. Looking around, there's nothing. Nothing as far as the eye can see. My heart sinks. I'm lost to Jesse now, and I need to come to terms with it.

"We should get inside," he says. "It's getting too hot out here." He makes his way to the two-story home. It's old. The white siding is chipped and peeling in places. It's not as sprawling as the farmhouse where we filmed, but it seems to be surrounded by a whole lot of vacant land. I can't even get my bearings. I don't know this place. I see no landmarks. No large boulders. No signs. But there is a fence. Barbed wire that surrounds the immediate area. Beyond that? Just fields. Unfarmed. Unused.

I follow Scott as he leads us inside the old house. The interior is just as plain and rundown as the outside. The living room bears only a faded green couch and a couple of mismatched side chairs, while the kitchen looks like it hasn't been updated since the 1970s.

He tells his men to keep watch outside, and then regards me. "How about a tour?"

I shudder, dreading whatever he has planned. I try to take in every detail inside and out, looking for anything I can use to my advantage or to aid in an escape. But the house seems completely isolated.

The wood floors are worn with deep gouges in many spots. Faded floral wallpaper adorns the walls, though it's peeling at the corners.

Scott places his hand on my hip, gripping it tightly and pulling me close. "Don't look so glum, sister. This will be your home now, at least until the new sanctuary is built. We have big plans for you." His voice drips with devilish affection that turns my stomach.

I jerk my shoulder away defiantly. "We might be blood, but I'm not your sister. And I'll never be part of your family."

His eyes flash with anger for a moment before his expression turns cold again. "We'll see about that. You have a purpose here with me, and you can't fight it forever." He motions for me to sit on the lumpy green couch while he confers with his men off to the side in hushed tones.

After a moment, he dismisses them, instructing them to stand guard outside. Now I'm alone with this psycho, the son of the cult leader my father brought down. Every ounce of me is consumed by terror, but I keep my face blank.

"Well, Kayla, it seems we have a lot to discuss," Scott says, turning his dark gaze on me. "But first, let's get you cleaned up and into some fresh clothes."

I begin to see his intent. He grabs my arm, his fingers digging into the soft underside, and leads me down the hallway to the bathroom. I try to pull away, but his grip only tightens.

"We need to get you somewhat presentable," he says, as he pushes open the bathroom door. The beige tiles are cracked and stained, the painted doors on the vanity sink hang loosely on their hinges, and the room smells of mildew.

Scott stands in front of me and rests his hands on my shoulders. I shudder at his touch. He pulls up the police T-shirt I'm wearing. "Raise your arms."

I wince in pain as he lifts it over my head, exposing my injuries — and my bra. He reaches around me and unfastens it. As it falls to the floor, his gaze is drawn to my bare breasts. His chest rises and falls with growing intensity as he stares at me. "I wonder what he saw in you. A tender young girl of only thirteen."

I know he's talking about his father, Lucas, and his desire to marry me.

Scott licks his lips and unbuttons my shorts next, tugging them down my legs along with my underwear. I stand there, naked and trembling before this monster, unable to contain my rising fear. I feel his hand brush my thigh, but he stops short of getting any closer.

His eyes travel over my body. I want to puke. I want to punch him in the face. "Please," I whisper through clenched teeth. "Don't."

He leans closer, and closer still, until our lips are almost touching. Then, he reaches past me and turns on the shower. "Get in."

I hesitate only a moment before obeying. The longer I can avoid provoking his rage, the longer I have to try to escape or be rescued.

As I stand under the icy spray, I feel his eyes still on me. He's turned it cold on purpose. The water washes away the dried blood. My bandages get soaked through, and my skin stings.

"Turn toward me," he says.

I do as he asks, the water running down me. It's so cold, my teeth begin to chatter. He stares at me with eyes that suddenly remind me of Lucas.

"That's enough," he says. "Turn off the water."

He's trying to humiliate me. That's all this is. A power play. I have to remain composed, refuse to let him see the truth of my fear. He grabs a nearby towel, holding it up before him. "Come on, now, sister. Let me dry you off."

I step out of the shower. He wraps the towel around me, pulling me against him. He's hard. I can feel it against my hip. My stomach turns.

"Now," he says, "doesn't that feel better?"

When he steps back, removing the towel from me, I stand naked before him once again. He reaches for what looks like fresh clothes on the edge of the vanity. "Here." He throws them at me. "Get dressed. I'll give you some privacy."

He smiles and steps out, closing the door as he exits.

I nearly collapse on the tile floor. Humiliated, ashamed. Pissed off. I can see the shadow of his feet beneath the door. He's waiting for me to break down. To prove to him that he has control over me, but I refuse to give him the satisfaction.

I dress myself in the clothes he provided. A pair of too-big denim shorts and a large T-shirt. These look like men's clothes. I glance at my reflection in the mirror. My body is covered in bruises, cuts, scrapes, bandages. At least the blood is gone. *Please God. Don't let me die here.*

I open the door, and there he is.

He gives me a thorough once-over. "Well, you look much better. Let's go. Still lots to do."

I follow him back into the living room. The men, his own private police force, are outside, standing on the front porch. "What do you mean?"

He walks into the kitchen and grabs a couple of bottles of water. I'm thirsty as hell, but I won't tell him that.

"Here." He returns, handing a bottle to me. "Drink up. You must be thirsty."

I take a long swig and he laughs.

"See? I knew it." Scott pushes me onto the couch before taking a seat next to me.

"Well, isn't this cozy," I say mockingly, so he doesn't think he's won.

"I know it's not much," he says, glancing around. "But it will have to do for now. I've got big plans for you, sis."

I ignore his comment, growing tired of him calling me 'sister,' hearing him talk of a future between us. That will never happen. Not as long as I still breathe.

"You must be hungry. Let me fix you something to eat."

"I'm not hungry," I reply, even though my stomach is growling. "What do you want from me?"

He gazes at me with a slight tilt of his head. "I used to watch you walk from your house into the center for school."

I crease my brow, wondering if he means from my aunt's house . . . then it comes to me. "At New Hope?"

"Of course." He rests his elbows on his thighs, turning his head toward me. "We're not so different, you know."

"Oh, I doubt that's true."

He chuckles, leaning back again. "Well, maybe you're right. I'm a lot more like Mom than you."

He's only saying these things to get a reaction. I can't let him. It's how he controls people. It's how he wins.

"I guess I could show you to your room, since you're not interested in eating anything. Let you get settled in."

"Will you be staying here, too?" I ask, almost smirking to show I'm not afraid of him.

"Of course. This place is all ours for tonight." He stands and offers a hand. "Come on. I'll show you."

My unease grows as we descend into a basement. The air down here is dank, tinged with mildew. Rows of exposed pipes line the ceiling. The only light comes from a single, bare bulb dangling overhead. "No. I'm not staying in here."

"It's the only way I can be sure you won't try to leave," he says. "You're a smart girl, Kayla. I underestimated you once. Trust me when I say, I won't do so again."

He shoves me inside the concrete room furnished with just a cot and a bucket in the corner. The door clangs shut behind me, the locks sliding into place with decisiveness.

This is where he intends to keep me until I submit — mentally, and maybe physically.

CHAPTER 33

Detective Burns

The next property is almost ten miles away, even farther out of town. It's becoming clear to me that Scott Shaw uses isolation tactics to convert his followers. Not uncommon.

From what I read in Dale Coleman's files, that was how they worked. Isolation. Forcing people to depend on Shaw for food, water, shelter. Convincing them he was their savior. I'd seen plenty of folks with a God complex in my career as a detective, but this was the worst kind. And only a sociopath could pull it off. That's what Scott Shaw is — a sociopath, a malignant narcissist. Turns out, the apple didn't fall far from the tree.

We drive up to the small home, surrounded by trees and more fields. The throbbing in my back and chest serves as a reminder I'm not one hundred percent. And to be honest, I was probably only seventy-five percent on a good day, in any case. Jesse's a young man, and while he suffers too, the heavy lifting — so to speak — I might have leave to him.

Daylight begins to wane. There isn't much time, because I suspect if we don't find Kylie today, we might never find her.

I don't tell Jesse this, of course. I need him to remain hopeful, even if I feel my hope slipping away with each passing moment.

I cut the engine and turn to him. "We found information in the previous home. There could be more here."

Jesse keeps his gaze ahead. "You sound like you don't think she's here."

"I'll be honest with you, son. If she was here, we'd probably see signs of Scott Shaw or his people. This place looks empty. The good news? There's only one other place after this. So, we get in and get out, then on to the next place."

I open the door and step out into the late afternoon sky. The air feels stifling and my wound throbs. But I can't stop now. I won't.

Jesse steps out and joins me as we approach the home. This one doesn't look in much better shape than the last. I wonder how Shaw got the money to buy these properties. Of course, it stands to reason his father left him a hefty sum. Probably hid it away in random places. Money he'd stolen from his followers.

The front door is a pale yellow, faded by the sun. A small stained-glass window rests in the center. I can't see inside, but it doesn't appear occupied. No sounds, no vehicles anywhere. "We need to get in."

"I'll do it," Jesse says, walking toward a nearby window. He finds a large stone on the ground. "This ought to do it." Drawing back, he crashes it into the window, his face twisting from the pain in his ribs. Glass shatters, echoing around us. "You ready?"

I nod, seeing in him a strength he didn't have only hours ago. I'm grateful, because we're going to need it.

With his elbow, Jesse knocks away shards of glass still attached to the frame and then he climbs inside, mindful of his current limitations. "I'll open the door."

I move back to the door and wait only a moment before hearing the click of a deadbolt sliding back and a turn of the handle. He opens it and behind him I see only shadows.

We step inside, my eyes scanning the dim interior. The air is musty and stale, as if no one has been here in a long while, not unlike the last property. But will we find anything here of use? Jesse flips a light switch, but nothing happens.

"No power," he says.

I pull a small flashlight from my coat pocket and flick it on, the narrow beam cutting through the gloom. The front room is sparse — just a ratty brown sofa, an old recliner, and a small coffee table. Dust particles dance in the flashlight's glow.

We move slowly through the first floor, room by empty room. The kitchen is bare except for some discarded takeout containers and dirty dishes in the sink. Must not have been too long since the place saw life. Upstairs, the two small bedrooms are devoid of any personal effects or furnishings.

"This place is a dead end," Jesse says, defeat creeping into his voice.

But I'm not ready to give up yet. Something about this house feels . . . off. Back downstairs, I notice scuff marks on the floor near the back wall of the living room, as if a large piece of furniture had been slid across repeatedly. Running my hand over the faded wallpaper, I feel a slight draft.

"Here," I say to Jesse, motioning him over. "Help me move this cabinet."

Together, we shove the heavy wooden furniture away from the wall, both of us grunting through our injuries. I'm sure I'll bleed out if I push any harder.

My flashlight illuminates a small door that had been concealed behind the cabinet. It blends seamlessly into the wall, only visible now as a thin outline. Jesse and I exchange a glance. This is what was setting my instincts on edge.

Without a word, Jesse grasps the edge of the door and pulls it open. A waft of cold, stale air escapes from a darkened passageway. Steeling myself, I raise the flashlight and step through the opening. Jesse follows close behind.

The passage leads to a narrow staircase that disappears into blackness. We descend slowly, wary of loose steps or other pitfalls. The deeper we go, the colder and more confined the air feels. At the bottom, the flashlight reveals a heavy metal door secured with a sturdy padlock.

Jesse clutches his side, firms his stance, then shoulders it with all the force he can muster. Again and again, until the rusted hinges finally give way. He stops and leans against the wall. I see how much pain he's in as tears well, but he says nothing. I'm left to wonder if he's only worsened his condition.

The door is open. Beyond it lies a small, windowless room lined with shelves.

"What the hell is all this?" I walk inside and begin examining the contents of those shelves. Mostly binders. A few small cardboard boxes. I glance at Jesse, who's sweeping the flashlight around.

I don't want to waste time, but curiosity gets the better of me, so I grab one of the binders and open it. Inside, I see pictures. And in almost every one of them is Kylie. Not when she was younger, before her family was slaughtered, but in recent years. "Jesse, you might want to take a look at this."

He walks over and stands next to me. His eyes go right to the photographs. "This is in L.A. Some of these are of Grace's home." He sets his gaze on me. "He's known all this time where she lives."

"Either he has, or it's possible he got these from Dale. Dale's been keeping tabs on Kylie for years, to help keep her safe."

Jesse continues to eye the photographs, then me. He knows I'm trying to keep him calm, making up a reason for these binders, which I suspect mean that Scott Shaw has been hunting Kylie Forbes for years. Waiting until he had both the means and the power to finally bring her to him.

I gently set down the binder, my mind spinning. This changes everything. Shaw had been planning this for years, slowly rebuilding his father's legacy. Kylie was the key all along. I turn to say as much to Jesse but stop when I see the look on his face. His jaw is set, eyes burning with barely contained rage as he continues flipping through the binders, each page revealing more evidence of Shaw's obsession.

I'm about to try and talk him down when a loud thud echoes through the hidden basement, followed by heavy footfalls upstairs. Jesse's head jerks up, fear mixing with fury in his expression now. We both know who it must be. Shaw's men have found us.

"Did you hear that?" Jesse whispers.

I nod, clicking off my flashlight and motioning for him to do the same. We're plunged into darkness as I draw my gun with renewed focus.

Another heavy thud, followed by the unmistakable sound of footsteps overhead. I grab Jesse's arm, pulling him back into the shadows behind the shelves, pressing a finger to my lips.

The footsteps grow louder, moving across the floor above us. I can make out two, maybe three distinct sets. They must have figured we'd come looking for Kylie, or they need something from this place. But with my car outside, they already know we're here.

Jesse shifts beside me, and I grip his arm tighter. We can't afford to make a sound. If Shaw's men make it down those stairs, we'll be trapped.

The footfalls stop, directly above us now. The muffled voices are too indistinct to make out words. After an endless, tense minute, they move again.

I tighten my grip on my weapon and usher Jesse behind me. He pushes back a moment. I shake my head until he concedes. Getting out of this without a scuffle seems impossible now.

We step back to the metal door, ears straining. More thuds sound, along with more muffled voices. I risk a peek upstairs. Through the crack in the hidden doorway, I can see two armed officers searching the bedrooms. Our men, still in uniform.

Jesse meets my eyes. With my injury, he sees I'll never make it up the stairs before they spot us. Our only chance is the outside exit at the top, meaning we're going to have to take these guys head-on.

As we climb the steps, I take another peek. The men are still there, but we wait a moment. And they carry on, looking for us, no doubt. "Now," I whisper to Jesse.

We climb back through the small opening into the living room. It's empty for the moment. I lead the way, moving silently, gun drawn and senses on high alert. Jesse follows close behind me. My eyes dart around, taking in every detail, ready to react in an instant.

As we approach the front door, still several feet away, I hold up a hand to stop Jesse. Voices sound from the other room. The two armed cops, they've heard us, and they're coming back.

I don't hesitate when I see the first one and fire two quick shots, dropping one of them. The other dives for cover, returning fire. Jesse hits the floor as bullets zing past overhead. I grab him and haul him to his feet.

"Go, go!" I yell. We burst through the front door as more shots ring out behind us. Sprinting for the car, I fire blindly over my bad shoulder to cover our escape. Jesse runs like hell, grabbing his side as though he was holding himself together.

The crack and snap of gunfire pursues us as the man gives chase. But there's only one of them now and I'm liking our odds. Jesse reaches the car first, opening the passenger door and taking cover. I scramble to keep up, heart pounding, back screaming, aware that I can't keep this up much longer.

I fall behind, slowing with each step, but I'm close to the car now. One of us has to make it out of here in order to find Kylie. And I don't think it'll be me.

CHAPTER 34

Kylie

He can't leave me in here all night. Can he? Or is this how he works? Is this another way for him to exert control over me? I do my best to rationalize my situation, knowing the odds of me being found at this point are growing increasingly slim. Jesse must be terrified. And Detective Burns . . . was there anyone he could trust to offer help?

No matter the cost, I can't let Scott think he's won. So I climb up the staircase and pound on the door, screaming, yelling. Anything I can do to get his attention. I refuse to submit.

But after ten minutes, I get no response. Either he's no longer here, or he's ignoring me. The idea that I'm in here alone, trapped, frightens me almost more than he does.

Defeated, I walk back down the rickety wooden steps, my bare feet echoing in the emptiness. I meander around the dark basement, running my hands along the cool masonry walls, looking for any sign of a way out. But there is nothing, only the blackness pressing in all around me.

Exhausted, I slide down against the wall. Every part of me hurts. My stomach, my arms, my chest. But I know one thing.

The fight is draining from me. I feel utterly alone, abandoned in this hell that Scott has created for me.

After what feels like hours, but was probably only minutes, a creaking noise startles me from my self-pity. I look up to see a sliver of light as the door at the top of the stairs cracks open. Heavy footsteps clomp down each step. I don't need to see his face to know it's Scott.

My body tenses, bracing for whatever plan he has for me next. As he reaches the bottom of the stairs, I lower my eyes in submission. The fire in me nearly extinguished.

Scott looms over me. I feel his gaze, but I don't look up.

"Are you ready to cooperate now?"

His words hang over me while I consider my options. Do I really have any? Submit or die seem to be the only two that come to mind, so I remain silent.

"Good." He lifts me by my arm,and pulls me toward the steps.

I stumble as he climbs, trying to keep up with him. I don't know what he intends to do, but I'll never get out of this if I'm stuck down here. So I trail him, my bare feet tentative on the creaky wooden steps.

At the top, he steps into the hallway and walks through, stopping at another door. He opens it and I see a sparsely decorated bedroom. Heavy curtains are drawn across the windows, cloaking the room in dim gray light.

He pushes me inside and closes the door behind us. We're alone now. My eyes dart around, searching for any means of escape. Maybe I'm not defeated just yet. I don't want to give up on Jesse. I can't give up yet.

"Don't even think about trying to get away," Scott says in a threatening tone, as though he'd heard my thoughts. "This house is heavily guarded. You wouldn't make it ten feet."

I don't give him the satisfaction of showing any sort of setback in my demeanor.

"Now, let's try this again, shall we?" Scott says, as he circles around to face me. "It's time you accept that your place is here with me, with your family."

"Like I said, you are not my family."

Scott rams his palms against my shoulders, slamming me into the wall. His fingers dig into my skin as he leans in close. "You will learn respect."

He pins me against the wall for a few more seconds before releasing me. I stand firm, my eyes boring into him.

"Now sit down and listen," Scott commands, pointing to the bed.

I obey, perching nervously on the edge of it. Scott pulls up a chair to sit facing me, uncomfortably close. Our knees are touching.

"It's time you understood why you're so important, why I've gone through all this trouble to bring you home," Scott says. His voice is calm, but his eyes blaze with fervor.

"You were chosen, Kayla. Born into our family for a divine purpose."

I stare at him in disbelief. "You're insane. I don't want anything to do with your delusions."

His hand cracks across my face, a stinging backhand blow. My head jerks to the side from the force.

"Don't speak to me that way."

I dab my fingers to my lips and see the blood on them. With a smile, I regard him. "You can beat me all you want. It won't change my mind or change what I know about you."

He leans back. "And you think you know me, do you?"

"I know you're just as crazy as your dad was," I reply. "He was nothing more than a fucking pedophile."

I glimpse a shadow cross in front of the curtains. "You need them to keep watch, huh? Afraid the people who are out looking for me will come here?" He doesn't respond, and I keep my gaze fixed on him. "Do you really think the people of this town, the government, or the feds are going to let you rebuild New Hope? It died because my father took a stand."

Scott aims a finger toward the window. "Those men out there? You know why I have their support?" He doesn't wait for me to answer. "Because they were there. They managed to escape the fire, but their families didn't. Parents, siblings, friends. They all burned to death."

"Am I supposed to feel bad for them?" I snap back. "My family was slaughtered in our home. I don't give a shit what happened to those assholes. Clearly, they're just as crazy as you are."

He backhands me across my face again. The sting hurts more than the first time, but I'll be damned if I show him my pain.

Scott takes a breath, as if trying to calm himself, and then stands. "Let me show you something." He opens the door and steps out into the hall.

I don't see him for a moment, but he quickly returns. He's carrying a small cardboard box as he walks back to the bed. He sits down, and with it resting on his legs, removes the lid.

"I'm not up to walking down memory lane, if that's what you're planning," I say.

He laughs, aiming his index finger at me. "You do have a sense of humor. That's good, because you're going to need it."

He turns serious again and retrieves a flash drive from inside the box. Then a laptop. He inserts the drive into his laptop and turns it on. After a moment, he smiles. "Take a listen, Kayla. This is important."

Scott plays an audio file, and I hear two men talking. One I recognize immediately. My father. The other is unknown to me.

"*I'm telling you, we have to do something about Lucas,*" Clarence says, an edge of anger in his tone. "*He's lost sight of our purpose. He's distracted by his desires. Children.*"

"*So you want to get rid of him?*" the other man asks.

"*I won't let my Kayla's future be destroyed by Lucas Shaw. She's meant for greater things. Lucas has become weak; he's unfit to lead us. We need to remove him before he destroys everything we've built.*"

There's a long pause before the other man speaks again. "*How do you plan to get to him? He keeps himself surrounded.*

You know that. And if you go through with it, the others, they still see Lucas as the chosen one, as a prophet. You have no idea the chaos this will unleash."

"I won't hand over my daughter to him. I promise you that. Evie doesn't know. She would never agree. She thinks Kayla's special because Lucas chose her. Bullshit." Clarence pauses. *"Will you help?"*

The audio stops. Scott looks at me. "You know who that was? The man your father was talking to?"

I shake my head, choking back my emotions, because I haven't heard my dad's voice in so long.

Scott aims his finger out toward the window again, to the guard whose outline is just visible through the curtains. "It was his father. So, it wasn't that hard to convince him and some of the others who'd lost family in the fire that I had the means for retribution."

He clicks on another file. "Lucas was a smart man. He had eyes everywhere. And recorded just about every conversation, as did the people who protected him. Like the man your father told about his plan." He presses play again.

I don't want to hear anymore. I can't, but I know the choice isn't mine. I feel my chest tighten and my heart begin to race as the next audio file starts playing. I don't recognize either voice.

"We have to tell Lucas," the first voice says. *"Clarence has gone off the rails. He's going to do something, and we'll all pay the price for it."*

"What about Evie?" the other man asks. *"Does she know?"*

"No. She's a loyal follower. He'll never convince her, even when it involves their oldest daughter."

"Then we have no choice but to tell Lucas."

It seemed everyone was against my father, yet no one was able to stop him.

Scott raises a finger. "You'll want to hear this last file." He opens another and presses play.

I'm growing tired of this game, and I don't want to hear any more. Reliving that nightmare is too painful. More painful than anything Scott Shaw could ever do to me.

This time, I hear a woman's voice. I feel a catch in my throat when I recognize it — my mother.

"I know you have a plan for her, Lucas, but Clarence . . . he's struggling with it. I've tried to remind him what an honor it is for Kayla, but he refuses to see it."

My stomach turns. "Jesus."

"Oh, it gets better," Scott says, a wide smile on his face.

His pleasure in causing me pain is what's driving him. He's doing this to punish me.

"*Evie, you and I share a bond. A strong bond that resulted in a son. He will take over for me one day. And God has spoken to me. He tells me Kayla will give me more children. And they'll grow, they'll learn, they'll help continue this way of life.*"

She wanted me to marry Lucas. How could any mother accept that? I want to cry, but I can't, even if my heart is breaking into a thousand pieces.

"Then maybe it's best to let Clarence work to expand what you've grown here," Evie says. *"Sending him away for a while could be exactly what he needs to understand the plan."*

"Why did they kill her too?" I ask, my voice barely a whisper. "And my siblings? They followed the rules. Even I followed them."

Scott nods. "Yes, but anger fueled the massacre. Once your father set his plan in motion, there was no turning back. Not even for our mom, who was still in love with Lucas."

I press the button to turn off the recording. "Why are you doing this? You could've accomplished your goal without me. I wanted nothing to do with any of this."

"True," he says. "But I need for the others to see that by having you at my side, my father is still with us. You were meant for him. And now, you're meant for me."

"I'm your fucking half-sister."

He looks at me, placing his hand on my knee. "You and I are the only people who know that now. The rest . . . are dead."

CHAPTER 35

Jesse

I left him behind. Burns returned fire while I managed to dart out into the nearby fields. I thought he might be able to jump back into the car and drive away. But that's not what happened. In fact, I don't even know what happened, but I've been huddled behind a cluster of trees on the far edge of one of the fields for hours. It's dark now. I think they gave up their search for me.

I can't go back there to look for Burns, because they could be waiting. I can't risk capture, or no one will find Kylie. It's up to me now. God, I hope Burns is okay.

Getting back to town, finding the third property, that's what I have to do. She must be there. But I have no one to turn to. Burns didn't trust his own people, so who the hell can I trust?

Captain Lyons. I stand up, my knees aching from crouching low. My side throbs as broken ribs poke at me. But I know it's far worse for Kylie. Maybe for Burns, too, if he's even still alive.

I walk through the thick grasses in the darkness, finally emerging onto a road. I'll be spotted easily if anyone drives by, but there's no place to hide out here. I don't have my phone, but I'm wearing my Apple Watch, which has a compass. But which way is town? I have no idea.

I can text from this, but text who? The crew is long gone. Could I ask Caroline for help? Maybe, but how long would it take for her to reach me? And I can't put her life in any more danger. No, it's best they're all gone now.

I squint in the darkness, trying to get my bearings as I follow the winding road. I check my watch again — the hands glow faintly, confirming I'm headed west.

West is good. Right? I just have to keep moving in this direction and I'll find help. My ribs ache with every step, but I force myself to keep putting one foot in front of the other. Kylie is counting on me. I can't let her down now.

In the distance, I finally see the warm amber lights of buildings, glowing like tiny fireflies inside a dense forest. I've been walking for two hours and must've traveled at least six or seven miles. This must be another town. There are so many small communities around here, I have no idea, but I'm grateful. My pace quickens, breaths coming sharper as pain lances through my side. Just a little farther. I'm almost there.

As I reach the edge of this town, I pause to catch my breath and assess the quiet streets ahead. Wait . . . is this Manning? I'm completely turned around, but is it possible I made it back here? I recognize this place. Holy shit. Okay. Okay, this is good. I know where I am.

The streets are empty. I keep to the shadows, making my way toward the buildings — the main street. I step into the pool of light under a streetlamp, eyes darting around. The diner is there, where we filmed a scene. And outside that diner is a phone booth. Grace? Could I call her? Could she help in any way, or would I only worry her more, because she'd know that Kylie was gone?

I need help, because I have no car to get to the last of Shaw's properties. What am I supposed to do, steal one? I recall Burns telling me the address and search my memory for it. How do I get there?

A car's engine rumbles behind me. I dart away, between the buildings. The diner on one side, the hardware store on the other. Is it Shaw's people? I wait, crouching low in the dark, not daring to move an inch.

I hold my breath as the car slowly rolls past the alley where I'm hidden. It's too dark to make out the driver, but my gut tells me it's no one friendly. The car continues down the street and turns the corner. I let out a shaky exhale, my heart pounding.

I emerge from my hiding spot and move toward the phone booth outside the diner. Time is running out for Kylie. I have to risk calling the police station, trying to get hold of Captain Lyons.

I pick up the phone and realize I have no idea of the number. I could dial 911, but just as I start, headlights flash at the end of the street. Another car is coming this way. I hang up, dashing out of view, just as the vehicle pulls up near me and a man steps out.

He's middle-aged, average height, wearing dark clothing. Could he be any more ordinary? But his eyes are alert, scanning the street. He moves with purpose — this is no random passerby. My senses are on high alert. Did they track me here already? Of course, it's the most logical place for me to go for help.

I shrink back into the shadows, praying he hasn't seen me. I press myself against the brick wall, barely breathing. The footsteps grow nearer, slow and steady. He's searching. Hunting. I take a glance around the corner. Who is he?

The footsteps start again, moving down the street. I exhale slowly, willing my pounding heart to quiet. I'm not in the clear yet. I inch along the wall, heading for the auto shop.

Almost there. Just a little farther. My shoe scuffs the pavement and I freeze, fearing the man heard me. The footsteps halt. He heard.

I still myself, slowing my breaths as I watch the man turn and walk into the darkness, searching for the source of the noise. I don't dare move a muscle. But it's too late. He sees me.

CHAPTER 36

Kylie

No one's ever accused me of being naive. And I know what will happen to me the longer I'm trapped here. Working in Hollywood has hardened me to the realities that exist for many women. But the question remains, do I give in? Let him do what he wants, and then, at the right moment, hit back at him hard enough to hurt? Do I have it in me?

Emotions aside, I don't see another way out. And even then, I'm not sure I'll get past his men outside. What can I do to get him to lower his guard? Is it possible to get his gun from him? Maybe.

Scott returns the items to the box. I know there's more inside, but he realizes his point is made. No use in beating a dead horse. I know the truth about my parents now. For years, I'd blamed the wrong one.

A desire to live up to his father's name is Scott's reasoning. I see that now and have no doubt, it's entirely possible. I push away thoughts of Jesse that creep into my head. I only thank God he's not here with me, fearing for his life, same as me.

Scott returns his little box of secrets to the closet and walks back. He stands over me for a moment, a clear attempt at intimidation. I don't give in and keep my eyes straight ahead. The tactic, I know, will cause me to suffer, but it's so worth it.

Scott must be close to forty, given the time frame in question. I consider where he'd been when I was there. I understand why Lucas kept the truth from his followers. "Where did you go during that time . . . when I was there with my family?"

He sits down next to me, his hand once again on my knee. "I didn't know she was my mother for a long time. Dad's other wives took care of me when Clarence took Evie with him, only to return years later with you and your sibling in tow. Of course, Katie was born in the compound."

I hate that her name spills from his mouth. My little sister, born and raised at New Hope, until she was stabbed to death at the age of four. My brother, Kyle, only ten. I was the oldest. I was supposed to look out for them. My new identity . . . an amalgam of their names, meant to honor their short lives.

"That was when Lucas told me about her. Our mother," he continues. "That was also when he started sending me off with some of the other members to grow the group. I came back several times, but again, I wasn't allowed contact with Evie. Or any of you."

"Weren't you angry about that?" I ask, trying to engage him, and get him to lower his guard. "Not being allowed to talk to your mom. Your siblings."

"No. I knew Lucas had a plan." He sets his gaze on me. "See, that's where your father didn't get it. He didn't believe."

I could easily come back with a smart-ass remark, but I would be defeating my goals, so I stay quiet.

"When I came back, just before your birthday." He looks up in thought. "I was almost nineteen by then. I knew Lucas's intention to marry you. He said, once all that was done, I could talk to Evie. But we never got that far."

Do I make the first move? Would he see through my actions? Maybe he was just enough of a sociopath to believe he'd converted me. But I need him in a weakened state. It's the only way I'll get the upper hand and maybe make it out of this alive.

The men outside? I'm not sure about them yet. There's a back door. I have no idea where I am, but if I can take cover until daylight, I will find a way out of here.

I take a deep breath and try to steady my nerves. Scott is watching me intently, waiting for a response. I know I need to tread carefully here.

"I'm sorry you didn't get to have a relationship with our mother," I say softly. "That must have been really hard for you."

Scott nods, seeming pleased by my sympathy. "It was. But it will be different for you and me. We can start over, rebuild what was taken from us."

His hand is still resting on my knee. I let my leg relax, just slightly, so my knee presses into his palm. Scott rubs his thumb over my bare skin.

"You and I will be so powerful together, Kayla," he says, his voice low and earnest. "Don't you see it? We're the rightful heirs to the legacy. With you by my side, we can make this family whole again."

I force myself to meet his intense gaze. "I want to believe that," I say. "But after everything that's happened between us, how can I trust you? You murdered my friends. Even made me think I was responsible . . . my shoes, the elevator, all of it." I raise my chin. "How did you do it? Why? Why not just take me instead of them?"

Scott holds my stare. "Everything that's happened has been carefully choreographed, from the moment I convinced the film scouts to shoot here, to when I had your shoes removed from your room. They were taken to where Brandon had pulled off the side of the road and pressed into the wet ground, leaving perfect prints for the detective to find. Even the elevator — the maintenance worker is one of us. So is the desk attendant who altered the surveillance video inside the elevator."

Anger knots in my gut. "Why?"

"The obvious answer is that by causing you to question yourself, it would force the detective to question you, too, taking his aim off us." He smiles. "But the real answer is that it was fun watching you unravel. Shouldering the guilt of your murdered friends. Your best friend. You see, Kayla, your father destroyed everything I held dear. And the last thing he ever wanted was for you to be with my father, and by extension, me. So, of course, I had to make that happen."

This was all a game to him. Maybe it still is. But how I handle myself now will make the difference in whether I live or die. "I need time, all right? You want me to fall in line, well, then you'll have to meet my demands."

"Such as?" he asks.

"Promising to never hurt Grace. Or Jesse. Or anyone I know."

Scott nods, a knowing smile spreading across his face. "Of course." His fingers trail up my thigh. "I think we can work out a deal."

I fight the urge to slap away his hand, my skin crawling at his touch. But I know I have to play along. "Okay, then." I let my legs relax.

He pushes them open and leans in, his lips nearly brushing my ear. "That's my good girl."

His hand cups my breast. It takes everything I have not to react. I fight back my tears, keeping my gaze firmly on him.

He slowly caresses my breasts through the thin fabric of my shirt. His touch makes me want to retch, but I clench my jaw and force myself to remain still. This is the price I have to pay if I want to survive.

"Stand up," he commands.

My pulse jumps with fear, but I know I have no choice. Slowly, I get to my feet. Scott's eyes never leave mine as he stands and circles me like a predator.

With a swift yank, he rips my shirt down the middle, exposing my bare breasts and the bandages on my stomach. The cool air sends goosebumps along my skin, both from the temperature and the knowledge of how exposed I am. He stares at me, his breathing labored.

"I knew you'd come around." He moves his other hand to my stomach, his fingers lightly raking over the bandages. "So much pain you've been through. So much loss . . . all for nothing."

His hands clutch my breasts again, squeezing hard enough to bruise. I bite back a scream, tears pricking my eyes.

"I've always wanted this. You're mine now."

He pushes me onto the bed, his weight pinning me down. I grit my teeth, every fiber of my being screaming to fight back. I have to play along for just a little longer. I force myself to meet his gaze, willing him to believe my submission.

"For our father," I whisper hoarsely, as he rips away my remaining clothes. "For us."

He caresses my cheek. "That's it, Kayla. You won't regret this. I promise."

As he leans in, I let my body go limp, feigning resignation. But inside, I'm plotting. Every second that ticks by brings me closer to finding an opportunity to escape this sickening hell. As Scott's attention moves lower, I scan the room for any possible weapons within reach.

A lamp rests on the bedside table. Will it be enough to do damage? If I'm quick about it . . . yes. Let him do what he wants, then, when he's in the throes of passion, reach for it and slam it against his head. I push aside the panic that grows in me. I need to be patient. I need to wait.

His hands roam my body, leaving a trail of revulsion in their wake. I can feel his erection pressing against my thigh, hard and insistent. My stomach turns and I swallow down the saliva that fills my mouth. That sensation you get just before vomiting. I can't afford to blow my one shot at killing this son of a bitch. Or at least, knocking him out. I'll worry about the rest later.

His fingers enter me, and I want to scream. My body tenses at his touch, but I have to convince him I want this.

"Don't fight it," he whispers. "The sooner you submit, the easier this will be for both of us." His fingers continue to probe between my legs.

No. I can't. I can't do this. I would rather die than let him inside me. In that moment, I find a reserve of strength. Summoning every ounce of energy, I arch my hips upwards. He thinks I'm giving into him. He relaxes, loosening his grip on me.

I reach out for the lamp, wrapping my fingers around the base as he kisses my breasts. Yanking it hard, the plug ripping from the wall, I bring it down, crashing it against his head. He clutches his skull, rolling off of me.

He's on his feet, but hunched over, as I scramble away. "You little bitch!" he seethes, advancing toward me.

I'm stark naked. About as defenseless as a woman can be, but I wield the lamp in front me and scoot off the bed on the other side. "Get away from me, you sick fuck."

CHAPTER 37

Jesse

Relief swells in my chest when the man steps back into his car and drives off. I thought he'd seen me, but I was wrong. His taillights fade in the distance. He must work for Shaw. How many more are out here? I have to get to Kylie. I have to find her.

My thoughts turn to the detective. I left him out there alone. Was he killed? Did he kill the second man? There could've been more; I have no idea. Now, I wonder how I'm supposed to get to Kylie? Walk?

The police station is about two miles ahead. I consider calling emergency services again, but I don't know who else I can trust. No, I have to go straight to the captain. I can't believe all of them are compromised. Burns isn't. I stand zero chance at finding Kylie without help. I'm going to have to trust someone.

I've never felt more helpless in my life, but if I give up, Kylie will have no one on the outside who knows what's happened here. That New Hope has re-emerged with Lucas Shaw's son at the helm.

My mind's made up. I force my legs to move as I head toward the police station. What choice do I have? I'm unarmed. I have no vehicle. And hell if I know what I'm doing, except that I have to try to help Kylie. I love her.

I hurry as quickly as I can along the dark streets, constantly glancing over my shoulder as I make my way to the police station. The feeling of unseen eyes watching my every move looms over me. I quicken my pace, nearly breaking into a jog despite my cracked ribs.

Finally, the lights of the station come into view. I force myself up the steps and push through the front doors, breathing hard. The officer at the front desk jumps at my sudden entrance.

My heart is pounding as I step inside, my eyes darting around the lobby. Hardly anyone is here. It's just me and the cop I startled. Burns warned me not to trust anyone but Lyons, that Shaw's influence had spread throughout the department. I don't know who I can turn to.

Taking a deep breath to steady my nerves, I approach the officer. "I need to speak to the captain."

The officer eyes me, his expression doubtful. "And who are you?"

I hesitate. Should I use my real name? There's no telling who might be listening. "Please, it's urgent. It's about Detective Burns. He's in trouble. He'll want to speak to me."

"Burns? Hang on." The officer picks up the phone, keeping his eyes fixed on me as he relays the message. "He says Burns is in trouble. You'd better get up here, fast." He ends the call. "Captain's coming up now, but you'd better start talking. If one of ours is in trouble, we need to know."

I swallow hard, trying to buy some time to think. How much should I reveal to this officer? If I say too little, he'll be suspicious. But if I say too much and he's with Shaw, I'm toast.

"Look, I'm not from here, all right? I'm with the film crew," I say. "You'll forgive me if I'm cautious. All I can say is that I believe Detective Burns, who's been working on the murder investigation of two of my friends, needs help. I know where he is."

The officer's eyes narrow, and he leans across the desk. "You'd better not be spinning some bullshit story here. Captain Lyons is on his way down. I'd suggest you tell him exactly what's happened unless you want to be booked for obstruction."

I hold up my hands defensively. "It's not bullshit. I swear, Burns is in serious danger. He needs help right away." I hold my tongue about Kylie and where I think she might be. That information goes to Lyons only.

The elevator doors slide open, capturing my attention. A tall, muscular man strides toward us. His brown hair is cropped close to his head. Wrinkles crease his eyes and lips. He looks about Burns' age.

He extends his hand. "I'm Captain Lyons. And you are?"

I glance back at the officer and step away from him. Lyons follows me. When I think we're out of earshot, I begin. "Look, Detective Burns was helping me find my girlfriend, Kylie Forbes."

"Yeah, I know all about that. I told Burns I have every available unit, those I'm sure I can trust, on the lookout for her and Scott Shaw . . . I know about him, too. Where is Burns now?"

"We were searching properties that Shaw owns, hoping to find Kylie, when we were ambushed." I look away, ashamed I left him alone. "I got away, he didn't. I can take you there, but then, I need your help, too."

"If we find Burns, we'll find Kylie, too." He stops and looks around. "Don't say anything to anyone else, you hear me?"

"I won't." Okay, it seems like he's someone I can trust. I hope.

"Burns told me what he suspects," the captain says. "I need you to take me to him. Now."

I lead him out to the parking lot, and we get into his unmarked SUV. As he pulls away, I give him hurried directions

to the house. What I can remember of it, anyway. And then I take a deep breath. "Have you heard of New Hope?"

Lyons grunts. "Everyone here has. And I'd just come onboard when it all went down. I know Scott Shaw is Lucas Shaw's son. And I know what he intends to do."

"Then you know he intends to do it with my girlfriend. Once we find Burns, we have to drive to where Burns thinks he has her."

The captain's knuckles tighten on the steering wheel. "New Hope. I thought I'd never hear that name again."

We drive on in silence with Lyons focusing on the darkened road ahead. "Here." I point my index finger at the windshield. "We were at this house when they came at us. I left Burns at the vehicle. But since the car's still here, God knows where Burns is." I look at the captain. "I swear, I didn't want to leave him."

Lyons pulls up to the house, right behind Burns' car. "How the hell are we going to find him? It's pitch-black out here."

"I don't see the car the men were driving," I say. "They might've taken him. Or he's out there somewhere . . . maybe dead."

"And your girlfriend, Kylie?" he asks. "You said there was a third location she might be?"

I nod. "Burns thought so, but we've struck out twice already."

Lyons opens the driver's side door. The interior light shines in my eyes. "Stay here, all right? I'll call out to him, and hope to God he answers. If not, we'll track down Kylie."

"No, I want to come with you. Please. I think I know where he would go if he was trying to get away from them." I open my door and he says nothing, so I get out.

We carry on into the fields. My thoughts are consumed with Kylie and what's happening to her. I need Burns to be alive. I need him to help me find her. I feel lost.

"Detective Burns?" I call out. "It's Jesse. Are you okay?"

Lyons eyes me, aiming his flashlight down at the ground ahead of us. He turns back and calls out to his partner. "Doug? You out here? We're coming, man. We're coming."

We trudge through the grass, heading toward the cluster of trees. He might've taken shelter there and maybe got too weak to get back. "Over here. This is where I ran. I remember the fallen tree here."

"This one?" he asks.

I glance back. "Yeah, I remember the house just there. This is it."

We make our way through the dense field. "Detective Burns? Come on, man. Please answer. I need you. We have to find Kylie."

We're met with silence, and I fear the worst. "I don't see him."

Lyons glances at me, then aims his flashlight at the ground again. "Where is he?"

I look back at the house. "Maybe he managed to get back inside?"

Lyons pinches his lips, and I see his face tighten in frustration. "Goddam it." He trudges back through the fields, toward the house.

I follow, both of us still calling out to Burns, but getting no reply. I wonder if he's dead, but don't dare say it out loud.

Within a few minutes, we return to the house and Lyons steps inside. "Doug? Doug, you in here?"

"Detective Burns?" I call out, knowing I'm not helping at all.

Lyons walks through the home and calls out my name. "Jesse, come over here."

"Oh God." I feel the worst has happened and Burns is dead. But when I reach Lyons, he aims his flashlight at the body, and it's not Burns. "This one of the guys who came after you?"

I study the figure, but only for a moment, because I remember him well. "Yes, sir."

He closes his eyes and presses his lips together. "That's Patrolman Garrett. He was in Shaw's pocket, by the look of it."

"The other man must've made it to his car," I say. "They could come back."

"Not if they know Burns is dead."

A rumble sounds. We both freeze. It's a voice, low, guttural. *Jesus. Is that Burns?*

We both listen for the sound again. There it is. "He's alive. Oh my God. He's alive."

"Doug, we're coming, man." Lyons marches through the hall, his flashlight sweeping back and forth until . . . "Here! He's over here."

I rush toward him as he stands in the kitchen.

Burns is on the ground, his leg bleeding. He looks up at us. "You have her? Is she safe?"

"We haven't found her yet," I reply.

"Then get me out of here, goddam it, so we can get her."

CHAPTER 38

Kylie

I tighten my grip on the lamp, sweeping it in front of me as we stand on opposite sides of the bed. I'm trembling, but I'm not sure if it's fear or because I'm completely naked. Scott's gaze bores into me, his chest heaving, blood spilling down his temple. How the hell is he not unconscious? I swung as hard as I could. The lamp's thick ceramic base cracked in my hands from the blow.

"Don't be stupid, Kayla," he sneers. "Put that down before you hurt yourself."

He takes a step around the bed and now stands at the bottom. I thrust the lamp at him again, knowing this is a feeble effort. I need something sharp. I need something that will kill him. "Stay back!" My voice comes out high and shaky.

Scott halts, raising his hands in surrender, but the glint in his eyes shows me his true intention. "Come on now, is that any way to treat your brother? I only want what's best for you. I thought we were on the same page now."

"You think I'd let you have me?" I spit out. "The only thing I want is to watch you die."

Scott shakes his head, clicking his tongue in disappointment. "Such harsh words. But you'll come to accept your place soon enough. After everything I've done for you, this is how you repay me? You ungrateful bitch."

He springs toward me, and I swing the lamp again, striking him hard across the face. Scott staggers back, blood dripping from his mouth.

"Stay the hell away from me!" I scream. His men will hear this and they'll come in to help. I have to kill him. Now.

Scott wipes the blood from his lips, an ugly grin spreading across his face. "Kayla. You've just made a big mistake."

He charges again and I swing with all my might. The lamp crashes into his shoulder with a sickening crack. It crumbles in my hand, cutting my palms. Scott howls in pain but keeps coming. I scramble backward, but he tackles me to the ground. I fall on the ceramic shards and he's on top of me, pinning me down.

"Worthless bitch." He straddles me, all his weight on my injured stomach. He clutches both my hands with his left and raises them over my head. With his right, he curls it into a fist and reels back, landing hard against my cheek. I feel a tooth dislodge in my mouth and tears fill my eyes.

But then he stops. He raises his hands as if surrendering. "I only want what's best for you."

I catch my breath, each inhale sending bolts of pain through me. His placating tone, meant to soothe, only makes my anger rise.

That's when I realize why he stopped. I look at him and I see it in his eyes. He needs me. He needs me to help convince the rest of his growing sycophant following that I'm with him. That I'm on his side. They'll believe that if he's able to bring me back into the fold — the daughter of the man who murdered Lucas Shaw — then he is the new prophet.

I freeze as the distant rumble of an engine drifts through the window. Scott's head whips toward the sound, his eyes narrowing. For a fleeting moment I feel a surge of hope

— could it be Jesse? But he has no idea where Scott has taken me. And this place is on total lockdown. No one gets in or out without Scott's say-so.

Still, someone is outside. I see a flash of uncertainty cross Scott's face. The rumbling stops, replaced by muffled voices, raising louder and louder.

"Don't get too excited, Kayla. No one's coming to save you." He grabs my arm and hauls me to my feet. I cry out as pain cuts through my battered body.

"How about we go see what's going on out there, huh?" He grabs the torn T-shirt and throws it at me. "Cover yourself."

I slip it on as he shoves me toward the door. I stumble forward, gritting my teeth against the ache in my jaw. Scott stays close behind me as we make our way into the hall and toward the front room.

Voices sound outside, but I see nothing through the window's closed curtains. I know two of them are Scott's people. Who does the other voice belong to? I can't make out what's being said. But my hope and fear of it being Jesse dwindles. And I'm almost grateful, though, because I have no doubt this monster beside me would kill Jesse right before my eyes to prove he can.

The handle turns. The front door opens a crack. "Scott?" The officer catches a glimpse of me standing in only the long, torn T-shirt, bloody and bruised. His eyes roam over my body, but then he turns back to Scott. "This guy says he knows you and that you'll want to see him. He knew your dad, too. We checked that he's unarmed."

Scott pushes me toward the sofa where I tumble over the arm and land on it haphazardly. I scurry back to a seated position, trying to pull my legs up to cover my exposed lower half, but I'm in too much pain to do so. I see a blanket on a nearby footstool and grab it, throwing in over my legs. The door opens farther.

Scott reaches for the gun on the kitchen table, holding it down at his side. I wonder who this mystery person is, and whether he'll participate in my murder, or torture. I see a foot through the door, then Scott steps back. His brow knits, and I'm not sure whether he recognizes whoever it is. The look on his face is . . .

"Hello, Scott. It's been a long time," the man says, still out of my line of sight as he stands behind the door. "You gonna let me in, or do I have to stand out here like you don't remember me?"

A strange expression crosses Scott's face, but he flicks the safety off the gun. Shit. Who is this guy? My pulse quickens and then finally — he enters.

I feel the blood drain from my extremities and my head grows light. I can't breathe; a vice grip tightens around my chest. I blink just to be sure my eyes aren't deceiving me.

He's older with gray hair and a weathered face, but those eyes . . . warm and kind . . . are unmistakable. "Dad?" I whisper. The man I thought was dead along with the rest of my family now stands before me, very much alive. "My God. Where have you been all this time?" I stare in shock, my mouth practically on the floor. How is this real? I'd run out of the house that night, escaping for my life. There's no possible way he could be standing here now.

But his eyes meet mine, and I see the truth. It's really him. After all these years believing my family was gone, my dad is here. He's alive.

"Hello, Kay," he says softly. He always called me Kay. I am his mother's namesake. His voice trembles with emotion as he takes in the sight of me.

I'm unsure if he's repulsed by my appearance, shocked at what Shaw has done to me, or if he sees past it. Sees me as his daughter once again.

I open my mouth, but no more words come out. A torrent of questions and emotions whirl inside me. Disbelief. Confusion. Heart-wrenching grief for all the lost years we can never get back.

Scott steps between us, his expression guarded. "I thought you were dead, old man. Lee took all you out, yet here you are."

Lee Stafford? He murdered my family? I knew him. He was a council member, along with my mother. He was one of the members who had committed suicide. The papers here were full of stories about what happened to the members. The ones who'd survived, and the ones who didn't. I, and my entire family, were among the ones who didn't. At least, that's what everyone believed.

"How did you get here?" My words come out slow, whispering.

My father looks at Scott, who now holds his gun at the ready, then he turns to me. "Dale. He sent for me."

"Well," Scott says. "I don't mean to interrupt this family reunion, but why don't you have a seat, Clarence?" He keeps the gun pointed at him. "Seems we got a whole lot to talk about."

CHAPTER 39

Detective Burns

The kid came back for me, the stupid son of a bitch. And he brought help. The only person I think I can still trust in that department, and Jesse managed to get to him. Guess he's smarter than I'd given him credit for. The problem is, he should've been looking for Kylie. Not me.

"Jesus, man, are you okay?" Lyons asks, squatting beside me.

"I gotta be honest with you, Cap. No, I'm not. The asshole shot me. That's twice now. But I got one of them." I look at the kid. "You shouldn't have come back."

"You're the only one who knows where she is," he says.

But that's not true, because I could be wrong. "She might not be there, son. It could be too late."

"No." He squats low, raking his eyes over me like he's a goddam doctor. "We have to get you to a hospital." He turns to Lyons. "Captain? Help me get him up?"

The two of them walk around either side of me, hooking their arms beneath mine and attempting to hoist me up. I grunt in pain, my shoulder and chest, stretching too far, but they continue. "Goddam it, that hurts."

"Stop complaining," Lyons says. "Be grateful we found you at all."

I am grateful; Captain's only talking bullshit. I know he's scared for me. So is Jesse. I can see it in their eyes. But I'm only scared for one person — Kylie Forbes.

"We go to the last house on the list first," I say. "We all know she won't survive the night. Not if Scott Shaw has any say in the matter."

"Fine," Lyons says.

The two drag me through the house. I try to ease the strain by putting as much weight on my legs as I can, but it's not easy. I know I need a hospital. My head grows lighter by the minute with how much blood I'm losing. But I plan to do everything in my power to get Kylie back. I won't see this town overrun by those people again. It's the least I can do for Dale Coleman.

The car appears as a shadow in the front yard. "Almost there, buddy. Hang on," Captain says. "We can get you to the hospital in twenty minutes and you can tell us where that other property is located. Don't be stupid, Doug. You're losing a shit ton of blood right now."

"Just get me in the car, would you?"

Jesse opens the rear passenger door. "This is going to hurt, Detective."

"Yeah, I figured."

He helps me inside. The pain is overwhelming now. I can feel more blood spilling down my leg. "Sorry about the mess."

"Don't worry," Lyons says. "It's the department's car. Not mine."

I chuckle, but then clutch at the pain. "Goddam it. Don't make me laugh."

He laughs at me anyway, then walks around and gets behind the wheel.

"You okay, Detective?" Jesse asks.

"As okay I can be. Get in, son. We'll find Kylie."

Lyons pulls away from the house and onto the road. "I need a destination, Doug. Where we headed?"

I relay the address. "He'll have protection. They already came for us once."

The captain glances through the rearview. "You got anyone else you can call to help us out?"

I capture his gaze. "No one I trust right now. We're on our own. And since I'm incapacitated . . . it'll be you two." I look at Jesse. "You know how to use a gun?"

"Yeah, I do," he says.

"Good. I'll give you mine," I reply.

Lyons asks, "And if this girl isn't there?"

It's the question I knew he'd be the one to ask, but I sure as hell didn't want to answer it in front of the girl's boyfriend. "We'll deal with that when we know for sure."

I thought I would die in that shithole of a house. Now, I'm not sure if I'll live to see Kylie Forbes returned.

CHAPTER 40

Kylie

The fact that my father I'd believed dead for the past twenty years is sitting next to me only makes me feel worse. The idea I might see him die all over again fills me with dread.

He said Dale sent him. How? When? Where has he been all this time? I look at Scott as he paces before us, holding his gun. What will he do now? My father murdered his father. Will he get his revenge now after all these years?

And then I wonder why Dad came here at all without a plan. He must've known I was here, and yet, he waltzes in and just lets Scott Shaw point a gun at him? I don't know what to do.

My father looks at me with those comforting blue eyes that I remember so well from my childhood. He seems calm, despite the gun aimed in our direction.

"Scott," he says in that deep, steady voice of his. "There's no need for violence here. I understand you're angry about your father, but Lucas brought that on himself. He was out of control, about to force your sister into a marriage she didn't want and was much too young for. I had to stop him before he destroyed everything."

Scott grunts, waving the gun. "Don't pretend you cared about my sister. You just wanted power, like you always did. That's why you took his eyes."

Clarence shakes his head. "No, son. I know it looked that way, but I was trying to protect the compound, protect our way of life." He leans forward, meeting Scott's gaze. "Lucas was going to lead us to ruin. The things he did, they were unforgivable. He needed to be stopped. Matthew Chapter 5, Verse 29 . . . *If your right eye causes you to sin, tear it out and throw it away.*"

My mouth drops. This was why he gouged out Lucas' eyes? A Bible verse taken literally? It had nothing to do with power, but . . . somehow cleansing Lucas of his sin?

"I'm sorry it had to end the way it did, but you have to see . . . I did it for the good of our family," Clarence continues.

Scott hesitates, confusion flickering in his gaze. He lowers the gun slightly as he considers my father's words. Conflicted emotions playing across his face. The gun wavers in his hand.

"You took everything from me," he says. "My dad, my home . . . you destroyed it all."

Clarence nods. "I know. And I'm sorry for the pain it caused you. But Lucas left me no choice." He gestures to me. "This is my daughter, Kayla. I know you think you have some claim over her, but you don't. She never belonged here. I won't let you keep her trapped in this madness."

Scott's eyes blaze with fury. "Madness? This is my family! Who are you to decide what's best for us?"

He thrusts the gun toward Clarence. My heart leaps into my throat.

Clarence raises his hands in supplication. "Scott, listen to me. I know you loved your dad, but he was ill. What he wanted for the compound was wrong. Let Kayla go. I'm here to answer for my sins. It's time to let all this end."

Scott wavers again, the gun dipping.

For a moment, my dad's soothing voice strips away the layers of resentment and vengeance Scott has nurtured all these years. But the moment passes. His eyes harden, jaw clenching with renewed fury. The dried blood on his temple seems to frame the anger on his face.

"No. You don't get to rewrite history, old man." Scott raises the gun, pointing it straight at my father's heart. "You murdered Lucas. Destroyed our family. And now you'll pay."

Clarence's eyes meet mine, resigned. After all these years of searching, our reunion will be short-lived.

I shake my head sharply, willing strength into my trembling limbs. No. I won't lose him again. I know the truth now. The truth that he tried to protect me when my own mother wouldn't.

The sound of tires screeching outside breaks the tension. Doors slam, voices shout. It sounds like the police. But how? Gunshots ring out, pinging against the house.

Scott darts to the window and peers out. "Goddam it." He whirls around, taking aim at Clarence. "This is your doing, isn't it? You led them here." He stalks toward my father, gun leveled at his chest.

Clarence raises his hands. "Scott, listen to me. This has gone too far. Surrender, before someone else gets hurt."

Shouts from outside grow louder. I think they're coming in. Scott glances around wildly, realization dawning on his face. But the madness in his eyes says he won't go down without a fight. His finger tightens on the trigger as he stares at the window.

I don't think — I just move. In an instant I'm across the room, crashing into him like an NFL linebacker. The gun goes off with a deafening pop. We slam to the floor. Somewhere, my father is shouting.

Scott and I grapple for the gun. He's stronger but I'm faster, fueled by adrenaline and desperation. With a guttural cry, I twist the gun from Scott's grasp. He swipes for me, but I scramble away, breathless, and point the gun at him.

"Don't move!" I shout. My hands shake but my aim is steady.

Scott freezes, eyes blazing. In the distance, the sound of heavy boots thunders up the porch steps.

Clarence stands slowly, one hand clutching his arm. Oh my God, the bullet hit him. Blood trickles from a gash on his bicep, but he's otherwise okay.

The front door bursts open and I see Jesse. In shock at the sight, I have to remind myself that Scott is still in my sights. *Don't screw this up now.* But Jesse . . . he has a gun, and he's aiming it at Scott, too. The man next to him . . . I don't know who he is, but he looks like a cop. Both take aim at the monster standing only feet away.

"Kylie!" Jesse's familiar voice cuts through the chaos. He darts around the other man and pulls me into his arms. I see him wince in pain. I cling to him, the gun slipping from my fingers and clattering to the floor.

"Put down the gun, Mr. Shaw," the other man says.

I look at Jesse, who shoves me behind him and raises his weapon again. I have no idea how he got a gun. And where the hell is Detective Burns?

Scott eyes me, then my dad. A closed-lip smile crosses his face as he raises the gun to his temple.

The other man lurches forward. "No!"

But Scott fires a bullet into his skull and collapses to the ground. I clasp my hand over my mouth as Jesse pulls me close. Scott's on the floor, staring at me, the life draining from his eyes. Only moments ago, I'd tried to fend him off, and now, he's taken his own life. Coward.

"It's over. You're okay," Jesse says, trying to draw my attention. "You're okay now."

I look at Clarence, still in shock at his arrival, and pull away from Jesse. Walking toward him, my rage turns to gratitude that he's alive. "Dad, how are you here? Why didn't you come find me? I've been alone all these years."

His eyes glisten as he holds my gaze. "I wanted to, Kay. I wanted to tell you so badly, but I was afraid." He looks at my dead half-brother, and then at the man I assume is a cop, because he's calling for an ambulance. "But the risk was too great. Dale knew Scott was getting stronger. I'm so sorry, Kay. I hope, in time, you'll be able to forgive me."

CHAPTER 41

Jesse and I arrive at the hospital, where Detective Burns is taken directly into surgery. I barely had a chance to tell him thank you. He'd lost consciousness just before the ambulance arrived. We're in the town of Carroll. It's closest to Scott Shaw's property. Which he owned thanks to Lucas.

My dad sits next to us as we wait for word that Burns will be okay. He'd lost a lot of blood. I still don't know what to say to Clarence. I called Aunt Grace to let her know I was safe and told her what happened. She never knew my dad had survived either. I'm not sure what to think about all this. Except that the man responsible for murdering my friends and Dale Coleman, Scott Shaw? He's dead.

I see a doctor walking toward us. He removes his skull cap and pulls down his mask. Captain Lyons, who sits across from us, gets to his feet.

"You're here for Doug Burns?" the doctor asks him.

"Yeah. He's one of my detectives. How's he doing, doc?" Lyons asks.

"He pulled through the surgery just fine. A transfusion was necessary, but he'll come through without any lasting damage, to his leg or his back."

My shoulders drop in relief. "Thank God."

The doctor glances at me. "He's still coming out of the anesthesia, so it'll be a while before anyone can visit him. In fact, it might be best for you all to come back in the morning." He peers outside to see a hint of light come through. "Which will be soon, by the look of things."

When the surgeon leaves, Lyons turns toward us. "There's a hotel just down the street. I can take you both there, if you'd like?"

I glance at Clarence, who remains seated. "Uh, yeah, thank you. I think we could use some rest."

Lyons appears to grow uncomfortable. "Well, I'll give you three a minute." He steps into the hall and disappears.

I wonder what will happen to Clarence now. He murdered Lucas Shaw. It wasn't self-defense. It wasn't an accident. So will he be arrested? I don't even know where he lives now, or how he got here. So many questions left unanswered. I turn to him. "Where is home for you, Dad?"

Clarence thrusts his hands into his pockets. "Small city, outside Chicago. Not too far from here. Although, I don't go by Clarence anymore."

"Right." I nod. "Makes sense."

I cling to Jesse, even while I'm certain his discomfort over this conversation grows. He knew nothing about any of this. Now, everything's changed.

"So, you work in the movies, huh?" Clarence smiles. "That sounds incredible. I'm so proud of you."

"Thank you. I enjoy it . . . usually." I crack a smile to relieve the growing tension. "Where do we go from here, Dad? What happens now?"

Clarence takes in a breath. "Well, I'm not really sure. I imagine I'll be tried for murder and spend the rest of my life in prison."

"I'm sorry," I whisper, my lips quivering.

"I'm not." He takes a step closer, gently gripping my arm. "Everything I did was to protect you and your brother and sister. Unfortunately, I couldn't prevent what happened to them. And I'll have to live with that for the rest of my life. I loved your mother and, well, I should've nipped all this in the bud, but I didn't. I knew she would've left me had we not returned to the compound." He waves his hand. "But none of that matters anymore. What matters is that you're safe. And you'll stay safe, now that Scott's dead." He stops and holds my gaze. A gentle smile pulls at his lips. "It's the best I could have hoped for, Kayla."

* * *

Jesse and I flew back to L.A. after making sure to see Burns and tell him that I owed my life to him. He knew where Scott would take me, and he fought to find me.

Now, months have passed, and my father stands trial for the murder of Lucas Shaw. It hardly seems fair. I get up from the couch and head to the kitchen. "You want a beer?"

Jesse glances over his shoulder at me. "Sure. Thanks."

I grab two from the fridge and return to the sofa, handing him one. After taking my seat, I twist off the cap and take a long gulp. The cool amber liquid feels good as it slides down my throat. Stinging just a little, leaving behind a hint of barley.

The newscast begins. A reporter stands in front of a courthouse in Sioux City and begins to speak.

"The trial of Clarence Skinner, for the brutal murder of Lucas Shaw, concluded last week. Today, the jury has finally reached its verdict. Twenty years later, Clarence Skinner is about to learn his fate. Defense argued Skinner committed the crime to protect his family. They were killed only hours after news of the death of Shaw spread through the New Hope compound, and eventually it was burned to the ground. And only one survived — the daughter Skinner was trying to protect."

I feel Jesse's hand squeezing my right shoulder as I cuddle next to him. "You sure you want to hear this?" he asks.

"Yeah. I do."

Several moments pass while the reporter rambles on, until finally, he stops. It seems the verdict is about to be read.

The next shot is inside the courtroom, where I see my dad standing next to his lawyer. He wears a suit, but has been held without bail for months, and it hangs off him, as he's so thin now.

I swallow my fear, waiting for them to speak.

"Has the jury reached its verdict?" the judge asks.

The lead juror stands. "Yes, sir, we have." He holds out a slip of paper, handing it to the bailiff. The bailiff then hands it to the judge.

I can't stand the suspense. I have to know what will become of my dad, the man I thought had been dead for the past twenty years.

The judge unfurls the paper and reads it.

"Come on, for Christ's sake, what does it say?" I ask. Jesse eyes me. "Yeah, I know. Calm down."

"Will the jury please read the verdict," the judge finally says.

A man in the jury box starts to speak, his shoulders back. "We, the jury, find the defendant, Clarence Skinner . . . not guilty on count one, first degree murder. On count two, manslaughter, we find the defendant . . . guilty."

I close my eyes, as they sting with tears.

"This is good, babe," Jesse says. "Manslaughter's a far lesser charge."

I nod. "Yeah, I know, but he's still going to prison."

"Thank you, jurors, for your service to this court. You are hereby dismissed." The judge slams down his gavel. "Sentencing will be issued on September twenty-second. The defendant will continue to be remanded in custody until that time."

"That's three weeks away," I say.

The shot cuts back to the reporter. "*There you have it. The verdict is in. Guilty on the charge of manslaughter. No doubt, the defense will file an appeal.*" He looks over his shoulder to see Dad's lawyers emerge from the courtroom and walk down the steps.

They approach a nearby podium, and the one in the blue suit speaks. "*We will clearly begin the appeals process in this case, as we firmly believe justice was not served for Mr. Skinner today. He is a man who protected his family from Lucas Shaw, a deranged leader of a dangerous cult. And he's spent the past twenty years ensuring what remains of his family stayed safe. We can only hope the judge, in his sentencing, remembers what happened that night at the New Hope compound. Thank you.*"

I lean back. My shoulders slump. The crowd in front of the courthouse begins to disburse. "I feel like I should've been there, Jess."

"Your father insisted you not be," he says. "He doesn't want anyone to know your face. To hound you over this for the rest of your life."

"Yeah, I know, but . . ." I stop cold and squint at the television screen. "The hell?"

"What is it?" Jesse asks.

I shoot up off the couch and march closer to the TV. "Oh my God."

"Babe, what is it?" Jesse moves in next to me.

"There." I point at the screen. "That man, right there. Look at his fucking arm."

He stares at the screen. "What am I looking for?"

I turn back to him. "It's the symbol." I take a breath, feeling my pulse rise. "They're still out there, Jesse. New Hope. For God's sake, how many of them are there?"

EPILOGUE

It was Dale Coleman who'd contacted my father when I'd returned to town. He knew all along Clarence Skinner was alive. And he knew about Scott Shaw. It was only when we returned to Dale's house after his death, and went through his things, that it became clear just how long he'd kept watch over my family, ensuring the threat never got ahead of him, until it did.

Dale and my father had worked together to bring down Lucas Shaw. And when things went south, and Clarence murdered him without Dale's foreknowledge, my father knew he was either going to prison or was about to be killed.

The man who broke into our house was Lee Stafford. He killed my brother first, near the kitchen, at the bottom of the stairs. Then he walked up to my sister's room. Finally, he reached my parents' room and stabbed my mother in the chest five times.

Dad had tried to escape, but Lee stabbed him too. But I managed to get out before he got to me. I never knew my father had survived the attack.

Dale had found him. He found all of them, and had helped Clarence get away.

My father was a murderer, and Dale made everyone believe he'd been killed, too, along with me. Dale kept that secret for twenty years.

He'd also kept tabs on Scott Shaw. Turns out, while Dale Coleman had been retired from the FBI, he'd kept in close contact with his colleagues, who used their resources to help him in his efforts.

I'd escaped the compound all on my own, hiding out until finding a safe place to call Aunt Grace. She arrived several hours later to save me.

According to Dale's files, Clarence told him Grace was the only family left and it was the logical place for me to go, so he set about finding me. When he did, he kept watch over me, relaying to my father how I was doing.

Dale helped my father escape his fate and did all of this while the compound burned to the ground. And the reason it burned?

Me.

I set the fire to the community center, the recreation room, the prayer center. All of it. That was how I got back at the man who'd planned to take me — a thirteen-year-old girl — as his wife. It was the only way I knew to avenge my family just before I made my escape. I didn't mean for all the others to die, but they did . . . by my hands.

But what I never knew was the part Dale Coleman played. And I never knew about Scott Shaw, or that our entire reason for being at the compound was a result of what my mother had wanted. I'm not sure I have the capacity to forgive her for what she allowed to happen. For what she did.

I've had a chance to study Dale's files. Detective Burns was good enough to copy them for me and send them to our home. Dale did so much to protect me and my dad. Even retired near where it all happened just to keep an eye out for a resurgence. And when that came to fruition, well, he tried to protect me again, only this time, it cost him his life.

Dad's sentencing came and went. The judge gave him five years, meaning with good behavior, he'd be out in three or less.

Did Clarence do the right thing? I don't know. I saw the monster that Lucas's son had become. Would that have happened otherwise? Maybe the two Shaw men were more alike than any of us knew. But I also know that Lucas's ideas, his teachings . . . they were dangerous. It took me a long time to realize that. Could any of his followers have come to that conclusion in their own time? Maybe.

But what I do know is that I'm a killer, just like my dad. Yet I've escaped my punishment. And if any of those sons of bitches from New Hope come for me again . . . I'll be ready.

THE END

THE JOFFE BOOKS STORY

We began in 2014 when Jasper agreed to publish his mum's much-rejected romance novel and it became a bestseller.

Since then we've grown into the largest independent publisher in the UK. We're extremely proud to publish some of the very best writers in the world, including Joy Ellis, Faith Martin, Caro Ramsay, Helen Forrester, Simon Brett and Robert Goddard. Everyone at Joffe Books loves reading and we never forget that it all begins with the magic of an author telling a story.

We are proud to publish talented first-time authors, as well as established writers whose books we love introducing to a new generation of readers.

We won Trade Publisher of the Year at the Independent Publishing Awards in 2023 and Best Publisher Award in 2024 at the People's Book Prize. We have been shortlisted for Independent Publisher of the Year at the British Book Awards for the last five years, and were shortlisted for the Diversity and Inclusivity Award at the 2022 Independent Publishing Awards. In 2023 we were shortlisted for Publisher of the Year at the RNA Industry Awards, and in 2024 we were shortlisted at the CWA Daggers for the Best Crime and Mystery Publisher.

We built this company with your help, and we love to hear from you, so please email us about absolutely anything bookish at feedback@joffebooks.com.

If you want to receive free books every Friday and hear about all our new releases, join our mailing list here: www.joffebooks.com/freebooks.

And when you tell your friends about us, just remember: it's pronounced Joffe as in coffee or toffee!

Milton Keynes UK
Ingram Content Group UK Ltd.
UKHW021937091224
452187UK00010B/52

9 781835 269060